Eric Ford was everything she wanted.

When he spoke, Camille had trouble hearing words because the deep timbre of his voice thrilled her so much, and that was a pity because he was so smart and she hated to look stupid. When he took her hand, her heartbeat faltered. It wasn't just because his hand was so big that it made hers seem dainty, although that was a delight.

She wasn't entirely blind, though. He had his faults. It was just that she loved them all. He was so big and blond that it took a moment to realize he wasn't classically handsome, or even spectacularly so. On closer consideration, it could be seen that his face was a jot too broad, his nose a bit too large. In fact, if he were a smaller man he mightn't be as eye-catching. But he dominated a room, and not just because of his size. A woman felt protected in his shadow, and she could be sure he'd move that shadow if he thought she wanted to be in the sunlight. Because he was as kind as he was bright.

No, she didn't worship him; she just wished she could marry him.

Other AVON ROMANCES

ALL MEN ARE ROGUES *by Sari Robins*
BELOVED HIGHLANDER *by Sara Bennett*
FOR THE FIRST TIME *by Kathryn Smith*
ONCE A SCOUNDREL *by Candice Hern*
THE PRINCESS AND HER PIRATE *by Lois Greiman*
SOARING EAGLE'S EMBRACE *by Karen Kay*
WICKEDLY YOURS *by Brenda Hiatt*

Coming Soon

ALMOST PERFECT *by Denise Hampton*
THE DUCHESS DIARIES *by Mia Ryan*

And Don't Miss These
ROMANTIC TREASURES
from Avon Books

THE PLEASURE OF HER KISS *by Linda Needham*
TAMING THE SCOTSMAN *by Kinley MacGregor*
A WEDDING STORY *by Susan Kay Law*

ATTENTION: ORGANIZATIONS AND CORPORATIONS
Most Avon Books paperbacks are available at special quantity discounts for bulk purchases for sales promotions, premiums, or fund-raising. For information, please call or write:

Special Markets Department, HarperCollins Publishers, Inc., 10 East 53rd Street, New York, N.Y. 10022–5299.
Telephone: (212) 207–7528. Fax: (212) 207-7222.

EDITH LAYTON

TO TEMPT A BRIDE

AVON BOOKS

An Imprint of HarperCollinsPublishers

This is a work of fiction. Names, characters, places, and incidents are products of the author's imagination or are used fictitiously and are not to be construed as real. Any resemblance to actual events, locales, organizations, or persons, living or dead, is entirely coincidental.

AVON BOOKS
An Imprint of HarperCollins*Publishers*
10 East 53rd Street
New York, New York 10022-5299

First Avon Books paperback printing: November 2003

Avon Trademark Reg. U.S. Pat. Off. and in Other Countries, Marca Registrada, Hecho en U.S.A.
HarperCollins® is a registered trademark of HarperCollins Publishers Inc.

Printed in the U.S.A.

10 9 8 7 6 5 4 3 2 1

For Valiant Stan,
the newest member of our clan.
With thanks to the good people
at Stray from the Heart,
who delivered him safely to Susie and Ed.
www.strayfromtheheart.org

Chapter 1

It was the hottest spot in London on the coldest night of the year. The humidity was so high that water dripped down the inside of the closed windows as the outside iced over. The dancers' armpits would have shown damp spots if there'd been room for them to lift their arms, but there was hardly room to move their feet. Still, they kept smiling. Because although it felt like a jungle, they were in a ballroom in the best part of London town, and for all their sweat and panting, they were happy to be there.

But one of the guests felt a chill and knew it was time to go home.

The problem was that he couldn't leave right away any more than he could stay. Eric Ford

looked around the crowded room and decided he
had a choice: he could remain and embarrass himself or leave and embarrass himself. He shuddered
again. That made up his mind. He recognized the
signs. He'd hoped it was over and done with, but
realized with sinking heart that it was not, and so
he had no choice. He'd have to be quick with a glib
excuse and leave as soon as he could, because he
began to think that this time, however hurt, feelings would mend faster than he would.

Eric scanned the room, seeing more than most
men would, if only because he was the tallest there.
The woman he was looking for was wearing gold,
he remembered.

There. She was with a young officer, romping in
a country reel.

Eric knew the tune, heard it winding to a close,
and knew the dance would soon be over. No matter
whose name she had on her dance card, he'd talk
her into letting him have the next one. He had to,
for he wasn't sure he could linger longer.

When the music stopped, she raised a flushed
face to her partner, and the two of them began to
leave the floor. Eric's head began to throb, but he
pasted on a smile and went to intercept them.

And the musicians struck up again, this time a
waltz.

Eric frowned. She had permission to waltz, but if
he tried to whirl around the room now, he was sure
his head would go whirling off his shoulders. Soon
it would feel as if it had anyway. But he couldn't

disappoint her. As he stood wondering what to do, he saw her being approached by another man. Eric grimaced and moved forward. This time, he'd have to be ready when the music ended. He'd given her his word.

"Two dances?" she had cried excitedly when he'd agreed to her teasing suggestion. She'd slewed around in her saddle. "Really? Oh, Eric! That would be wonderful! Won't that open their eyes! To see me, a great gawk of a girl from the country, snaring *you* for two dances! I'll have a partner for every dance for the rest of the Season, much less the night!" She'd whooped with laughter before he could make a comment to take the sting from her words.

"What a bag of moonshine!" He'd laughed in return, angling his horse closer. "You've been a success since you appeared on the scene. I wonder how many likely lads I'll have the threaten in order to even get my two dances."

"They'll have to deal with me if they try to interfere with you," she'd said immediately and then laughed again, a little shamefacedly, when he grinned at the thought of her having to help him.

Because while Camille was a fine figure of a girl, he was almost a giant, with enough muscles to give his tailor fits. Current fashion wasn't happy with gentlemen built along the lines of Hercules, but Camille obviously was. Still, she was young, and he was her brother's friend, and she adored her brother, so that probably accounted for it. But she was also bright, so Eric was sure that sooner than later she'd see that was the extent of her interest in him and go on to fascinate more suitable beaux. That would be especially true now that she was in London at last. Still, the least he could do was to make her feel comfortable in her new setting, and if two dances would do it, he was happy to oblige.

She had flashed him a brilliant smile that day, nudged her horse forward, and they'd gone galloping down the riding trail, each too pleased with the fine afternoon and their plans to say another word.

When he'd seen her tonight, he'd actually stopped in his tracks, confused, as though he'd seen a familiar face in an unfamiliar setting and couldn't quite place it. His jolly companion on horseback was now a vision, with her hair done up like a lady and the thin gold gown showing how much of a woman she'd become. He was used to seeing her romping with her dogs or riding her horses, always dressed in comfortable old clothes. He didn't know if her new gown was comfortable, but it made him uncomfortable to see the young lady she had suddenly become.

She'd opened her arms to show him all her new splendor and then sank into a deep curtsey. When she rose, she grinned her old familiar grin at him. "I clean up nicely, don't I?" she said with her usual cheeky good humor.

Her brother sighed, her sister-in-law rolled her eyes, and Eric laughed. "You certainly do," he said, and led her into his first promised dance.

But tonight Eric realized his own personal David was in the room with him and he didn't have long before he'd be felled as certainly as Goliath had been. He wondered if he could last until her waltz ended, and forced himself to stand up straight. He would endure because he had to. A soldier was trained to stand firm against his enemy, even if that enemy lived in his own head. The pain in his head began to throb in time to the music, and it seemed to him that the waltz would go on forever.

Finally, the music began to wind down. He stepped forward again, steadfastly ignoring the shivery feeling of icy fingers trailing down the considerable length of his spine. Now too, in the perverse spite of the malady he suffered from, he felt the heat. But he wasn't sweating yet so judged he still had time.

The couples on the dance floor were glowing from exertion. When the music stopped, the ladies began fanning themselves vigorously, some discreetly lifting the sheer fabric of their gowns so the breeze could touch their flesh. The gentlemen, sealed in their fashionable high neckcloths and tight-fitted waistcoats and jackets, were red-cheeked, some blowing hard as spent racehorses.

One of the dancers wore her exertion like a cosmetic. Eric smiled in spite of his pain, because although she was disheveled, Camille's high spirits were irrepressible, and dishevelment suited her. Her curly cinnamon hair was coming down in tendrils all around her face, and her eyes were sparkling. Her amazing gown pointed up the gold in those merry eyes. She looked wonderful, and obviously every man she'd danced with tonight thought so too. She hadn't stopped dancing since he'd arrived.

No, she didn't need his escort to give her the social boost she claimed she needed. But he'd promised, and he would deliver that second dance, then leave as soon as the music stopped. That should give him enough time to get safely home.

But as the dancers began to leave the floor, the music suddenly picked up again, as though it had never stopped. The couples turned to each other; shrugged, laughed, and stepped right back into the dance.

"Damn!" an aggrieved male voice complained close to Eric's ear, "some curst fellow must have greased the fiddlers' palms to keep them sawing so he wouldn't have to let his lady go! I'll bet it was that blasted Harcourt, so he wouldn't have to give the fair Lucinda up to me now!"

"It ain't him," another male voice said. "Everyone knows he don't have tuppence to spare. Look at Burke and how he's smirking at Leigh over the top of the youngest Swanson girl's head as he's twirling her round the room. Ten to one he's the one who slipped the musicians their gold."

The music played on until the dancers began to look as though they were suffering. Then the host strode over and had a quick, harsh word with the musicians, and it came to an abrupt halt. The sudden ending of the waltz was met with laughter and groans from the exhausted dancers.

Eric was waiting at the edge of the floor as Camille sauntered over with her partner. Her eyes lit up when she saw him.

"Drat!" she said as she noted his flushed face and glittering eyes. "You've been dancing with everyone else and now you'll be too tired to collect your dance with me."

He bowed. "I'm never too weary for that. Shall we?"

"But this is *my* dance," a spotty young fellow whined from behind Eric's shoulder. He stood on his toes and bobbed up and down, trying to see Camille, as he made his claim.

"It's no one's, I'm afraid," she said with regret. "See, the musicians are resting, and the doors to the dining room are being opened. Midnight supper, gentlemen. We'll have our dance afterward," she assured the spotty youth. Putting a hand on Eric's arm, she added, with a bright glance up at him, "but I'm already promised for supper."

The younger man frowned, bowed, and left them. She looked up to see a look of pain on Eric's face. She dropped her hand. "I didn't mean to presume," she said quickly. "You can dine with whomever you like. It's just that I didn't fancy taking my mutton with that fellow."

He managed a smile. "Mustn't say 'taking my mutton.' Your mother would skin you for it."

"Yes," she said smugly, "but she's at home, and

I'm here, and besides, it's only for your ears, and you know me." She looked up at him with troubled eyes. "You're frowning. Does it bother you too?"

"No. But my headache does," he admitted, because he could no longer deny it. He looked down at her and tried to frame a crooked smile. "I'd have liked to take supper as well as dance with you, but I'm going to have to be a complete cad. I must leave now. I'm sorry."

"Oh!" she said quickly. "Is there anything I can do for you?"

"Forgive me," he said and, not trusting himself to say another word, turned and blindly walked away, leaving her standing, biting her lip as she looked after him.

He collected his greatcoat and hat and left the house. Once out on the front stair, he stopped and breathed in the icy air. It felt wonderful, like a dash of ice water on his flushed face. He felt his body and his worries cooling down. The blast of wintry cold was a relief; it calmed his nerves and cleared his head.

Maybe it wouldn't be so bad, he thought. After all, it hadn't been so bad in over a year, and the doctors said that sometimes the intensity of the fever diminished the longer one was away from the source of contagion. Tonight the tropical heat of the ballroom had reminded him of the past. He decided that might have added to his symptoms, because he was a firm believer in the mind's influence over the body. He'd had to be.

And too, this was London, not India. Men didn't contract the malarial fever in London; this was where a fellow came to get away from it. At least, he had, and it had done him good. He'd had some small bouts of fever but hadn't been really sick since he'd first come home to England a year ago.

"Your carriage, sir?" a footman asked, seeing the big gent paused on the front step. He raised his hand to signal for whichever carriage Eric requested.

"I don't have one," Eric said. He'd walked to the ball because he enjoyed the exercise. Taking a carriage would have been more prudent, because he never knew when the fever would strike, but a man couldn't live in constant fear of disaster. At least, he refused to. And now he did feel better. He breathed a small sigh of relief. A fine thing if he collapsed on his host's front step! He'd done that when he'd first returned to London from his tour abroad, and he never wanted to be that helpless again.

"Want me to call a hack for you then, sir?" the footman asked. "It'll take a bit of time, since there ain't room in front of the house for nothing but personal carriages. This is a real squeeze," he said with pride at how successful the ball at his master's house was. "But we got hired hacks at the ready a few streets down. I just have to send somebody running for one."

The flaming torches in front of the house added to the glow of the new gaslights on the street, so

Eric could see down the long line of carriages waiting for their owners. One thing was certain: a coach that wasn't already in that line didn't stand a chance of getting near the house tonight. He'd have to walk a way to get into one even if it drew up closer. What was the difference between walking along one street or two?

"Don't bother," he told the footman, tossing him a coin for his trouble. "I'll walk."

Hoping his luck would hold, Eric took a deep breath of cold air and strode off into the frigid night.

Camille stood looking after Eric's broad back as he disappeared from sight. She frowned. He hadn't been himself. She ought to know. She always watched him closely, far more than he knew. It wasn't only his abrupt departure. His smile had seemed forced, and worse, his usually tanned face had looked curiously sallow. Was he ill? Of course, she knew he'd been mortally sick when he'd first arrived home from India. Her brother had mentioned it often enough. Still, she'd discounted it. Anyone could get sick, and Eric had obviously fully recovered. But now the way he'd so abruptly deserted her made her remember the stories. They said he'd been sick unto death then.

Her heart began to race. She looked around the crowded room for her brother. She saw his lovely wife, Lady Annabelle, chatting with a clutch of ladies. Then she saw Belle look up, as though someone had touched her on the shoulder, and gaze across the room. Camille narrowed her eyes, trying to see through the heated shimmer of candle glow. Belle stared and then exchanged a small secret smile with—*there*. Miles was talking with some of his friends but, as always, with his eyes on his wife, as hers were on him.

Camille quickly made her way through the crowd to him.

"Miles," she said immediately. "Eric has just left very abruptly."

"He probably felt all the joy went out of the night after he'd had his last dance with you," he teased, with a grin at his friends.

"No," she said. "That's just the point. I thought he was going to dance with me next."

"Oh. Well, maybe he had another important engagement," he began to say evasively, but she cut him off.

"No need to sugarcoat things," she snapped. "I don't expect men to give up anything in order to dance with me, especially men like Eric. But Miles," she went on anxiously, ignoring the other men as they began gallantly to contradict her, "he was green around the gills."

"Any fellow can drink too much, even experienced troopers like Eric, right, Rafe?" her brother commented, turning to one of his friends, Raphael, Lord Dalton, an ex-army man.

"Eric doesn't have a vigilant lady to keep him in line, as I do," his friend answered proudly.

"But you don't understand," Camille said impatiently. "He'd *promised* the next dance to me."

Miles's smile faded. He put down his cup. "Tell my lady I'll be back soon," he commanded her, turned on his heel, and headed for the door, Rafe following closely.

"When did he leave?" he asked Camille over his shoulder, as she trotted after him.

"Just five minutes past. It took that long to find you in this crowd."

As the two men strode into the outer hall, Miles turned his head to find her still right behind him. "Camille," he said, "I said, go tell Belle and the other ladies where we've gone."

"Have a footman do it," she said. "I'm coming with you."

He scowled, and Rafe frowned, but they didn't break stride. They sent for their coats and made inquiries as they waited for them. A footman reported that a big, fair gent had just left and had been seen walking off alone toward the west. Miles called for his coach and left the house with Rafe. Camille followed, her heart pounding with nervousness.

Nothing they could have said or done would have stopped her from joining them. But they didn't even take the time to argue. That frightened her even more.

Eric felt light-headed with relief. The shakes had stopped, the aches were gone, his head had cleared.

The long strides he was taking seemed to be leaving his sickness behind. He felt so good he didn't want to stop and so walked right on past the line of waiting hacks and headed toward his own lodgings. They weren't far, just straight ahead six streets and then up three more twisting ones, around a corner, and he'd be home. Since the bracing air had helped so much, he was sure more would do him further good.

But when he got home, just in case, he'd have his valet mix up some quinine in lemonade, the potion his doctor advised him to take for the fever. Then he'd have a jot of hot buttered rum. It was cold and getting colder, and he felt it in spite of his exercise.

His symptoms began to plague him again as soon as he'd gone three streets, once he left the crowded, well-lighted pavements behind.

Rome and Paris were said to be cities of churches, because there seemed to be a church every few steps. England was called a nation of merchants for equally good reason. By day London's shops were open, and so was trade in the streets. Pavements were thronged with street criers and peddlers dealing goods from pony carts, dogcarts and pushcarts, barrows, even trays hanging from their own neck.

By night other vendors sold more intimately attached goods. Once the sun set, the same streets filled with prostitutes. It was one of the reasons decent women never walked alone by night. And also the reason why so many gentlemen did.

So a man walking alone, especially a well-dressed one, drew London's host of whores from the shadows like pigeons to strewn seed. They came up to the big, blond man—but once they got a look at his face, most drew back. He kept his gaze forward, offering them no encouragement. Besides that, his looks made them hesitate. Because he was such a magnificent-looking fellow, they doubted he'd have to buy his night's pleasures.

Tall, broad, and blond as the Viking invaders who had coursed over this same ground an age before, Eric Ford bore himself with the pride of the military man he'd been and the grace of the gentleman he'd been educated to be. His face had the strong features seen on ancient coins, his figure was that of a gladiator, and he had the height of a colossus. He would have appeared intimidating but for the humor and humanity that gleamed in his hazel eyes.

The next woman who approached him spoke for her sisterhood.

" 'Ere, milord," she murmured as she stepped from an alley to confront him. "I'm as cheap as I'm fun. . . . Aw, blimey, never mind." She laughed when she saw his face and the thick honey-gold hair under his high beaver hat. " 'Ow much do *you* charge, luv? It's been a good evening. I might just buy myself a treat!"

"At any other time I might have spared you the expense," he lied in his deep, even voice, "but I have to get home straightaway tonight. But thank you."

"And a gentleman!" she exclaimed, with a hand to her heart. "Luv, your courtesy is as good as your kiss—well, mebbe not. But I'll take what I can get from you, sir. Godspeed to you and whatever lucky lass awaits you!"

He managed a smile and strode on. He never bought street women but was experienced enough to know that rebuffing them was a delicate art. Though they had a price, they had pride too, and they could make a man's life hell if he refused them rudely. Apart from the fact that he saw no reason to abuse women already degraded by their livelihood, now he felt his head beginning to ache again and didn't think it could have borne the catcalls and abuse that have would followed him down the street if he'd been impolite.

Eric lengthened his stride. He was headed toward a quiet, wealthy residential area where the street women seldom tarried, because they wouldn't find much trade there. He was relieved to find himself increasingly alone. Shaking his head "no" was beginning to make it hurt, and speaking required effort. Now he realized his old foe had only been lying low. He prayed he could make it safely home.

Only two more streets, then a turn to the right. . . . He was sweating but freezing cold. His shirt was damp, his face clammy. Only one and a half streets and then a turn to the right. . . .

He almost walked straight into her. A woman had been shoved into his path. Eric stopped abruptly, nonplussed. A heavyset man in dark clothing accompanied her. Eric got a glimpse of a white, frightened face, big dark eyes . . . and tears? It hardly mattered. He had to go on before he fell down. He stepped aside, but now the man was in his way.

"Here's a treat, sir," the man said, his harsh voice so loud Eric winced. "I keeps her covered to keep the mob away. Take off your shawl now, girl," he roared, snatching it from her head. "Look, sir, fair as the dawn, ain't she?"

Eric frowned and tried to step around the girl, but the man shoved her at him.

"You could take her home or here, it don't matter. She don't come cheap, but I seen you turned down all them cheap whores, and who's to blame you? But look at her! Fine as she can stare. And modest," he said through gritted teeth as the woman pulled up her shawl and ducked her head. He forced her chin up. "A picture, ain't she? And believe me, her body's good as it gets. A regular Venus, this one is. She's untouched too, so a gent like yourself don't have to worry none about disease. You'd be the first, a rare treat. It'd cost, but you'd know a bargain, wouldn't you?"

Eric drew in breath to say no, but she said it instead.

"No," she cried. "Oh, please, no, sir. Help me!"

He could have been on his deathbed and he'd

have responded to that. "Are you here unwillingly?" he asked her.

She nodded.

"Want to talk to her, do you? Fine!" the man said quickly. "Do what you want with her once you pay for her. Give us a guinea, then. For that much, she'll talk your ear as well as your pants off."

Eric knew he had to end this now. He had no time to argue, no time to think it through. It would be easier to throw money at the problem and let it go away. He'd pay the villain and be done with him, then let the girl go on her way. He reached for his wallet—but so did the other man, because the moment Eric had his wallet in his hand, the man grabbed it.

The woman cried out. The man cuffed her. She cringed and cried out again. Eric swung a fist, but the woman now had a death grip on his arm.

"Don't let him take me!" she sobbed.

The man held Eric's wallet in one hand, the woman's hand in the other. He took a second to make up his mind, then gave up his hold on the woman, spun on his heel, and ran. Or tried to, because Eric grabbed his shoulder. The fellow ducked and twisted, but it was like trying to escape being caught in a fissure in a rock. He snarled, pulled a short club from his belt, turned, and swung it hard, connecting with Eric's ear.

Eric heard an explosion of sound and saw the light splinter. The pain was sudden, shocking, and blinding. Stunned, he went down to one knee.

Then he bellowed and grabbed at the hand that
held the club. He caught the hand hard and twisted
and didn't stop until the man screamed. He
wouldn't have stopped even then, but the fellow
dropped to his knees.

The moment Eric relaxed his grip, the man
bounded up. Bent double, he rushed forward and
butted Eric in the forehead with his own head. The
sound was sickening, the surprise and pain sent
Eric sprawling. His attacker turned, grabbed the
woman, and tried to drag her away with him. But
she'd managed to keep hold of Eric's arm and was
hanging on for dear life.

Now they all heard the sounds of an approaching carriage rushing over the cobbles, hoofbeats,
and loud, outraged shouts. Eric heard his own
name called.

The man cursed, abruptly let go of the girl and,
clutching the wallet, took off at a stumbling run
into the darkness.

The coach clattered to a stop. Eric heard horses
whinnying, their brasses ringing, coach doors
slamming, more shouts, and many footsteps
pounding toward him. Then the footsteps stopped.
He heard worried voices exclaiming over him, but
was still so dazed and sickened that he couldn't
gather his breath or wits enough to open his eyes,
much less move.

"Damn! Is he dead?" a voice asked harshly.

He felt a cool hand on his cheek, then on his
forehead.

"No," another voice, this one soft and shaken, said. "Just . . . damaged, I think."

"Here," an impatient voice commanded. "Let me see. I have experience." There was an exasperated sigh. "Would you please get back, Camille? Take her, Miles. A mad start for her to be here at all," he muttered.

"Did you ever try stopping her, Rafe?" a strained voice answered. "Eric? Can you hear me?"

Eric managed to open one eye.

"Good evening, Rafe," he said to the man kneeling beside him. He looked up and recognized the worried faces peering down. "Oh, lord. Camille!" he groaned. "In the gutter with me? What are you doing here?"

She raised her chin. "You left so suddenly, I worried. It wasn't like you, and you didn't look well. I told my brother when I remembered you sometimes suffered—"

"Malarial fever," Rafe interrupted angrily. "Another attack? Of course! Look at the color of his skin, yellow as a cheap candle. And he's shaking. Just like old times. Idiot," he told Eric through clenched teeth. "Why didn't you say something? But look at that egg rising on your forehead. Like you're growing another head. Now, tell me so I know what to do first. Eric, listen," he said as his friend's eyes began closing again. "Tell me. What's worse, the fever or your forehead? Or did that whore's son hurt you some other place too?"

"It's only both, I think," Eric murmured. "Head

and fever. But I'll do till I get home. Give me a hand and I'll get up and go."

"In my coach," Rafe muttered. "Thank God we'd the sense to drive after you."

Another man came trotting up, breathing hard. "He got away, milord," he reported in disgust. "The villain slipped off into the shadows."

"With my wallet," Eric said sadly. "I'm sorry you didn't nab him."

"You live, Eric," Rafe said. "At least we have that. And who is this you've got attached to your sleeve?" he asked curiously, looking at the drab, who knelt at Eric's other side and still clung to the big man's sleeve. "Let go, girl, if you please!"

"Yes, who is she?" Camille couldn't help blurting as the woman shrank back.

Eric was helped to his feet. He tried to regain his balance—mind and body—as he squinted at the cringing woman they were all staring at. She'd let go of his sleeve but hadn't moved far. She crouched at his feet and stared back at him.

"Oh," Eric said. "Yes. That's what started this. I've just bought her."

Chapter 2

Camille hoped they'd think it was the cold wind making her eyes water. She was horrified to find she felt like bawling and quickly wiped away the embarrassing moisture on her cheeks, glad everyone else was too stunned to look at anyone but Eric—and the draggle-tailed slut he'd just said he'd bought. She wasn't weeping because of that, Camille told herself. She was upset by how Eric looked compared to when she'd last seen him a scant half-hour ago. Who wouldn't be?

Eric was wavering on his feet. A frighteningly huge lump, already turning blue, was on his forehead. Just looking at it made her stomach feel as if it was turning over, and she was not a missish girl. There was an angry welt rising along the side of his head as well. He was drawn and sallow, obviously suffering from more than the beating he'd taken. It was a remarkable and terrible change.

Could a man change as drastically mentally from one minute to another? Camille stood staring at Eric. He had left a glittering ball so he could rush out into the dark, cold streets and buy himself the services of a whore? She shook her head. No, she wouldn't believe he'd do that even if he'd been feeling well, even if he did say so himself.

Obviously, neither could his friends.

"How many times were you hit on the head, Eric?" Miles asked.

Eric squinted at the speaker. "Miles? You really are here too? Lord Dalton *and* Viscount Pelham? The Swansons will never forgive me. I've ruined their ball for certain."

"Where else were you hit?" Miles persisted.

"Only the head, twice." Eric said, gingerly touching his forehead. "There's no blood or anything broken, I think. The bastard—" Eric paused, remembering his audience. "Your pardon, Camille. The villain offered me the . . . wench," he said, with another sidewise glance at Camille. "I thought to pay him just to . . ."

He stopped talking as a long rolling shudder shook him. He wrapped his arms around his chest as though he were holding himself together. As the shivering finally subsided, he added bitterly through clenched teeth, "I paid him to be rid of him. The wench objected to the bargain. She cried for help. How could I just walk away? But I knew I couldn't settle it with words or fists. The damned—sorry, Cammie—deuced fever was back, and I knew I didn't have much time. I had to get home. I should have known appeasement never works."

He shook his head, grimacing at the pain that caused. "When he saw gold, he struck, grabbed, and ran. He tried to take her with him, but she had my arm and clung like a winkle to a rock. Now, will you help me home?"

"He's as good as blind now," Rafe muttered angrily. "I've seen him like this before. The fever's on him. Here, lad," he told the footman, "get on his other side. We'll lead him to the coach and get him home. My home. You need care," he added over Eric's mumbled protests. "I've done it before. And think on, your sister would slay me if I sent you home alone. Want to face my wife's wrath *and* your fever? I didn't think so. Miles, there are too many to crowd into a coach with a sick man with a head injury. I'll send another coach to take you and your sister back to the ball."

"As if I could dance now!" Camille scoffed. "Surely there's something I can do!"

"Yes. Stay with your brother," Rafe said, "and when you can, tell my Brenna what's toward."

The two men put their arms around Eric and began to guide him to the waiting coach. Another female voice made them pause.

"You can't leave me!" the drab cried. "I'm not what I seem, none of this is." She stepped forward, throwing back the shawl she'd been huddling under. "Oh, have pity! He'll take me up again if you leave me now."

They stopped and stared, and not just because of her words.

She was lovely, even in the inconstant moonlight, perhaps even more so in its thin, luminous glow. She was young, with a pale, white, oval face surrounded by hair so black the moonlight silvered and shimmered in its shining coils. Her tilted eyes were dark, her nose, small and shapely, and her lips, even in the bleached light, were plump, pale pink, and exquisitely shaped. Once she'd cast off her covering shawl, they could see that her slender figure was covered by a simple, modest, round-necked white gown, the kind any well-brought-up young woman might wear.

If her looks hadn't stopped the men in their tracks, her voice would have. It was low and husky, her accents refined.

Camille blinked and stood staring, as arrested as the men were. What was such a lovely creature doing selling herself on the streets of London?

The plots of dozens of Minerva Press novels she'd read on all those long nights at home in the country sprang into Camille's mind, a welter of evil uncles and wicked stepmothers, displaced heiresses and lost princesses. Surely this lovely young woman was some sort of heroine rescued from a dire plot.

Camille's heart sank. The way the radiant young woman was gazing at Eric made it evident that if she was the princess in peril, he was the rescuer-knight.

"No time to sort this out now," Miles said, breaking the spell the young woman's outcry had cast. "Don't worry," he told her. "You won't be left alone. Rafe, Godspeed. I'll be at your house as soon as I can."

"Good. But I'm driving home," Rafe said, signaling the coachman to step down from his box. "I don't doubt you can take on villains, Miles, but with two females to protect, I'd feel better if the odds were more in your favor until reinforcements come. John Coachman may have driven a mile or two, but he's still got a few tricks up his sleeve, right, John?"

The old fellow grinned down at them. "Aye, milord, a few tricks and a stout cudgel as well!"

"Right," Rafe said. "Now, come, let's get him in the coach."

They guided Eric up the steps and into the carriage. Rafe climbed up to the driver's seat and took the reins so the coachman could clamber down.

Eric's face appeared at the window. "Take care of her, Miles," he said, as the coach started to pull away from the curb.

Miles nodded. The young woman stepped closer to him. Camille stood watching the carriage leave, too distressed to speak. She was worrying about Eric and about what he'd just said: wondering bleakly which of them was the *her* he meant.

After the coach rattled off down the street, Camille

finally turned to her brother. But Miles had literally turned his back on her. The coachman, hands fisted, stood opposite him, the two men facing out with the women between them. Camille started to speak, then held her tongue. Miles's expression was grim; he was watching the street intently. She realized he did so for good reason. It was late and the streets were empty. They were in a good district, which meant it was a quiet one where the residents went to bed early. If there was a watchman nearby, he hadn't appeared, and lately there'd been violence done. The quietness increased their danger, as did the absence of passersby and their party's seeming vulnerability, because it consisted of two young females, an old man, and a tulip of the *ton* who looked as much prey as protector.

Her brother Miles was a slender man of average height, exquisitely dressed tonight as befitted a gentleman of means and leisure. There was no way a casual observer could know that he'd served as an officer in His Majesty's Royal Navy or that his lean body was well muscled and agile. Camille knew he could hold his own in a fight; the problem was that villains might not. She prepared herself. She wasn't so used to being a lady that she wouldn't fight to her last breath, if she had to.

"Thank you, sir," the unknown young woman whispered to Miles. "I was so afraid. You won't leave me here, will you?"

"No," he said, never taking his eyes off the shadows. "But don't speak now. We'll discuss it all later."

Camille hadn't realized how shallowly she'd been breathing until after what seemed like hours but must have only been minutes later, she saw her brother's carriage come down the street.

They boarded in silence.

Camille got in first. The young woman came next and immediately huddled by the window beside her. Miles took the seat opposite. He held up a hand.

"No need for explanations yet," he told the young woman, though she hadn't offered any. "You'll only have to repeat them all later. But your name, if you please."

"Nell," she answered. "Nell Baynes, sir. From Kent."

"I'm Pelham. This is my sister, Camille. Now, sit back, we'll be home soon."

"Your home?" the girl asked quickly.

"Yes. But no need to worry. I'm married, and happily, to the most beautiful woman in London. After I know how my friend is doing, be sure I'll want to speak with you. I'm going straight to Rafe's, Camille. You needn't get out of the carriage. After I get out, I'll send you back to the ball. You were looking forward to it, no sense in disappointing all your beaux."

"Just you try, Miles!" Camille said, sitting up straight. "I want to know how Eric does too. I'll go with you to Rafe's house now, thank you very much. You'll need someone to stay with Miss Baynes anyway. We can send word to Belle from there. I just hope she doesn't feel she has to leave on my account. She was so looking forward to this ball."

"Only for your sake," Miles commented. "She felt bilious all day but wouldn't stay home and let you go it all alone."

"Well, if that don't beat all!" Camille exclaimed angrily. "I told her not to set foot out the door if she didn't feel perfectly right. She said she did! I asked if she was casting up her accounts because she was anticipating and told her not to worry because, if she was, she'd stop once the baby was set in nice and tight, and she nearly bit my head off. She said it was just something she ate. She didn't tell me she was still feeling green by the time we left tonight."

"Two socially suicidal mistakes in two sentences," Miles said on a groan. "Or maybe three. I don't know how you do it. A lady doesn't use slang, and she pretends she doesn't know a thing about gestation, and she doesn't discuss digestion. If Belle heard you talking like a stable boy again, she'd have your head. I think that's why she went tonight despite how she felt—to keep you in line."

"I told her she didn't need to," Camille said hotly. "I had my dance card filled the second I got there."

"Oh, we know you have dozens of admirers," he said. "It's not your getting proposals we worried about."

Since they were sitting side by side in a small

space, Camille couldn't miss feeling the unknown woman's start of surprise when Miles mentioned her popularity.

"It's the sort of proposals you'll get," he went on. He saw Camille's expression in the coach lamp's light and flung up one hand. "Peace!" he laughed. "We know no one would be fool enough to offer you a slip on the shoulder. If I didn't kill him for it, Eric, Rafe, or any of your other self-appointed warriors would—if only to keep you from doing it yourself." He stopped chuckling and added, "But seriously, we wanted to make sure you didn't say something that would bar you from Almack's and such finicking places this Season. Once you're married, it won't matter, but it does now."

Camille lifted her chin. "I may be country bred, but I'm not ignorant as a milch cow, Miles. I don't discuss either pregnancy or digestion in public, and I'm only doing it now because it's just us. And Miss Baynes here," she added belatedly, realizing she hadn't cared what the girl thought of her. "I can behave well in Town, you know."

She refused to acknowledge his laughing apology and sat in offended silence as the coach rolled on. Her silence wouldn't last, and they both knew it. Brothers forgot their sisters had feelings as easily as sisters forgot they had to mind their manners around their brothers, and they both forgot to be angry with each other as quickly as their tempers had flared.

More troublesome were her thoughts about Eric. Although she knew it didn't matter, she was unhappy because of how the wench next to her had stiffened in surprise when she heard that Camille had many suitors. She wasn't insulted so much as hurt. It wasn't impossible that she was so popular—though she granted it must seem improbable.

After all, Camille knew too well that she wasn't lovely. Not like Mama, who'd been a famous beauty and never let anyone forget it. Nothing like her sister-in-law Belle, who was most amazingly beautiful, nor like any of the women Miles's friends had married. Not like any beauty, actually, Camille thought glumly. Because she simply wasn't beautiful or lovely or even handsome, and that was that.

Not that she was a medusa, she thought defensively. She wasn't shrunken or bony, fat or misshapen. She was of average height, and though her shape was sturdy, she had a waist and good breasts—at least, the famous modiste who had designed her London wardrobe had complimented her on them. Camille had thought her head would catch fire from her flaming cheeks, but the improper compliment had been nice to hear. True, she also had hips, which fashionable ladies did not, but hers weren't that wide, at least, she didn't have to turn sideways to get through a doorway. And it was a great pity that a woman's legs were never seen. Because hers were long and as shapely as any gentleman's who was proud of his, as so many men were.

Her brown hair curled, her nose didn't look like a carrot or a mushroom, her mouth was as well shaped as either of her brothers', and they were good-looking fellows. She had good teeth too. Although she regretted her eyes were merely brown, they were said to be her finest feature. But she was not beautiful.

Worse, she wasn't very feminine, at least, not the way admired women in Society were. While she could appreciate fashionable gowns, she only wore them sometimes, because most of the things she enjoyed doing required old clothes. After all, she couldn't go to the stables or a trout stream or romp with her dogs in a fine gown.

The truth was, Camille admitted, she was more at home on a horse than in a parlor. She could dance the night away without treading on any toes, but conversation was another matter, because she was too candid and forthright, and it was the devil of a thing to try to hold her tongue. Worse, she had a hard time listening starry-eyed to nonsense, no matter how handsome the fellow spouting it was. And if politics were being discussed, she had to put her oar in, even though she knew a woman was just supposed to agree with whatever a male was saying.

She wasn't a bluestocking, because she enjoyed sports as much as books. Sometimes her speech was rough, she admitted. But she'd spent more time with boys than girls when she was growing up, because she had more in common with boys. In all, she was definitely an oddity in fashionable London and had to work hard not to embarrass her beloved brother and sister-in-law. It pained her that she might have failed.

"Camille, honestly, I never meant to wound you," Miles suddenly murmured, mistaking her silence for continued insult.

"Oh, I know that," she said, surprised. "I'm brooding about something else."

"Eric will be fine," he reassured her. "Rafe will know what to do."

"Yes, I know," she said. "Thank you."

She felt warmed. She loved her brothers, though neither had been close during her lonely childhood. Miles had been at sea, trying to repair the family fortunes, and Bernard was sent away to school early. Her mama had little time for any of her children; she'd lavished all her love and attention on first one husband and then the other. Even now she was in Bath, hoping to find a third husband. Camille's childhood companions had been her pets, dogs, cats, and horses. They'd given her love in return, but no guidance on how to be feminine.

Still, for a wonder, no man had ever run screaming from her. Just the reverse, she thought smugly. She'd garnered her share of offers even before her brother had made enough money for her formal come-out and had already gotten five decent offers of marriage in this her first Season.

But though the proposals she received were

heartfelt, they were never ones she wanted to hear.

"*I say, Cammie, you and I deal so well together, let's get married, what do you think of that?*"

"*What fun we'll have together Miss Croft. You know horses as well as hazard. In short, you understand a chap and don't kick up a fuss over nonsense like other girls do. And you've got a sense of humor. You don't need the flowers and the poetry. You're sound as a winter apple and sane as you can hold together. I ain't so bad, neither. So will you marry me?*"

"*A fellow doesn't have to worry about minding his manners around you, Camille, he can be himself. I'm tired of doing the pretty for all these Incomparables with their temperamental fits and starts. I want to go home. I've got parents itching for grandchildren, a good income, and a fine estate. How about it? Want to get shackled?*"

Those were the more romantic offers. But she hadn't got even a hint of that from the one man she most wanted to hear it from. He could have asked her any old way. Sometimes, when reality rode her hard, she doubted he ever would. But she wouldn't accept anyone until he at least asked someone. So long as he was free, she was caught.

It could happen, she told herself fiercely. Hadn't all the men who'd offered for her been friends? Anything could come from friendship. She had to believe that.

Eric Ford was everything she wanted. When he

spoke, she had trouble hearing the words because
the deep timbre of his voice thrilled her so much,
and that was a pity, because he was so smart and
she hated to look stupid. When he took her hand,
her heartbeat faltered. It wasn't just because his
hand was so big that it made hers seem dainty, although that was a delight.

She wasn't entirely blind, though. He had his
faults. It was just that she loved them all. He was so
big and blond that it took a moment to realize he
wasn't classically handsome or even spectacularly
so. On closer consideration, it could be seen that
his face was a jot too broad, his nose a bit too
large. In fact, if he'd been a smaller man, he mightn't
have been as eye-catching. But he dominated a
room, and not just because of his size. A woman
felt protected in his shadow, and she could be sure
he'd move that shadow if he thought she wanted to
be in the sunlight. Because he was as kind as he was
bright.

No, she didn't worship him; she just wished she
could marry him. The effect he had on her was tu-
multuous and had been since the day she'd clapped
eyes on him at her brother's wedding. It only inten-
sified when she'd seen him at her first formal appearance in London.

When Miles had come home and restored their
fortunes, he had promised her a Season, complete
with gowns and parties. A Season hadn't tempted
her that much, but oh! Eric did. She'd come to Lon-

don to please her brother and her sister-in-law, but she stayed because that was where Eric was. She'd immediately quizzed her brother about him, trying to be casual so he wouldn't know how his friend had affected her.

"Did you meet him when you were in the navy, Miles?" she'd asked at breakfast the morning after she'd met Eric, sifting in her questions about him along with comments about the ball.

"No, he was army. We met years before, at school."

"Why did you never bring him home?"

"He spent vacations at his own home. He's devoted to his family. They live in the country. His father's a retired colonel. His stepmother, a charming woman, is like his sister, Rafe's wife, Brenna, in looks. It's strange to think of them as brother and sister. She's as dark and exotic as her Welsh mama. They say Eric is as fair as his late mother was. Different as they are, both he and Brenna are handsome as they can stare. But then," he'd added, because of his wife's raised eyebrow, "of course I'd notice that. I have a fondness for exotic ladies. Luckily, I got the best one for myself."

"Why isn't he married? Something deep and dark and secret? Did some exotic female break his heart?" Camille asked with mock melodrama and was instantly sorry. Her sister-in-law, Belle, looked stricken.

Miles reached out and took his wife's hand. "As

a matter of fact, he had a fancy for our Belle," he told Camille, though his eyes never left his wife's. "Who would not? But my luck held. As you can see, she preferred me."

Camille had felt ill. Not only would she not hurt Belle's feelings for the world, she herself was as far from exotic as she could get without leaving the country.

"No, not so," Belle said softly. "Eric never meant it. All that flirtation was merely for effect. In fact, it seems to me that he's always preferred whomever he thought he couldn't get."

Camille had turned her face away, afraid her sudden joy at hearing that Eric hadn't really succumbed to Belle's dark charms might be noticed.

She'd seen him often since then. She made sure of it. "Of course I could go with other men," she'd told Miles and Belle in as pitiable a voice as she could muster, "but I feel most comfortable with Eric, because he's your friend." It was a gamble. They might guess how she really felt. She couldn't help that. But they loved her, and she could trust them to keep their knowledge to themselves.

And so, as a friend, and one of Miles's few unmarried ones, Eric came along with them to the theater and the opera and for walks and drives. Once he'd even invited her for an afternoon all by herself, with her maid for propriety, of course. They'd gone to Astley's Amphitheatre to see performing equestrians and trained horses. Camille hadn't slept the night before and had been light-headed with happiness when she got there—until she'd looked around and seen that it was exactly where a kindly uncle would take a child who was visiting the city.

The more she found out about him, the more he delighted her. His likes and dislikes dovetailed with her own. He was athletic, he liked animals and the countryside. He read books and cared about politics and never minded that she did too. But however he looked and sounded, Camille was no fool, and she'd learned in a hard school. Her mother's second husband had been a handsome, charming villain. Camille knew how to judge a man. She judged Eric one of the best.

She had nothing to offer him but conversation, laughter, friendship, love, and devotion. She knew that. But she dared dream that would be enough, and all the novels she'd read fueled that dream. Now she had her chance.

Eric hadn't found someone else to love in London, at least, not yet. He didn't seem smitten by the recent crop of Incomparables, nor did he have a current mistress. She knew, because she'd asked every gossip she'd met. Little by little, her dream had grown ever more possible—until tonight.

She believed he would survive the beating he'd just received. After all, he was still walking and making sense. Nor was she daunted by his illness— malaria might be dreadful, but she refused to believe he could be felled by it. If it was chronic, it didn't matter. She'd see him through that and more. The question was whether he'd want her to.

Camille stole a glance at the perfect profile of the girl Eric had rescued. She sat gazing out the window at the darkened city, her secrets still as mysterious as she was. Young, beautiful, a tragic victim saved by a gallant stranger. They'd been thrown together by fate. And fate had a way of uniting chance-met lovers, or at least, it did in every novel Camille had read.

She swallowed hard and prayed her own fantasies were more powerful than the fictions she imagined, because she was so weary of fantasy and so very eager for life. And she couldn't see how her life would mean very much without Eric in it.

Chapter 3

There was nothing to do but wait and worry. Camille was good at the worrying, if not the waiting.

"Rafe will not enjoy your pacing a hole in his carpet," her brother commented, looking up at her as she passed by him again. "Would you care to sit? Or else stalk somewhere else? Like at home?"

"Oh, bother!" she said, plunking herself down into a chair. "You wouldn't say that if I were a man. Why is it only the women who are supposed to sit calm and collected when they're not?"

"Do you see me stalking the room like a caged cat?" he answered mildly.

"Well, if you think quarreling like cats will pass

the time better, I'm at your service," Camille said too brightly.

"Camille!" Belle exclaimed with a frown.

"I'm sorry," Camille said, burying her face in her hands.

"It's all right," Miles said gently. "If tearing each other to pieces would help Eric, I'd be glad to let you have at me."

"It won't, I'm sorry," Camille said miserably.

"All's forgiven and forgotten."

"We're all worried," Belle said. "But if pacing makes you feel better, Camille, do it."

"Yes, only do it in the hall," Miles said. "There's a nice long one out there. Mind you don't frighten the footmen. That Rafe mightn't forgive you for. Good help is hard to find."

Camille smiled. The tension in the room lifted. But only for a moment.

The physician had been up there with Eric for nearly an hour, and Rafe and Eric's sister, Brenna, hadn't come down yet.

As soon as Brenna had got word of her brother's condition, she'd fled the ball, along with Belle. They'd gotten to Rafe's house only moments after Eric had been settled in a bed there. Brenna had gone immediately upstairs to join her husband and brother. Moments later the doctor arrived. No word from them had been heard since.

Rafe Dalton, his wife, and infant son lived in a lovely house in a prime part of London, near a green square, around the corner from the park.

The spacious rooms were beautifully furnished with modern furniture in the Egyptian style. High windows let in air and sunlight during the day; new gaslights high on the walls provided a warm aura by night. Those walls were covered with stretched silks in shades of light blue and green—to compliment Lord Dalton's blazing red head, his friends always joked. But not tonight. Now the house was filled with suspense and dread. No one raised a voice lest they miss hearing anyone come down the stair. Conversations stopped and eyes looked up whenever there was a footfall in the outer hall. So far, those footfalls had only been from the servants coming into the salon where the guests sat, with offerings of food and drink.

Miles and Belle passed their time in murmurous conversation.

Camille was too preoccupied with thoughts of Eric to be sociable, and because she hated the fact that she could do nothing, she again got up to pace. She glanced over at a chair near the window. The unknown girl Eric had rescued sat there so quietly it was easy to forget her presence. She'd been given a glass of something fortifying, told that she was safe, and advised to relax. Then she'd been left alone in her shadowy corner. She still sat withdrawn, acting more like a criminal than a victim. Even though she'd been told her story would be heard and help would be forthcoming, Camille belatedly realized the poor creature must be worrying herself to bits, wondering about her fate.

Camille went and perched on a chair next to her. "Do you need anything?" she asked. "I know you told us you hadn't been hurt, but we've been so busy worrying about Eric that we hadn't thought to ask. I mean, do you need to use the convenience? Would you like something to eat? There's cakes and wine, but maybe you want something more substantial?"

The answer came soft and low. "No. Thank you."

"Well . . . Oh, my goodness!" Camille said, as the thought occurred to her. "Is there anyone you'd like us to send word to? We never thought of that!"

Miles and Belle looked up sharply at Camille's exclamation.

The girl seemed to shrink from their stares. "No, thank you," she whispered, drawing the hem of her skirt in. "I don't know anyone in London. That's part of my problem."

"Camille," Miles said sharply, "I told Miss Baynes there would be time for that later. Let her be."

"She wasn't troubling me," the girl said quickly.

Oh, wonderful, Camille thought glumly. *Now the heroine has to protect me from my own brother.* "I wasn't bothering her, Miles," she said defensively. "I just asked if there was anything she needed."

"I suspect she's a bit overwhelmed," Miles said. "Don't worry, Miss Baynes. When Lord Dalton comes downstairs, we'll hear you out and try to resolve your problems. It's just that there's a more pressing one now."

Even her happily married brother was quick to defend the unknown chit, Camille thought glumly. Beauty was obviously as powerful a defense for a woman when she was among gentlemen as it was a danger when she met up with rogues. That was a thing she herself would never know.

She looked at the girl again and felt guilty. Maybe this poor creature didn't know that either. Maybe she'd never been among gentlemen. The girl was watching her, wide-eyed and wary.

"Well, then," Camille asked her, "is there *anything* I can do for you?"

"You're very kind," the girl said softly. "I didn't think that a woman of your class would be that kind to me . . . after the way we met."

"A woman?" Camille blurted, flustered. Surely she and this Nell were of an age? Was she being insulted? She met the slight the same way she'd meet a compliment, straight on, with incredulous honesty.

"Well, first off," she said a shade too heartily, "I'm not a woman exactly. That is, I am. But I'm only just turned twenty-one. You see, a woman is usually someone who has at least a decade more to their name. Well, at least, that's how I . . ." She paused, flustered, as it occurred to her that she really was now legally a woman and not a girl anymore.

"Oh! I'm so sorry. I thought you were older," the girl said.

Camille felt even worse. "Well, there you are," she finally managed to say stupidly. Not wanting to show her hurt, she added, "And our class is like any other, you know. There are good and bad people in it. How old are you?"

Now was it Nell who hesitated? A second later, she said, "Eighteen, my lady."

A beautiful younger girl, Camille thought sadly. "I'm not a lady. My brother's a viscount, but he inherited that title from an uncle. I'm plain Miss Croft, Camille Croft."

Nell nodded. It would be easier chatting up a clamshell, Camille thought. At least then she wouldn't expect an answer. The girl sat straight, her slender hands twisting in her lap, clearly apprehensive, as though she were being threatened. It was odd how one's companions changed one's sense of self, Camille thought. Because if Eric Ford made her feel dainty, this delicate creature made her feel like a hulking brute of a girl—woman, she corrected herself with painful honesty.

"Well," she persisted. "If there's anything you want, you can tell me, you know."

The girl nodded.

"Don't hesitate," Camille added.

"I won't," Nell said, ducking her head. "Thank you."

Camille rose, tired of feeling like an ogre.

Then Rafe Dalton came striding into the room.

"He does well," Rafe reported.

It seemed everyone in the room let out their breath.

"That is to say," he went on, "he has the fever

and the blasted shakes, but I've seen him worse, and so has Brenna. It appears the intensity of the fever is abating over time. But he still suffers from it. Even so, we can expect him to get better faster and for the effects to be less each time he has an attack. As for that other attack . . ." His eyes slid to the corner of the room where Nell sat. "The beating he got dazed him, but no real harm was done. He didn't lose consciousness and is in no way addled. He'll ache, but he'll do. And he's staying on here until he's well enough to fight me with more than words for the right to go home. So don't worry. Now," he said, openly looking at Nell, "let's find out more about it.

"Miss Baynes," he said, turning his full attention on her, "how did you come to be on the street and why did you accost my friend?"

"Rafe!" Miles exclaimed as the girl shrank back. "Couldn't you phrase it a little more gently?"

"Well, I said it as best I could," Rafe said with a scowl.

"That's probably true," Miles said with a smile, "but she doesn't know that."

"Sorry if I frightened you," Rafe told Nell roughly, "but I'm trying to get to the bottom of this."

"Perhaps I might try?" Miles asked.

Rafe shrugged.

Camille gaped. They were not only arguing about whether the girl was insulted but also wondering how to talk to her! Though Nell might well be the innocent heroine of some romantic tale, the girl had, after all, caused Eric's injury, and they had a perfect right to ask her any questions they wanted to. But the men were tiptoeing around her, and these were men who had sometimes worked for the War Office during the late wars, men accustomed to dealing with all sorts of spies and double-dealers. Camille was astonished. She looked at Annabelle and saw her amused smile.

Of course, Camille thought with a twinge of sadness, she was the only one who was surprised. Beautiful women expected that sort of treatment and understood when it was offered to others of their fortunate sisterhood, whatever their social station.

"Miss Baynes, please don't distress yourself," Miles said. "Lord Dalton is a man of few words, and those always to the point. But though his question might not have been phrased delicately, it is the one on our minds. Could you please tell us the details of your meeting tonight with our friend Eric? And don't worry. We aren't here to condemn you, only to get at the truth. The damage to our friend is done. We only want to prevent more."

That was fairly said, Camille thought, and waited for the girl to speak.

"I am so ashamed," Nell said. She ducked her head, and when she looked up again, there were tears tracing down her lovely pale cheeks.

"If you're in any pain," Miles said quickly, "we can go on at some later time."

"No, no," Nell said with a weak and wavering smile. "Nothing hurts but my feelings, and that isn't your fault. You see, I came to London only a week ago—only a week!" she murmured, as though in disbelief. She straightened, locked her fingers together, and held her hands in her lap, like a little girl giving a recital in class.

"I was born and raised near Eastwell, in Kent."

Belle interrupted, "That's where I heard the name! I thought it sounded familiar. Are you related to the Baynes of Rye? Viscount Baynes was a schoolmate of my father's."

Nell shook her head. "I can't say. My father didn't see eye to eye with his family after his marriage to my mama, so I don't know any of them. And now Papa can't tell me, as he's dead. Nor can my mama, though she's alive but not—in her right mind. She became ill a few years ago and is getting feebler every day. That's why I came to London. When she no longer recognized me, I knew it was time to seek help from any relatives I could find." She looked down, as though shamed.

It was remarkable how her long lashes formed fans on her pale cheeks when she did that, Camille thought, as fascinated as she was envious that the girl's sorrow became her so well.

"My mother didn't have a big family," Nell went on. "At least, I don't think so. I never saw them any more than I did my father's. Her side were prosperous farmers, but his were of higher rank. Neither married where their families wished, so they were estranged. Papa started a mercantile business, but when he died, it was sold. We lived on the profit, but when Mama began to fail, I went through her dower chest and found letters. She had an older sister, who lived in London, and they'd corresponded years ago. I thought if I came in person I could find her and appeal to her for Mama's sake. She needs more care than I can give her now.

"I arranged for a neighbor to look after Mama and took the mail coach to London. When I arrived a week ago," she said, looking up, eyes wide, bright with fear, "I was met at the coaching stop by the kindest little old woman. I thought my aunt had sent her, because she seemed to know so much about me."

Miles frowned. Rafe nodded. Belle sighed.

"Yes, I was a greenhead," Nell admitted sadly. "She asked as many questions as she answered, but I didn't see that, not then. She said she'd take me to my aunt, but instead she took me to a terrible place—a brothel! She locked me in a room and wouldn't let me out, although I cried and screamed."

"What is the name of the place?" Miles asked.

Nell shook her head. "I don't know. I saw the women and heard men coming and going, but I never heard any names. They brought me food, but I wouldn't eat. I only drank from the wash water they brought me too. I had sense and remembered things I'd heard, if too late."

"Good thing," Rafe said darkly.

"Yes," Nell agreed, looking up again. "I was afraid they'd drug me."

"They likely would have," Miles agreed.

Nell bowed her head and went on. "They took away my traveling bag and left me only the clothes I stand up in. I begged to be let go, but no one listened. I prayed the rest of the time. And then, just last night, when the old woman who brought me dinner said I'd better eat fast because they were going to send me company that night—I knew I had to do something. So when she turned her back to set her tray down, I pushed my handkerchief into the doorjamb so it wouldn't close tight. After she left, I drew the door open, slipped out, and made my way down the stair.

"I got out through the back door, but I didn't get far. The streets were so dark and frightening, I started running. I supposed I shouldn't have done that, because it drew attention. That's how I met that man you saw tonight. He asked if he could help me, and I told him my whole story. I said my aunt would reward him if he took me to her. But he said I'd be a better reward.

"He dragged me with him along the street and said he'd kill me if I fought or screeched for help. The next thing I knew he was offering me to your friend. I didn't know that's what he meant to do, but I hoped that would be my salvation. Your friend looked so strong, and he appeared to be a good man . . . one who wouldn't need to buy . . .

company. You know the rest. Ah, but it's been such a terrible time!"

The room was quiet.

Yes, Camille thought with sinking heart, there sat a bona fide heroine.

"We can find the aunt," Rafe finally announced to the room, "but the bast—villain who attacked Eric is likely long gone."

"Yes," Miles said thoughtfully. "He probably wasn't in the trade, only an opportunist. As for the madam, there are too many like her in London. If the girl never heard a name, we'll never find that house."

"So," Rafe said abruptly, "what do we do with her until we locate this aunt?"

"I don't want to be any trouble!" Nell cried.

"Can't see how you won't be," he said in his usual abrupt way. "We're certainly not going to turn you out on the street again. No insult meant, but you wouldn't have a chance here in London by yourself. Make no mistake, if we let you out, you'll only get into trouble again. Can't put you in a hotel either, you're too pretty for your own good, and you haven't got the sense . . ."

"She can stay here with us," his wife interrupted quickly.

"That she cannot!" Belle exclaimed. "With Eric so ill? And you with an infant to tend? You already have your hands full, thank you. We'll take her."

"With you? Not likely!" Brenna protested. "You

don't feel at all the thing in the mornings as it is."

Belle laughed. "The mornings are soon over, and besides, the girl won't be my responsibility. The housekeeper can look after her."

Camille felt terrible. They were arguing over the girl as if she were no more than a servant. But, she realized, that was after all almost the case. An impoverished country girl, however lovely, was lucky to have found herself even in the company of ladies and gentlemen of wealth and breeding, let alone those willing to take her under their wing. It didn't matter that she'd been badly used; uncountable women of London were misused every day of their lives. So if any of these noble persons let an unknown commoner share a bed in the attic with the servants or a pallet on the floor in their kitchen, it would be both kind and generous of them.

But Nell was a heroine, and her bravery should be rewarded. And she might after all be of good family.

But men noticed her, and so if she stayed in his vicinity, Eric certainly would.

Camille always faced head on whatever frightened her. Eric had seen beautiful women before, and he was a gentleman, not a seducer.

But since he didn't have either a title or a toplofty family, he could also marry anywhere he chose. And beauty was a powerful lure.

That frightened Camille. So she knew what she had to do. And if a pretty face meant so much to him, it would be better for her to know it now.

"Yes. Let her stay with us," Camille declared. "I'll look after her."

"You?" Miles asked, with a grin. "Aren't you too occupied with conquering all London?"

"I've already done that," she said, grinning back at him. "So why not? After all, everyone else has something important to do. Brenna has Eric to take care of as well as an infant to tend. Belle has to be careful of herself. You and Rafe and your friends from the War Office will doubtless find Nell's aunt. Everyone else has responsibilities," Camille said. "And so I'm the only possible one to look after Miss Baynes and show her the proper way to get on here in the polite world of London."

As she hoped, they began to laugh.

She just wished she felt like joining in.

Chapter 4

Morning sunlight edged in silver the margins of the draperies covering the windows, but the bedroom remained dim. Still, it was light enough to wake the man in the tall-canopied bed. At first, the only evidence was the change in his breathing. Then he cracked one eye open, then another. He looked around. His chest rose and fell in a deep sigh of relief.

He was safe . . . and comfortable, he realized.

Eric lay quietly and took stock of his body. The tremors had stopped. His head didn't ache. He felt cool. The fever was gone. It was over for now, at least. But this wasn't his bedchamber. He slowly remembered how often he'd seen Brenna's and Rafe's worried faces through the wavering mists that clouded his perceptions when he woke between the damnable bouts of shivering and burning. So. This must be their house.

Eric grimaced. It was painful to know he was a bother to his sister and his best friend again. Still, that sort of pain was easier to bear than what he'd just been through. He raised himself to his elbows and tried to look out a window. He couldn't see much but their pale outlines. Past dawn, he'd guess, and past time to get out of bed and go home.

He sat up, grimacing at the effort, and swung his legs out from under the coverlets. Then he sat on the side of the high bed, his head whirling, waiting to be sure he could step down. He'd learned the hard way that getting up and around after one of his attacks wasn't as simple as he wanted it to be. How long had he been here? He ran a hand over his chin and found it smooth-shaven. He grimaced again. He was blond, but his beard grew in quickly. And his sister wasn't a fusspot. If Brenna had sent for a valet to have him shaved, it meant he'd been here long enough to grow a significant beard. His spirits sank.

His last attack a few months ago had been brief, and he'd recovered from it quickly. He'd begun to hope—and now those hopes were dashed. Being stricken for a long siege meant that coming home to the cooler climate of England hadn't changed things. He was still firmly in the grip of his disease. The doctors on both sides of the ocean had agreed on one thing besides quinine for the fever and shakes.

They'd all said there was no way to know the course of malarial fever any more than they knew a cure for it. The disease might slowly lift, or it could grow slowly worse.

Eric hung his head. His feeling better now meant nothing. He still didn't know what would happen next time, or when that next time would be. Even more worrisome, how long could he keep suffering these attacks before they did worse things to him?

"Lie down before you fall down," a familiar voice said with irritation "Can't leave you alone for five minutes without you getting into trouble."

"Hello, Rafe," Eric said without looking up. He lifted a hand. "Don't worry, I won't fall. I'm feeling better. The best thing for me is to start moving again before my muscles turn into something like those damnable milksops you were spooning into me. I remember it now. Gads, Bren! You wouldn't dare if I were half in my right mind. Pretty bad this time, was it?"

"How did you know I was here?" his startled sister asked as she came through the door behind her husband.

Eric laughed. "Tick and tock, that's you and Rafe. If I hear one, I know it won't be long before I hear the other."

"Yes, wonderful, isn't it? But you weren't sick that long this time, Eric," she said eagerly. "Only a few days."

His head shot up. "Truly? How many?"

"Don't bark at her," Rafe said. "She was out of

her mind with worry. But yes, only five days, old lad. Much better than the last time you stayed with me."

Eric grinned. "That time I almost didn't wake up, but that was over a year ago. Only five days? That's no time at all."

"Even better than last July," Brenna said happily, "and since that only lasted a little over a week, we didn't even tell Mother or Father."

"Better than in September too," Eric said, doing rapid calculations, "This attack is the best one yet. Though it didn't feel like that when I had it, I promise you."

"When in September?" his sister asked. "I thought you hadn't had an episode since July. You had another and you didn't send for me?"

Eric's cheeks grew ruddy. "Well, no. I'm not even sure it was an attack of the fever, you see, it was over so fast."

"Oh, Eric," she sighed. "We had an agreement. You gave your word."

He sat up straighter. "That we did not. My word is my bond. I just said that if I got sick again I'd send if I needed you, and I didn't. I had Watkins, who's more than a valet. He's an old army man, very capable of taking care of me. Speaking of which, if it was only five days, why did you have me shaved?"

"Watkins," she said. "He came at once. He's been staying here. He never left you for a moment, but this morning he saw you were without fever at last, so he went back to your house to pick out some clothes for you. Well, he didn't leave so much as we sent him. He needed some fresh air himself. We promised we'd look in while he was gone. He'll be delighted when he—*Oh!* That time last summer when you sent word you were going to visit an old friend—that was when you were sick again?"

Eric shrugged. "So I was visited by an old enemy instead. It hardly matters. I told Watkins that if it lasted above a week, you should be told about it. It didn't, so we didn't. No sense in scaring you for no good reason."

She started to argue but stopped when she saw his expression. He was smiling almost shyly. His bout of fever had left his cheekbones more pronounced, and he was still very pale. But his face looked younger, joyous and full of hope. She realized she hadn't seen him like that in a very long time, not since they'd come home from India. He'd almost died on that voyage. Rafe's unexpected hospitality might have been the only thing that saved him then. It had certainly saved her, for staying with Rafe had been the beginning of their life together.

Eric had healed in body since and also had seemed to return to his former self. He'd gone about his normal life in the country with their parents as well as his social life in London with no apparent problems. But she hadn't seen him this happy in a long time. Brenna smiled back at him. It was impossible not to. She finally realized what had been missing since he'd come home. His buoyant spirit had been gone. She loved her grave, responsible older brother but had never known how much she missed the blithe and merry boy she'd known until just now, when she got a glimpse of him again.

"Only five days," he said with wonder. "It might be, it just may be that the damned thing is loosing its grip! No, don't shoot off any cannons," he said with a wave of a hand. "It's not time to celebrate yet. The doctors said there'd be many a false start and stop." He looked at her, his eyes glowing. "But Bren, it *is* lasting less time each time—so far."

"It will be gone by spring," Rafe said decisively. "Then you'll have to find another reason to get the ladies dancing attendance on you. As to that, what should we do with the chit you saved?"

"The chit?" Eric echoed in puzzlement. Then his eyes opened wider. "The whore—the woman—that bloody—that blasted ponce tried to sell me?"

"Oh, don't start tying yourself into knots on my account," Brenna said with a laugh. "Not only am I the daughter *and* the sister of an army man, I married one. Remember?"

Rafe grinned. "No one talks warm around you, my girl, and we aren't starting to now. Wouldn't want the babe to hear," he added, with a fond glance at her midsection. Since the fashion was for high-waisted gowns, only a gentle swelling beneath her breasts hinted at what Rafe was smiling at.

Eric ignored them, his brow furrowed. "The woman? She's still here?"

"No," Rafe said. "She's bivouacked with Camille."

Eric's expression grew grave. "*Camille?* That will never do. What could you have been thinking of?"

"Wasn't us," Rafe protested. "Camille leapt in like a mama cat whose kit was threatened, volunteering to take her in. Volunteering? Insisting! Try to get that filly's head turned when she's got the bit in her mouth."

Eric's grin was warm and reminiscent though his words were not. "That girl's altogether too headstrong."

"You encourage her," his sister said, and paused before she added, "You could do more for her, you know."

"For her or to her?" Eric asked, cocking an eyebrow. "Are you matchmaking, Bren?"

"I just thought since Camille obviously—or rather," she stammered, "seems to—care for you, that—"

"That an older man with a debilitating disease that can strike him down at any moment should encourage an impulsive girl who's simply feeling the effects of first infatuation?" Eric's smile was twisted. "I don't think so, Bren. I like Cammie too well for that. And I like her too much to be easy about her landing herself with an unknown from the gutter."

"You risked your neck for her yourself," Rafe reminded him.

"You'd have done the same," Eric said. "She was hopelessly outranked and appealed to me for help. Whether she was a nun or a tart, I had to step in."

"Don't judge without facts, Eric," Brenna warned him with a significant look. "You know how wrong that can be."

"Thing is," Rafe told Eric, "there's no saying the girl's guilty of anything but being a country miss in the big city. Can't say she's an innocent, mind. But can't say she's a harlot either. She tells quite a tale anyway. I haven't been able to investigate it yet, what with you landed on me," he added with a smile. "But Drum's on it, so we'll know more soon enough."

"We'll know more even sooner if I can be up and at it," Eric said, and stepped down from the bed. Rafe started toward him. "And I can!" Eric said triumphantly, as he stood tall.

"You can," Rafe admitted. "But you won't until the doctor tells you so."

"Want to take it to the court of fives?" Eric asked, balling his fists and taking a boxer's stance.

They crouched and faced each other, holding their fists high.

Brenna laughed. Rafe looked dangerous even against her mighty brother, especially since that mighty brother was wearing a nightshirt that stopped at his calves. She put her hands on her hips.

"If you take one step out the door without the doctor's permission, I'll mill you down myself, Eric. It was you who showed me how, when I first came to you, crying because a bully hit me. Remember? You said any woman can protect herself against any man, the same way that an axe that only weighs a few pounds can fell the tallest tree. And I've practiced since."

"You wouldn't do that to your own brother," Eric said, pretending to be terrified.

"I would if I had to, but I doubt I will. I don't think you'll leave us now, unless of course you're vainer than I remember and want to show your lovely legs to the world."

Eric glanced down at his naked legs and grinned. "Not a thing to be ashamed of," he said staunchly, wriggling his toes to prove his point.

"Maybe not. But can you say the same thing about your other nether parts?"

He looked puzzled.

"We *do* have all your clothes," she reminded him.

He stopped grinning as Rafe began to laugh.

"We can visit him in three days!" Camille said, turning from her mirror as Nell entered her room. "That's when he goes home."

"Are you sure?" Nell asked. "Will it be safe for us to visit him? He does suffer from a fever."

"Yes, but it's the malaria. He caught it in India. You can't get it from people, only from hot places

near swamps and the evil miasmas that flourish
there. There's none of that in London."

"Then I'd like to go and thank him. It's only . . .
I'm grateful for the clothes you've lent me, but it
would be nice to have my own bag back. My clothing is in it."

"Well, not much hope of that," Camille said,
turning back to look at herself and frowning at the
bonnet she had on her head. "Miles said it's probably been sold three times over by now. We'll get
you other clothes, never fear. Speaking of which,
what do you think of this bonnet? Do I look as
though I'm wearing a chicken on my head? No,
don't say it. Blast! Why do bonnets have to be covered with poultry feathers? They're fine in pillows,
but why have them on hats? Maybe I'd look good
to a rooster but not anyone else."

She snatched off the bonnet, gave it to her maid,
and took another from her. "And this one. Ugh. Pa-
per roses. I'd look as if I was wearing a garden. In
November? Oh, damnation!" she cried, flinging it
on her bed. "Why do I have to wear a hat at all? It's
not like we're meeting in a park. I'll be inside when
we visit."

Nell quickly stepped to the bed and scooped up
the bonnet. "It's bad luck to put a hat on the bed,"
she said.

The maid nodded agreement.

"It will be worse luck if I can't find something to
wear on my head," Camille said. "I can't go hatless
but I want to look . . ." She paused, suddenly self-

conscious. Useless to say that she wanted to look especially good for Eric, at least to Nell. She wouldn't understand. The girl would look fine whatever she clapped on her head. Anyway, she didn't want Nell knowing how much Eric's opinion meant to her. Bad enough it was possible that Miles and Belle had twigged to how she felt. Worse if this lovely little creature knew it. Camille could deal with anything, but pity was unendurable.

But Eric himself didn't pity her. He really enjoyed her company, she knew that. Whether he'd ever see her as more than a jolly companion was the problem. Well, Camille thought philosophically, time would tell. And now she had that time!

"Lady Belle picked this one herself," her maid said, offering Camille another bonnet. "Remember? A variation of the coalscuttle style, she said. You liked it when you bought it."

Camille plopped the bonnet on her head and groaned. "Belle could make me buy anything. But it makes me look like a mushroom."

"That's because you have all your hair hidden under it," her sister-in-law said as she walked into the room. "Tug some of your lovely curls out and let them frame your face." She came to Camille and deftly teased some ringlets out from beneath her bonnet. "There. Charming. What's the sense in having such abundant curls if you don't show them? Ladies spend hours with curling irons, and you have curls naturally and hide them. Folly. Now look," she said with satisfaction. "Not a mushroom anymore but a pretty young woman instead. The bonnet's charming. The gown," she said, narrowing her eyes, "is not."

"I wasn't sure I was going to wear this one," Camille said.

"Good. You shouldn't. The blue with the little pink rosebuds that we had sent the other week," Belle told the maidservant.

"That one? I'll freeze!" Camille protested. "It's so thin!"

"Eric heats his rooms," Belle said calmly. "Anyway, I thought you were made of sterner stuff."

"I am!"

"Good. It's just that we don't always want the gentlemen to think of that. Ah, yes," she said, as she saw the gown the maid took from the wardrobe. "Perfect. Try it on. Let me see."

"Such a fuss about a friendly visit, you'd think I was going to see the king," Camille grumbled, but let her maid help her change gowns.

Then she stared at herself in the glass again. The gown's low neck gave it sophistication, and the long, close-fitted sleeves were elegant. The soft blue wool felt as good as it looked, and the artful way the rosebuds marched up and down the line of the frock gave her figure definition. Her shape wasn't really that sinuous, but the gown made her look almost like a siren.

"Yes," she said with immense satisfaction. "Thank you, Belle! I don't know what I'd do without you."

Her sister-in-law's pleasure in the simple compliment gave her face a peachy blush, making her even lovelier. With her raven curls and alabaster skin, Annabelle was a famous beauty. And while people might whisper she had a history of being vain and toplofty, Camille had never found her to be either.

"Now," Camille said, turning her attention to Nell, "what do we have for Nell to wear?"

There was a sudden silence.

They all looked at the lost girl they'd taken in. Nell had pulled her smooth inky hair up high, so it showed off the smooth camellia-colored skin on her long neck and pointed up the beauty of her face. The gown Camille had given her was a bit short, but that only showed glimpses of her shapely ankles. The plain cream-colored gown didn't look at all simple on her, not with her elegant, high-breasted, slim figure. She looked cool and refined and yet sensational. That, Camille thought with a curious pang, was really what sinuous meant.

The silence threatened to become rudeness. Camille spoke up quickly. "Nell and I are different shapes and sizes. That gown is fine for about the house, but she needs another for going out."

Annabelle's lovely face suddenly went still. The maidservant pursed her lips. Though they didn't know it, they were of a single mind: a strange penniless female of unknown origins did not merit being dressed as well as her betters.

But if Camille didn't know, it seemed Nell herself did.

"You mustn't worry about me," Nell said in her soft voice. "I'm pleased to have anything to wear at all. I'm lucky to be here to wear it."

Belle's smile was forced. "No, Camille's right. We can't have you going about with your legs showing. I'll have another gown altered for you, either one of Camille's or one my own. My maid is a marvel with a needle and a flatiron. A hem can be let out in no time."

"But I thought Nell could come with us to walk the dogs now," Camille said. "It's so early no one will see us."

Their daily jaunt with Camille's pair of dogs was a tradition with them, stemming from when Belle had been a newlywed staying at Miles's country home.

"Early or late, she can't go out with her ankles showing," Belle said briskly. "She'll have to wait until we have something decent for her to wear."

"Please don't trouble yourself," Nell said. "It's kind of you to care, Miss Croft, but I'm a bit afraid of dogs."

"Do you still want to go?" Belle asked Camille.

"Of course!" Camille said.

"Then give me a moment to change my gown."

Camille looked puzzled. Belle's delicate complexion grew rosy. "This one isn't warm enough," she explained. "I don't know what I was thinking when I put it on. I'll be back soon," she said, and left the room, her skirts swirling against her legs as she hurried out.

Belle stormed down the hall toward her own chamber and almost walked straight into her husband. That pleased him very much. He folded her in his arms and whispered, "So eager? But alas, we have to wait until dark. That's the only time we can decently be alone. Another reason to get Cammie married off," he breathed as he nuzzled her ear.

"We never will if she keeps dragging strays home," his lady said angrily.

He could feel the tension in her body and reluctantly let her go. Holding her at arm's length, he tried to look into her eyes. "What is it? What's got you so upset?"

"That—that woman we brought to our house."

He became alert. "She's been caught stealing?"

"No. Except perhaps . . . Oh, Miles, do you know, I had to leave the room just now I was so angry. Camille's taken her so to heart she even invited her along on our morning walk. And I was jealous! Nonsensical, isn't it?" She sighed. "Will I ever learn to share? But I'm trying."

"Oh, good. That means I can take another wife?" he asked, and was rewarded by a look of mock outrage and then a giggle. "Don't worry," he said softly. "Camille loves you above all others, as I do. But she does take in birds and dogs, starving cats, and now she's graduated to forlorn humans. It was only a matter of time."

"I know. But this girl . . . Miles, I have the worst feeling about her. I cannot trust her. Yes, the chit is quiet-spoken and we haven't found a thing against her. And she may be well born. That's the only reason I finally took her in, aside from the fact that I saw Camille wanted to. But it's one thing to house the creature, another to take her to the bosom of the family as Camille's done. We can't board her in the attics, but we can't invite her to parties or teas either, because though she might actually turn out to be related to *somebody*, until we know, we can't foist an unknown on Society, and even Camille knows that.

"But that means Camille won't go out, because she doesn't want to hurt the girl's feelings. And she plans to take this Nell with us when we visit Eric! The girl says she wants to thank him. I know that sounds proper, but . . . what man wouldn't be interested in such a beautiful little baggage? And your daft sister is dangling her in front of Eric like—like a shiny prize."

"And you think Eric will grab at it? I didn't know you thought so little of him."

"No, I don't—but oh! I don't know. Why tempt him?"

"London is full of temptations," he said, putting his arms around her again. "A man who cares for one woman won't be tempted by any other. Just look at me if you doubt that."

"But we're married. And Eric is not. And I'm not even sure if he thinks about Camille that way. You know, I believe that's why Camille is fostering that girl, whether she fully knows it or not. She wants to give him every chance to hurt her now, before she lets her desires entirely run away with her good sense."

"No," he said thoughtfully. "I think it's just her way. She never retreats from fear. If there was a noise in the night, she'd go downstairs with a candle—and a cricket bat." He chuckled. "She'd rather seek out danger and defeat it than huddle under the bedcovers. Giving Eric enough rope to hang herself may be part of it, but I don't think it's all a test for him. Much of it is just her way. Strays gravitate to her, and she treats them royally."

His wife remained silent. But something about the girl rankled Belle. It wasn't just because she was a real beauty. Perhaps that was *part* of it, she'd silently admitted when she'd capitulated and given Nell a room she'd offer any guest. After all, she'd always hated competition. Even now, secure as she was, she had to guard against that base emotion. Still, her worst fears were for Camille, her devotion to her sister-in-law surprising even herself. She didn't want to see her hurt. She herself had once been a sort of stray, and Camille had warmly welcomed her into Miles's family. In doing so, she taught her how wonderful the friendship of another female could be.

"Camille's generous to a fault," Miles said. "She's also brave, honest, and kind. Those are just some of the things that make her the remarkable woman she is."

Belle looked up at him. "Will Eric know? Will he appreciate it?"

"If he doesn't, then she's better off knowing that now, isn't she?"

"But why does she fling temptation in his face?" she asked peevishly.

"The girl lives here. Am I tempted?"

She grew still. "Are you?"

He answered her promptly and exactly as she would wish: fully, convincingly, and at length, and with his lips—although he never spoke a word.

Chapter 5

The first thing Camille saw was that illness became Eric. His face was a bit gaunt and he seemed tired, but his newly lean face made his cheekbones seem even higher and the weariness made him look seductive. In any case, he looked even more handsome than ever to her. *The wretch!* she thought, eying him, *he'd look wonderful on his deathbed.*

She grew a tremulous smile when he stood as they entered his parlor. As an invalid, he was permitted to dress comfortably for their visit, and he had taken advantage of it. His honey-colored hair was a little overlong but neatly brushed, and he was clean-shaven. He wore no jacket, waistcoat, or neckcloth, only a dark-gold patterned dressing robe over a white shirt and tan breeches. Most gentlemen of the *ton* used their clothing to emphasize their figure or their rank. Eric didn't need to do either. He didn't require a neckcloth to hold up his proud head or a carefully tailored jacket to nip in his trim waist or padding to emphasis his wide shoulders. Freed from the strict rules of fashionable gentlemen's clothing, he looked clean and correct and incredibly virile.

"My lady," he said, as he bowed over Belle's hand, greeting her with easy grace. Then he turned his attention to Camille and grinned at her. Finally, he noticed Nell. He stared. Camille's smile slipped as he kept staring.

"I see you are well," he told Nell gravely as he took her hand.

Anyone could see that, Camille thought, with a funny feeling in her stomach. After all, Nell wore one of Belle's old frocks made over until it looked like new. The cast-off gown showed off Nell's figure and its pink color gave her face a lovely glow. Her hair was done simply under the bonnet Camille had discarded, the one with feathers. Now Camille wished she'd never given it up. She also wished Eric would release Nell's hand. Just looking at that big, strong tanned hand swallowing up Nell's was like watching the two of them making love, she thought, suddenly stricken as well as sickened by the thought.

"I am well, thanks to you," Nell said softly, gazing into his eyes and then shuttering her own with her long dark lashes.

Thanks to me too! Camille silently shouted. *Unworthy,* she chided herself. *Fool for harboring her,* another, more practical voice in her head said scornfully, *and folly to have brought her here. But if he's never meant for me, I have to know it,* she argued. *That doesn't mean you have to give him your rival,* she answered herself.

But she couldn't be that petty. After all, if she and Eric had a future outside her dreams, she didn't want to look back one day and wonder what would have happened if she hadn't turned away the girl he rescued. Would she always wonder if he'd have preferred Nell? She had to know. *Well, now you do,* she thought in despair.

"Cammie?" Eric said again, because she hadn't taken the chair he'd just offered her. "Aren't you going to sit? Beg pardon, miss. Are you there? I thought I was the one who got knocked in the head."

"As to that," she said quickly, recovering herself, "how's your poor head?" She was so eager to know that she kept her eyes on his face and found a place to sit only by putting her hand on the seat of the chair behind her and following it down without looking, only belatedly aware that a lady was supposed to settle into her chair like a butterfly on a rose petal.

Eric didn't seem to notice. He smiled at her. "My head?" he said as he sank to his chair again. "It's hard enough on the outside. It was the fever that leveled me, not the villain. I'm better now. In fact, I'd have been out riding with you already if it weren't for Rafe's setting a watch on me. He let me come home, but he's in league with my valet. One misstep, and Brenna would know it and lecture me to death. I'd rather die of fever. Which I won't!" he said hastily, when he saw her expression. "In fact, the evidence is mounting. It seems that though I keep getting these attacks, I'm also getting better every day I stay here in England. So how was your ride this morning?"

"Fine," Camille said, and then, greatly daring for someone who tried to never let him see how much he meant to her, she added, "but dam— deucedly lonely."

"Terribly," Belle corrected her in a weary whisper, "or *mightily.*"

"Aye. Mightily lonely," Camille agreed with a vigorous nod.

Eric grinned. "But why?"

"Well, you know Belle doesn't care to ride," Camille said.

"What about your guest?" he asked. "Don't you care to ride, Miss . . . Baynes, is it? We really were never properly introduced."

"There was hardly time," Nell said with a tilted smile. "No, I never learned to ride, Lieutenant Ford. I lived in the country, but in a little town, not on a farm."

"No, not 'lieutenant' if you please. I'm done with the army now, or at least it's done with me," Eric said ruefully. "The war's done, and my fever put paid to that career. So a mere 'mister' will do."

"There's nothing mere about you," Camille said staunchly.

Belle stopped herself before she actually rolled her eyes, and suppressed a small sigh of frustration. She'd seen spaniels keep their adoration for their master more of a secret.

"Yes," Eric said, deliberately misunderstanding her, "I am much too big for a mere anything."

"And your house!" Camille said in awe, looking around. "It's just—well, it's not at all what I expected. It's lavish, elegant, and—"

"And not what you'd think to find me in?" he asked.

"Right," Camille said.

This time Belle's sigh was heavy enough to send a toy sailboat across the pond in the park across the street.

"I didn't mean anything rude by that," Camille added, looking at Belle. She hesitated as she considered how to answer his question more tactfully. His lodgings were in a house in a fine district opposite the park. She gazed around the splendidly furnished salon, taking in the tasteful display of antique figurines on the rose marble mantel over the hearth, the peach-colored stretched-silk walls hung with exquisite etchings, the celestial-blue ceiling with gold carvings at its margins, the priceless vase filled with hothouse roses on a fine French table by the window.

Eric was a big, masculine man. She'd expected huge old chairs and stuffed elk heads, tiger skins on the floor, sporting prints and stray riding crops strewn about—the clutter of a man home from the hunt. This room was more of a connoisseur's retreat, artful and filled with rare prizes. While not feminine, it was delicate and subtle in style. And yet it suited him perfectly.

"No," she finally said flatly. "It isn't what I expected at all. But it's grand. Who are you leasing the place from?"

"You think I'm that much of a barbarian?" he asked, one brow raised. "But even the Vikings carried home loot they admired." She looked so confused that he relented. "I'm not a tenant," he explained. "This is actually my house. Drum advised me to buy a place when I came back to London. I'm grateful to him for it. Now my lodgings are not only for comfort, they're an investment. Rental money goes out, never to return. When you own your home, you're able to live not only with, but also in, your assets. I had it decked out the way I always wanted a house to look. The manor is stuffed with my father's mementos. These keepsakes are mine, picked up on my travels. I got something besides my malarial fever when I was abroad, you know. I got an education in the way other people live and a taste for some of the finer things. Some of my curios are ancient and worth a mint, some only cost pennies, but they remind me of where I've been."

"I'm sorry," Camille said, "I didn't realize—"

"No need," he said quickly. "I surprised myself when I bought and fitted out this place."

Camille nodded, embarrassed by the sudden look Nell gave her. Because when Nell had asked about Eric in idle conversation, Camille had told the girl that though he was the only son, his father was just a retired army officer, and so he wasn't particularly wealthy. She hadn't lied, she just hadn't known. She realized now that there were many things about Eric that she didn't know.

"It's very lovely," Nell said.

Camille was grateful to her for saying something to break the awkward moment.

"And I'm glad I had the chance to visit," Nell went on, "because I finally have a chance to say thank you, Lieutenant—I mean, Mr. Ford."

"You're welcome, Miss Baynes."

She cast her gaze down again. "But please call me Nell."

"Well, Nell." He paused to grin and went on, "You've a euphonious name as well as a pretty face. You can make a poet of any man."

Camille stopped breathing until he continued more heartily, "At any rate, Nell, we hope to have good news for you soon."

Her gaze flashed to his.

"Drum, Rafe, and other friends of ours in high and low places are searching for your relatives. There is no one of that name at the address you provided. Nor has there been, so far as anyone knows."

Nell's eyes grew wide. "But that's the last address I had!" she cried. "It was from some time ago, because it's been a while since Mama could write, as I said. Oh, my! So that's why they never answered my letter saying I was coming to London. I decided not to wait a moment longer and got on the coach for London. Oh, I've been so foolish, but what else was I to do?"

"Don't be distressed," Eric said quickly. "It means nothing. The address was that of a hotel. Many people come to London and stop there before moving on to more permanent lodgings. That's what they must have done. There's no forwarding address, but if they'd left a while ago, it would have been discarded. Don't worry. If your aunt and cousins are to be found, we'll find them."

Nell sat back and fell silent.

"In the meanwhile," Eric said, "I believe you're well situated."

"I am," Nell said shyly. "Everyone's been so kind to me. But you have every right to dislike me. If it weren't for me, you wouldn't have been hurt."

He laughed. "The fever was already on me when you appeared on the scene. The dunt on the head was merely a finishing touch. If it hadn't been for that fever I'd have been able to stop that lout who had you in his clutches even if he'd butted me a dozen times. We're looking for him too," he added more seriously. "I'll be able to take an active role any day now. Speaking of active . . ." His expression brightened. "What do you say we all go riding when I can? In my new carriage," he added, before Camille could decide who he wanted to answer him. "That way we all can get out and enjoy the day, even the horse haters among us. What do you say?"

"Your carriage is for two," Belle reminded him acidly. "Have you bought another? If not, how are you going to choose between us? Or are you planning on us competing for your charms?"

"My new carriage is also a phaeton, that's true. But I can rent a nice big lumbering coach for us, my dear Belle, complete with footmen *and* foot warmers. We can all take a turn around the park, top down if the weather permits. I certainly could use the air and the diversion. And your charming company, of course. Miles too, if he insists," he added with a grin. "It would do me a world of good. Be charitable. What do you say?"

"First let's hear what the doctor says," Belle answered primly.

"He'll probably say I can run around the park if I want. Aha!" Eric exclaimed as a servant came in with a laden tray. "Look here! You get cakes and wine as well as tea, and all I've gotten are gruel and lectures. You must visit more often. Will you

pour?" he asked Belle. "And tell me everything I've
missed while I've been out of combat?"

"What can I tell you?" she asked. "I'm sure you
see the newspapers and broadsheets. And I know
this place is filled with your friends every night,
because my Miles is often among them. At least,
he had better be, since that's what he's been telling
me."

"As if he'd dare lie to you," Eric scoffed, and
then, seeing the militant look in her eyes, flung up a
hand and, laughing, added, "Don't throw anything
at me, I'm an invalid! I was only joking. The man is
your slave, and you know it. But I meant the things
that don't go into the papers. The libelous stuff I've
missed because I can't leave these rooms of mine.
Things my friends don't tell me because they don't
know them. How can they? They've been here with
me every night, as you say. You know the type of
thing I mean, Belle—what's being said at dinners
and dances."

"You mean gossip. You're bamming me, my
dear sir," Belle said with a smile. "You don't care
for gossip."

He put a hand on his heart. "I do, if you're
telling it to me."

"Have a care," she warned him, her eyes
sparkling, "Miles is a very jealous man."

"He has reason. He's a very lucky one," Eric answered gallantly.

They both grinned. So did Camille. They were

playing at flirtation. Camille enjoyed their word-play as much as they did.

But the looks Eric kept shooting at Nell, where she sat silent and yet always aware, didn't amuse Camille at all.

Chapter 6

Belle found Camille in her room two mornings later, sitting in the window seat with a book in her lap but obviously not paying attention to it. She was gazing out the window into the distance, looking forlorn.

Belle grimaced. "It is not the end of the world," she told Camille. "It is, in fact, a lovely morning."

Camille nodded.

Belle sighed. "I *had* to refuse Eric's offer of a carriage ride, Cammie. It was kindly intentioned, but it just wouldn't do. Nell's a guest but not ready to be introduced to Society—if indeed she ever will be. It's one thing to include the girl in our daily walks," she added in exasperation, "quite another to have her carried about in a gentleman's carriage as an equal. We aren't sure of what she is. But we nonetheless are being both civil and kind. The chit's being fed and housed, not beaten or starved. In fact, she's being fitted into one of my gowns at this very minute. That's going beyond charity. And you know how I feel about my gowns."

"Yes," Camille said, looking up, her expression brightening. "I suppose you're right." She frowned again. The thought of an insult to Nell had been lifted from her conscience, but she remembered the reason for her sorrow. She had so wanted to see Eric again.

"Come," Belle said suddenly. "Get up. We may not go riding with Eric, but the park is still there and it's a glorious day. We'll walk. My maid is almost done pinning Nell's gown, so we can include her if you like. Well, are you coming? You're the one who said there's nothing like exercise to get a mare in shape for foaling."

Camille laughed out loud. "You'd slay me for saying that to you."

"So I would," Belle agreed calmly. "Now, get your bonnet. The new one."

Camille breathed deep. London usually smelled of smoke, coal, and horses. But the air in the park was fresh, crisp and cold as a winter apple. Though the sun was bright, it had no heat, so they walked quickly: Camille, with her arm in Belle's, Nell and a maid behind them. It was too cold for much conversation, but Camille's eyes sparkled. There was so much to see. The park was alive with strollers, horsemen, and carriages. It might be frigid, but it was clear, and that was a rarity at this sullen time of year.

"Ho! I spy treachery," a deep voice called.

They stopped and turned around in time to see Eric pull his high-perch phaeton to a halt at their side. "You couldn't come riding in a nice warm coach with me," he said, "but here you are braving the elements on foot. Do I never speak to you again or merely go home and weep? Or," he asked in mock shock, "do I go look for a new mouthwash?"

"You know very well why we couldn't come with you," Belle said. "As I said in my note to you, Miss Baynes only finished with her dress fitting a half-hour ago. In fact, we came out late and are returning early. But I see you're hardly languishing. Nice equipage," she added, eyeing his phaeton. "I wish I could try it. Miles would murder me, or you, if I dared, of course. Nor would I be so foolhardy. Such dashing vehicles are not for me these days."

Eric's high-perch phaeton was the last word in style, Camille thought, looking at it with awed admiration. Gold with yellow trim, its wheels were huge and skeletal, so thin as to look fragile. The driver's seat was so far from the ground that it seemed precariously perched above the body of the coach. In fact, the whole equipage looked as delicate as some fantastic mechanical daddy long-legs. But Camille knew it was as well balanced as a fine watch and equally well sprung. It was built for comfort and speed and would be safe enough in a good driver's hands. She could guess that Eric was that.

His highly bred white horse snorted and pawed the ground in his eagerness to be off again.

"Cammie looks as though she'd venture a whirl round the park in it, though," Eric said. "Would you permit? I promise not to break my neck with her beside me. And there can be no scandal. It would take a more creative man than I to get up to any nonsense while tooling around in this kind of rig. I promise to keep moving until I set her down. May she?"

Camille held her breath.

"You didn't ask if she'd care to," Belle said.

Eric laughed. "You're right. I presume. Miss Croft, would you care to ride with me?"

"Would I?" Camille breathed. "I mean . . . Why, yes, thank you, I should."

"Very well," Belle said.

Eric sketched a bow. "I do not forget you, Nell," he added. "But there's only room for two. After I take Camille for a spin, I'd be delighted to show off my skill to you. If you care to wait."

Nell flushed with pleasure but shook her head. "Thank you, but it looks too—I'm not used to horses or such carriages," she murmured.

"And it's far too cold to wait here for you to finish tooling around the park," Belle said. "We'll be going back home. Please deposit Cammie on our doorstep, intact, when you're done."

Eric put one hand on his heart. "She shall be returned without so much as an eyelash missing," he promised. Then he held his hand out to Camille. "Come on, Cammie. See how we can fly."

Camille might moan that she wasn't ladylike and despair of her manners in the parlor. But she ascended to the seat beside Eric with consummate poise. She put a foot on a rung of Eric's rig, took his hand, and sprang to the seat beside him with the ease and grace of the athlete she was.

"Now, this," she said, turning a glowing face to him, "will be something. Let's see what this rig can do."

Eric grinned, shook his reins, and the phaeton rolled off down the lane into the park.

Camille held on to the seat with one hand and her bonnet with the other, even though her bonnet was tied under her chin. The wind was trying to tug it off.

"We must be going at fifteen miles an hour!" she cried in delight.

It was both terrifying and exhilarating. The phaeton rode smoothly, but she'd never sat so far from the ground or gone so fast in such a fragile vehicle. The height was dizzying, the speed amazing. She felt as though she sat atop a juggernaut and felt a frisson of terror in the pit of her stomach. It made the ride even more exciting. Because though she was frightened, she didn't for a moment think Eric would bring her to harm.

All too soon Eric slowed his horse, and they be-

gan driving at a more sedate pace. "Enough showing off," he said. "The road winds here, and we'll
take it more easily."

But it was still thrilling for Camille. Because she
was riding beside Eric, and they were alone together.

"So what do you think of it?" he asked her.

"Wonderful," she breathed, and then sat back
and listened as he proudly explained the finer
points of his new rig.

Now that they were riding more decorously,
Camille could see others in the park eyeing them,
and she sat up straighter. She wished that the cold
were as kind to her as it was to Nell and Annabelle.
The icy breeze was a cosmetic for them, teasing
color into their cheeks and making them look like
freshly blooming roses. The chill wind wasn't as
kind to Camille. She knew she must have grown a
cherry nose and tomato red cheeks, and her eyes
didn't sparkle so much as water. But nothing could
ruin the fact that she was here with Eric.

"So don't think I spring my horses all the time,"
he was saying. "I was just having some fun. Believe
it or not, safety is as important to me as speed."
His smile slipped as he added, "Being confined to
bed by causes I can't help is one thing, and I refuse
to arrive there through my own folly."

"Are you feeling better?" she asked softly. That
gave her another excuse to look right at him.

He was vivid as an autumn sunset on this bleak
December day. His thick hair under his high beaver

hat gleamed molten honey in the sunlight. He wore his greatcoat open, showing his dark-gold jacket and buff breeches. In spite of the cold, or maybe because of it, he looked so vital, so vividly alive, Camille had the feeling he'd have unbuttoned his jacket and tossed aside his high neckcloth too if he could. Color had returned to his face, his hazel eyes shone like topaz, he looked magnificent again. She hoped it was a true reflection of his health.

He smiled. "I feel perfectly better, little fusspot, I assure you."

She ducked her head to hide her foolish pleasure. Who else could call her little and not seem ridiculous or condescending?

Eric looked at her downcast face and saw the edges of her smile. He didn't have to ask if she was enjoying herself, for Camille's emotions ran clear in her eyes. And so he was surprised to see her pleasure suddenly fade.

"Bother," she said, frowning. "This isn't at all the thing, is it?"

"Why not?" he asked, puzzled. "You heard Belle. It's perfectly respectable. We're alone, but we can't so much as sneeze without the polite world seeing it."

"That, yes," she said gruffly. "But I'm grinning from ear to ear, and a young lady is supposed to be calm and cool at all times. Moderate, as Belle keeps telling me. I look about as moderate as a child at Astley's Amphitheatre. Remember how they jumped and squealed when they saw the horses go through their paces?"

He laughed. "Believe me, it's a delight to take someone for a ride who doesn't squeal or shriek. Besides, it frightens the horses."

"That's just it," she eagerly agreed. "Behaving naturally makes more sense, but it isn't what's done. I just can't seem to do what's done," she complained. "Not because I'm stupid but because it seems foolish to me. Why, did you know a young lady of fashion is supposed to rap a gentleman on the knuckles with her fan if he says something warm? Did you ever hear such nonsense? I wouldn't like being smacked for something I said when I tried to be clever. I don't care if men are the stronger sex, a rap across the knuckles hurts."

"I assure you it's uncomfortable," he agreed, with a straight face.

"Why, yes. Do they think men have no feelings?" she said indignantly. "And since you're laughing, think about that. You don't have to, right?"

He raised an eyebrow.

"If something's amusing," she explained, "you just laugh. As do I, although in my case, admittedly, sometimes too loud. But a young woman of quality is supposed to study laughing and practice it. Can you believe that? She's supposed to trill up and down the scales when she laughs. How can you enjoy anything when you have to concentrate on how to do it? Does that sort of thing matter to you? Do gentlemen of fashion really care how a girl laughs?"

Her eyes were wide and sincere, they glowed

clear gold in the sunlight. Clear and pure, like Cammie herself, Eric thought. There was no artifice in her, no deceit. Most young women of good breeding acted just as she said when in the company of a man, reacting to him with pouts, squeals, giggles, or trills of practiced laughter. But not Cammie. It was what drew him to her; it was what kept him back from her. Her pleasure in his company was flattering, the more so because he knew none of it was artificial. She was utterly unaffected. And inexperienced, he reminded himself sharply again.

"Look there," he said, looking out over the park in order to divert her and himself. "Lady Philmont and her pugs. Good God, she has five of them now. A herd. By the way, where are your pups?"

"Belle stayed in this morning, so I took them out earlier," Camille said. She turned a radiant smile on Eric. "Wasn't that lucky? They couldn't have gone riding with us, and Belle couldn't have managed them on her own. No one really can but me."

He smiled, thinking of Belle trying to handle the wayward setters. "They listen to me," he said, and then his eyes narrowed as he gazed at a group of horsemen clustered down the lane. "Speaking of hounds, there's Dearborne. What the devil is he doing here? I thought he was gone to the Continent for good."

"He was never anything good," Camille said, turning her head from the dark horseman Eric mentioned.

But the dark man fixed his stare on their phaeton and didn't look away until he saw Eric's expression. Then he turned his horse so his back was to them. Camille knew of Lord Dearborne, though they'd never met. From all the stories she'd heard, she didn't want to meet him either.

Her brother and some of his dearest friends had each once had dealings with him, all harrowing. Lord Dearborne was said to be a cheat. That would have been enough to repel her, since her stepfather had been one. But the dissolute nobleman was also vindictive and cowardly. Her heart always went out to the underdog, but there was a world of difference between a misunderstood rogue and an out and out villain.

They said Dearborne had been devilishly handsome once. It seemed to Camille that his terrible career was now written boldly on that devastated face. That was especially clear to see here in the brilliant winter sunlight. He looked dashing from a distance, but closer, she could see how haggard he was. The patrician nose had been broken, and the power of the dark eyes was eclipsed by the lines around them and the dark circles beneath.

"We saw him earlier," Camille said as they drove past Dearborne and his party. "Nell was fascinated by him, and he kept looking at her. She said he was handsome. Maybe from afar, but from near?" She shuddered. "All I can say is ugh! How could they say he's attractive?"

"Once he was," Eric said. "He began as a wild, spoiled young gentleman much like many another. His crimes were the usual for youths of great privilege and few morals. But he went from mischief to cruelty and violence in short order." Eric fell still. He wouldn't tell Camille how the man was famous for his treatment of women. Dearborne started as a jilt and seducer of well-born young ladies and gone on to be "difficult" with prostitutes. Eventually even his friends fell away as his occasional drunkenness became perennial and his wit turned to spite. He'd gone to the Continent a few years ago for his health. Rafe, among others, had threatened to kill him if he did not. Dearborne had obviously only lately returned. Everyone knew Rafe's temper cooled down as fast as it boiled up.

"We told Nell not to look at him," Camille said on a sigh. "Might as well tell water to run uphill."

"She's young and new to Town," Eric said gently.

Camille felt her face grow hot. "I don't blame her. I know it's not her fault," she said defensively. "We also told her not to speak to him ever." She didn't want Eric thinking she was careless or cruel to her guest and struggled for the right thing to say. Nell had disappointed her. She'd hoped for a friend to share experiences with. But the girl didn't like anything she cared for, except, of course, for Eric. "I try to give her good advice, but she's unaccustomed to Society. Lord," Camille said weakly, "but there are a lot of rules here in London."

"You've been very kind to Nell Baynes," he said softly. "You've got a good heart, Cammie."

She tried to look pleased. But it was hard to hear him complimenting her heart when there was so very much else she longed for him to notice and admire.

"I can't help you down," Eric said when they rolled up to Miles's house. "There's no one to hold the horse."

"You don't need to," she said on a laugh. "Thank you, I had a wonderful time." Then she jumped down to the pavement as lightly as she'd gone up to the high driver's seat.

"I can't leave until I see you safely home either," he told her. "Go in. And thank you for the pleasure of your company."

She was still smiling when the footman closed the door behind her. She took off her coat, went up the stair, and felt like she was floating. It had been such a glorious morning. . . . Her smile faded when she saw Nell waiting at the top of the stairs, her face sad.

"Did you have a good time?" Nell asked.

"Grand," Camille said, feeling guilty. It must have been a boring morning for Nell, or worse. If she'd been Nell, she'd have been agonized, thinking of what she was missing. "But I don't know if you'd have cared for it," she added quickly. "We positively raced along."

"I'm sure I wouldn't have enjoyed that," Nell said. "Still, it must have been wonderful to pass the morning with Eric by yourself. You told me there was no way a proper young lady could see a gentleman by herself, but I see there is." There was only a hint of reproach in her voice.

"I suppose that's so," Camille said awkwardly, feeling like a wicked stepsister from a fairy story. "And as time goes by, you'll have more freedom too. Remember, Miles said it was best for you to lie low until we found your relatives."

"I know," Nell said, "I agree. Who knows what could happen? But could you tell me what you saw in the park?" she asked wistfully.

"Right," Camille said, eager to make amends. "Come to my room, I want to get these slippers off. My feet are frozen."

After Camille had her slippers off, she sent her maid away and sat back on her bed, wriggling her toes. Nell perched on the edge of the bed and watched her.

"Lovely to be warm," Camille declared. "Now, then, what did I see? To tell the truth, Nell, I was more tickled at being seen than seeing. Eric's new rig is so sweet! The last word. The suspension is brilliant and the speed it can approach is dizzying. Everyone was looking."

"So then maybe you can tell me more about what we saw this morning?" Nell asked hopefully. "I mean to say, why did Lady Annabelle refuse to answer my question about the beautiful woman in the white carriage that we saw? Remember? The blond woman in the carriage pulled by white horses, who had all the gentlemen on horseback as well as on foot milling around her? She looked right at us and smiled, but Lady Annabelle turned her head away and then refused to discuss her."

"Oh, her." Camille shrugged. "Of course we couldn't acknowledge her. She's a demirep." She saw Nell's puzzlement. "A Paphian. A Cyprian. Nell, whatever fancy names they give it, she's just a whore. Lily Pearl, they call her. She used that name when she was on the stage, I think. They say she was an opera dancer until she found her true calling. Actually, I don't know which of us she was smiling at," she said thoughtfully, her expression growing dark. "She's a bold piece and might just have done it to pull Belle's tail, because she knows what real ladies think of her, and Belle's even better-looking than she is, but—"

"*Lily Pearl!*" Nell said excitedly. "Really? That was the famous Lily Pearl?"

"Infamous, more like," Camille said, looking at her curiously. "Where did you hear about her?"

"Is it true she keeps company with the Prince himself? And some of the richest men in London? And that she has jewels big as eggs? And is her house really all done in white, with a bed made of silver and blankets of ermine?"

"Well, I wouldn't know that!" Camille said, startled by Nell's enthusiasm. "How would you?"

"She's very famous," Nell said in suddenly dampened tones.

"Cut line," Camille said.

She always tried to be polite, even if Belle wasn't there to caution her. She knew she needed to be more ladylike, because otherwise she could sound rough or curt. So she took extra care to mind her manners. But when she didn't, she was impressive. Nell's eyes widened.

"Out with it," Camille said. "How do you know about that woman Pearl?"

"A woman at home told me," Nell said evasively.

Since they met, Camille had felt inferior to Nell in so many ways. But now she saw the girl was as bad a liar as she was. That was heartening. So she just stared at her, because she knew liars always felt impelled to defend their worst lies.

"Well," Nell finally said, fidgeting with the sash around her waist, "the woman knew because . . . She'd been a friend of Lily Pearl's, she said."

Now Camille's eyes widened. Nell's grew bright again when she saw Camille's reaction. "Yes," she said eagerly. "See, I did errands for her and we became friends. She was lonely, I suppose. No one else wanted anything to do with her. She moved to our village when I was twelve. A friend left her the grandest house in town, but no one spoke to her unless they had to. I did, because she'd give me an extra penny whenever she came into my papa's store. Soon she was asking me to run errands for her, and then we had tea together sometimes, and later I spent time with her whenever I could. She had *such* a sense of humor, and she was generous too. She gave me money and trinkets and told me stories about London and the fun she had there. The other women in town snubbed her, but I liked her from the first. She wore such beautiful clothing and smelled better than any woman I knew!" Nell laughed.

"How did she know a woman like Lily Pearl?" Camille breathed with startled amazement.

Taking her obvious shock for stunned admiration, Nell smiled smugly. "She'd been a woman like Lily Pearl, that's how. One of the best and most sought-after courtesans in all London, she said, and I tell you, she certainly had the jewels to prove it. I saw them with my own eyes: diamonds and sapphires and rubies, necklaces, bracelets, and rings. That's how she got her name. She was ever partial to rubies, she said."

"Didn't your parents object to your friendship?" Camille asked in bewilderment.

"What people don't know doesn't hurt them—or you," Nell said with another laugh. "That's what Ruby said, and she was right. At any rate, my mama was sick and my papa too busy to notice what I was doing. I spent a lot of time with Ruby and here I am, none the worse for it. That's why I can't understand why 'good' women turn away from them. They have an awful lot to teach, you know." She giggled.

"Ruby always said she wouldn't have been as rich if the 'good' women didn't have so much to learn."

"But she—she was like the women in that vile house that you were taken to and escaped from!"

Nell shook her head and smiled a superior little smile. "No. Different as chalk from cheese. Those were poor sluts. Lily, Harriette Wilson and her sisters, that la Starr woman, and that kind, they're not sluts. They're worldly women of business and property."

"They all sell their bodies to men," Camille said, not believing she was having this discussion.

Nell nodded. "Yes. But the difference between by the hour and by the month is what makes all the difference in the world, Ruby always said. Of course," she added, showing a dimple, "sometimes one night can be worth three months, if the demand is high enough."

"Oh, Nell," Camille wailed, so appalled that she was bereft of words. She just sat down and stared at her guest.

Nell's smug expression slipped. She cocked her head to the side. A moment later she was smiling again. "Oh, Camille, forgive me. I was only funning."

"But you think it's a good occupation for a female?" Camille persisted.

"No," Nell said quickly. "Oh, I don't know why I said all those things. I suppose I felt bad about the way everyone ignored the beautiful woman in the carriage."

"But you were friends with a courtesan?"

"She wasn't that when I knew her," Nell said. "She was just a jolly old woman. Why, who knows if she was even telling me the truth?" she said with a forced laugh. "I quite liked her. She was kind to me when I needed a friend, whatever she'd been. Anyway, she was past that when I met her. She couldn't get a dustman to wink at her by then. As I said, she was just a friend when I needed one. Can we forget it, please? I didn't mean to upset you."

Camille took a deep breath. She wasn't a fool and refused to be played for one. "Nell," she said bluntly, "give over. Is that why you came to London? To set yourself up in that trade?"

Nell's head came up; her eyes were filling with tears. "I was only joking. I came to London to find my family!"

Camille didn't have the gift of tears, but her mother could weep buckets whenever they would serve her well. Because of that, Camille still couldn't bear to see a woman cry. "I suppose it doesn't matter what I think," she said gruffly, "so turn off the waterworks, if you please, and let's talk about something else, shall we? Do you really want to learn how to ride? Now, that's something I can help you with."

Camille found her sister-in-law in her sitting room an hour later, stretched out on a French-style backless couch with a book and a box of candied cherries. She looked very much more like the famous untouchable beauty Lady Annabelle than her friend Belle. That was daunting, because she needed to ask Belle for advice.

Camille came into the room slowly, looking for a light way to start the conversation. "I don't know how you do it," she finally commented, when Belle looked up. "You could drape yourself around a fishing pole and look comfortable. You have more ways to relax than a cat."

Belle put her finger in the book to mark her place. "You can't get rid of her now without you being the one who looks like a cat," she said, and put another cherry in her mouth.

"How did you . . . ?" Camille gasped. "Oh, lord love a duck! Am I that obvious?"

"Only to me," Belle said. "And please leave colorful phrases about ducks to the servants. An 'Oh, La!' or 'Oh, lud!' will do to show your surprise."

"His inviting her for a ride through the park this morning. And the way she looks at him. She worships him. Belle?" Camille asked in such a hurt little voice that her sister-in-law put down her book altogether. "Do you think he's interested in her too? I mean, besides being interested in what happened to her?"

"Eric? Nonsense! He was just being courteous."

"But she's very lovely."

"So are many other women. Don't regard it."

When Camille spoke again, she avoided Belle's eyes. "Does everyone know how I feel about him?" she asked quietly.

"How could they?" Belle asked in return, in order to avoid a direct lie, because it was plain as the nose on Camille's face. Miles said that of course Eric knew Camille admired him. But he also said Eric believed it to be calf love, a fleeting fascination that would be over as soon as she met men nearer to her own age here in London.

Camille nodded. "But that's not why I came to see you. I confess it's getting difficult and not just because of Eric. You see, Nell and I . . ."

She paused, suddenly hesitant to bring up Nell's comments about courtesans. She didn't want to sound like a cat or a prude. And if she told Belle, there was the distinct possibility that Nell would be told to leave. Apart from maybe being unfair to Nell, Camille knew enough of gentlemen to know that would be disastrous. Eric would certainly feel sorry for the girl. He'd rescued her once before, hadn't he?

Camille decided to let the matter rest for now. "Nell and I have little in common," she finished lamely.

"No, you don't," Belle said bitterly. "You have much in common."

Camille looked up.

"Eric," Belle said bluntly.

"Oh!" Camille swallowed hard. "What shall we do?"

"We have to go on as we began," Belle said forcefully, picking up her book. "And hope that Miles and his friends have as many acquaintances in low places as they think they do. I begin to believe that's where we'll find our Mistress Nell's proper—or, rather, improper—place."

Camille drew in a startled breath. How could Belle know what Nell had just confessed to her? She wasn't superstitious, but she was ready to believe her sister-in-law was a witch until she spoke again.

"I don't know why I don't trust her," Belle mused. "But I know a conniver when I see one." She sighed. "Oh, lud. I suppose once I was one myself. I wasn't happy unless I won every masculine heart I came across. I didn't like myself much then, but I certainly didn't care for anyone else either, not even the men I was after." She turned a sober blue stare on her sister-in-law. "Let's get our heroine united with her family, Camille. I'm willing to bet anything that Eric won't think twice about her after we do."

Chapter 7

The summons came at dinner.

Miles took the note from the silver salver his butler brought him. He read it and smiled. "It seems we're invited to Eric's house this evening," he announced.

"Is he sick again?" Camille blurted, starting up from her chair, her face growing pale.

"He'd scarcely send us an invitation to view that," Belle said, giving Camille a pained look. Camille sat down, though she didn't give up the white-knuckled grip she had on her napkin. "But it is late, Miles," Belle said, turning her attention to her husband. "Why does he want us to fly over there now, at the drop of a hat?"

"He apologizes for that," Miles said. "But it's a

very nice hat, one I don't think you'd want to miss seeing. He's also invited Rafe and Brenna. And our old friend Drum. The earl of Drummond," he explained to Nell, who was watching, wide-eyed. "Seems he just arrived in London for the Season. He and Rafe were thick as thieves in the old days. Come to think of it, the rumor is they were thieves and worse—or better, in their case—in the service of His Majesty in the wars. They have many a tale to tell and as time goes by they tell more of them. So shall we go there even at such short notice?"

"Of course," Belle said eagerly. "I'll just change my gown."

"You look very well," he said.

"But you know I always want to look very, very well," she laughed. "Don't worry. I'll be quick about it. I'm as curious as you are." She narrowed her eyes. "Or are you? You know something I don't know. Confess!"

"And take the fun out of it? Never. Coming, ladies?" he asked Camille and Nell.

"I wouldn't miss it," Camille said excitedly. "Can I wear this, Belle? Or should I put on the pink? Or my new ice-blue or—"

"The new blue," Belle said.

"Am I invited too?" Nell asked timidly.

"Oh, I don't think we could get in without you," Miles said. "You see, the other guest will be your cousin Dana."

Nell went stone-still; her face became impassive.

"Dana?" she finally said. "I didn't know I had such a cousin."

"You do," Miles said, offering the note to her. "We're very sure of that, and so is he. He'd be in a position to know. Your cousin, Dana Bartlett, is a barrister. A lawyer, Nell."

"How very . . . how very wonderful," Nell said, although the look on her face was not glee.

Camille was beyond gleeful. She was ecstatic. Nell's family had been found! She'd be leaving, they might not see her again, and there was every chance that once she was gone, Eric wouldn't be seeing her again either. Camille's racing pulses slowed. Well, maybe he would. And if he did? There was nothing she could do about it. She had to deal with what was. And what was—was that she was free again. She didn't have to look after Nell or feel guilty for not doing so, and best of all, there'd be less opportunity for Eric to look at her at all.

She whirled in front of her mirror, dancing in place with her new blue gown held up in front of her. The family had planned a quiet evening, so she'd given her maid the night off. But she wasn't such a grand lady that she'd call her maid back for something as trivial as putting on a gown. Although, she thought as she stopped prancing, now she wished she had her maid help's in dressing. She wanted to look so fine tonight.

She lowered the gown and stared at her reflection. It was daunting. She wanted to see a vision. She saw only her naked self with a really nice gown in her hand.

"Are you ready, Camille?" Nell asked from outside her door.

"Just a minute!' she answered. She raised her arms and dropped the gown over her head like a curtain and wriggled until it seemed settled in all the right places. She did up her buttons, hopping in place as she sought her slippers and slipped her feet into them. Then she drew her sash tight and tied it. She glanced in the looking glass. It would do.

Camille pulled up her hair, hastily tied it with a ribbon, then shook her head like a dog shedding water, trying to get her curls to bounce the way her maid did when she made up her hair. She blew out a breath and sent a strand up off her face so she could see how she'd done.

Her hair looked tousled, as though she'd just gotten out of bed. But men were said to like that. She could only hope the style looked casual instead of sloppy. She took a deep breath, noted how that made her breasts rise and fall, and nodded to herself. There was no more she could do. The rest was up to fate. And Eric.

"Right," she called. "Come in."

The door opened and she saw Nell. Nell's gown was blue too. It was another of Belle's cast-offs, but it suited Nell perfectly, making her eyes seem to gleam bright as sapphires. Her hair was drawn back in a smooth ebony sweep, making her look cool and pure, like a medieval portrait of the Madonna. But her figure made her look more like Mary Magdalene.

Camille forced a smile. "I'm done," she said, repressing the "for" that almost slipped from her lips. "Let's go."

Eric himself greeted his guests at the door.

"Mission accomplished," he told Miles. "Little girl found. Nell," he said gravely, taking her hand in his, "we've located your cousin Dana, your nearest kin. He's here, and he's anxious to see you."

Nell, Camille thought, merely looked anxious. Understandable, of course. She was about to meet the man who would have absolute control over her life for the next three years and possibly forever. This was the fellow who was her male next of kin. As such, if he consented to take her in, he would have the power to dower her, marry her off, or force her to remain a spinster. That was enough to make anyone anxious. What if he was an opportunist? Or a monster?

Camille bit her tongue. She tried to force herself to stifle all the plans that flew to her mind, plans to rush to the rescue if the man seemed unfit. Eric, Miles, and Rafe would be very capable of doing that. Nell was in good hands, no matter whose hands they placed her in. Given the girl's recent outrageous comments about women and their choices, Camille couldn't help thinking that was a very good thing.

Eric showed them into his salon. Nell stood staring, seemingly dazzled by the company. Camille knew almost all of them. Two she hadn't seen in a while, her brother's friends: the dark, lean, elegant, long-nosed earl of Drummond and his lovely wife, Alexandria.

But another dark gentleman was far more interesting to Camille, because he was a stranger.

He turned to look at them as they walked into the room. He was as well dressed as the other men, if a little more soberly, all in black, except for his high white neckcloth. Though not as tall as any of them either, he looked extremely fit. His black hair was brushed till it shone. Though his aquiline nose was a trifle large for his face, his other features were regular and his mouth well shaped. In all, he was handsome enough, but the intelligence in his expressive dark eyes made him strikingly so. Those remarkable eyes fixed on Nell, and he smiled, showing small even white teeth.

He immediately came forward and bowed over her hand. "Cousin," he said. "I would know you anywhere."

Nell bit her lip. "I'm afraid I wouldn't know you," she said. "Have we met?"

"No. I regret not, but you look very like my mother did. I'm sorry to tell you that she has passed away."

Nell looked startled and began to murmur condolences.

Her cousin cut them short. "Thank you. It was

two years ago, so I've grown accustomed, if not reconciled, to her loss. But I wish I'd known you were coming to London. It would have prevented the misfortune that befell you. Still, I'm grateful that though you almost met disaster, you also met these good people. Ours is a small family, but at least now I am here to see to your welfare. How awkward," he said with a smile. "Allow me to present myself. I'm Dana Bartlett, your aunt Clara's only son."

"I'm so sorry about your mother," Nell said again.

"As am I," he said. "But seeing you returns her to me in a way. She was also considered a great beauty in her day."

Nell dropped her gaze and blushed.

Camille felt joyous relief tainted with a twinge of jealousy, and it wasn't because she herself looked nothing like her mother.

"And you must be her newfound friends," Dana went on, bowing to Miles and Belle. "Lord Pelham, Lady Annabelle. Thank you for taking my cousin in. It was kind and generous of you. And this," he said, turning his attention to Camille, "must be Miss Croft. I've been hearing stories about your generous championing of my cousin, and believe me I am infinitely grateful to you too."

He took Camille's hand and smiled at her

Camille found herself a little flustered by the enormous warmth and approval in that smile as well as the strength in the blunt-fingered, warm hand he offered.

He blinked as though against a blinding light, shuttering his brilliant eyes with long dark eyelashes and, after a long moment, slowly released Camille's hand.

Eric looked at him oddly and stepped closer. But Nell's cousin immediately assumed his urbane expression again.

"Well, cousin," Dana Bartlett said briskly, turning to Nell again. "I think we've taken up enough of these good people's time, don't you? I'm solely responsible for you now. I know, I've consulted all the family documents, and as I'm a man-at-law, I looked extensively, believe me. You're connected to Viscount Baynes of Rye on your father's side, but distantly, very distantly. I'll write to him and see if he's willing to assume any familial responsibility for you, nevertheless. Don't worry," he added quickly. "It's not that I'm reluctant to become your guardian, but I want to be sure to do everything legally, and being a guardian is a new role for me. I've been responsible only for myself for a while now. I confess that bearing responsibility for any young woman other than my eventual wife is something I never expected."

He looked at her steadily. "I'll try to see to your welfare in the future as well as your saviors here have already done, I promise. Bear with me; I'm sure that I'll get it right in time. The only thing left to discuss is where to take you now." He heaved a sigh. "I'm a bachelor and live in rooms by myself. That isn't a fitting accommodation for you. And even if I had the room, I don't know where I can find a chaperone for you as yet. I'll look for one as well as for new lodgings. In the meanwhile, I was thinking of maybe a suitable hotel or respectable boarding house for you."

He turned to the company. "You've all been so kind. I hate to impose on you further, but can you recommend any such hotels or boarding houses?"

"There's Stephens," Rafe said. "And my brother stays at the Pulteney. They set a good table."

"Yes, Rafe, Stephens is excellent." Eric laughed. "For us army men."

Miles smiled. "And the Pulteney will put Mr. Bartlett in the poorhouse if he keeps her there above a month."

"There's Limners," Rafe persisted. "I'd an aunt swore by the place every time she came to London."

"But not for a young woman alone, Rafe!" his wife protested. "All the other guests are elderly and bring rafts of servants."

"Ah, yes," Dana said, "I suppose I'll have to hire a maid as well."

"One wouldn't be enough for that place," Brenna said.

The room was still for a moment, with everyone deep in thought. It was so still that they could all hear the muted sob. Nell bent her head and scrabbled in her pocket for a handkerchief. Her cousin handed her one, and she dabbed at her eyes.

Even with all her reservations about Nell and the boredom she found in her company, still Camille felt like a beast. Worse, she realized she must look like one for not speaking up. She exchanged an agonized look with Belle, all her inner turmoil in her eyes.

Belle saw it and sighed. "She can stay on with us until you find more suitable accommodation, Mr. Bartlett," she said evenly. "If that's all right."

"All right?" Dana said, one hand to his heart. "My lady, you must know it's far more than that. But we couldn't continue to impose."

"I don't see how you cannot," Belle said, giving her husband a secret poke in the ribs when he turned to stare at her. "And it isn't an imposition. I'd want the same for our Camille should she ever be in a similar position, which I pray to God she never is."

"It's the only solution really," Miles said, giving his wife's hand a squeeze to show he understood. "So take your time, find a chaperone and the right kind of lodgings. Until then, if she wants to, Nell can stay on with us. In fact," he went on with a grin, "I assure you that if we didn't offer, there'd be no living with my sister. Right, Camille?"

Camille nodded, too embarrassed to lie straight out.

"Very wise of you," Eric said, laughing. "I wouldn't want to risk Camille's wrath myself. Are you agreeable, Nell?" he asked more gently.

She hung her head. Belle and Miles made polite protests until Nell finally gave them a watery smile. "Thank you," she whispered.

"Yes, thank you," Dana said, "but," he added with troubled frown, "this is awkward. . . . Please don't think I'm not grateful. I really wouldn't feel right about this unless I spoke to my cousin about it first. May we have a brief talk in private?"

"You may be a man-at-law, but you'd make a fine judge," Eric said. "Of course. There's no one in my study. Please feel free to have your conference there. If," he added with a wry smile, "Nell herself agrees."

"Thank you," Dana said. "Cousin?"

Nell hesitated and then gave him a shy smile. "Of course, cousin," she said. And bowing her sleek sable head, she took her cousin's arm and went into Eric's study with him.

It was a small room framed in dark wood, with books lining the walls from the floor to the ceiling moldings. A fire snapped and sang in the hearth, and heavy draperies were closed over the frosty windows. Dana Bartlett took it all in with one sweeping glance as they entered the room. He shut the door behind them.

"We'll have privacy here," he said. "Nothing we say can be heard. It wouldn't be proper if we were acquaintances, but it's all right because we're family, after all. Aren't we, Cousin . . . Nell, is it now?

Nell eyed him warily

He circled Eric's desk, picked a pen out of an ornate inkstand, and stood, legs apart, pretending to inspect it. "And you are eighteen, they tell me. Interesting. By my reckoning, you're twenty-one. But people are so much kinder to young women aren't they, Nell? Nell instead of Helen," he said thoughtfully, gazing at the pen in his hands. "After your idol, Nell Gwyn, King Charles's favorite mistress?"

"I prefer the nickname Nell," she said in a reedy little voice. "No one minded me using it at home."

"Especially not your poor dear daft mama, I suppose," he mused. "How could she, after all? My condolences on your witless parent, by the way. I heard all about her from your new friends. But that's odd too." He raised his brilliant black eyes to Nell. "She wrote to my mother for years, and her letters were models of clarity. Too clear for your comfort, I imagine. Mama wasn't terribly fond of her niece—especially after she heard about all the things wicked little Helen was doing. So though I didn't expect it to turn out this way, I wasn't surprised to find you were in London after I was told you'd run away from home, almost as surprised as you must have been to discover my existence. Yes," he said as he saw Nell's face grow pale, "your poor daft mama wrote to tell me."

"Then why didn't I hear about you or any letters from you?" Nell challenged him.

"Unlike my mama, I never write back. I merely send money. After all, I've little but blood in common with your side of the family. But there's not a thing wrong with your mother's mind. Except that it's heavy with sorrow over you."

"Well, I suppose that puts paid to my plans, don't it?" Nell said, taking a seat. She shrugged. "Nothing ventured, nothing gained," she murmured. "It was a good beginning, but I can make another. I'm staying in London whatever happens, but I guess I'll have to move on now. Mama told you everything, did she?"

"Enough," he said, watching her closely from under his eyelashes, though he kept toying with the pen. "The history of your transgressions wasn't significant at first—at least, not to me, although they troubled her, of course. They were simple indiscretions that grew as you did. At first, petty thefts from her purse when you were a girl. Later, as you matured, rather more significant ones, of other women's husbands, not to mention your flings with local boys and men and the scandalous friendship with that courtesan. Speaking of losing one's wits, your notorious friend must have been the one who was doing that. It was idiotic of her to set up a knocking shop in such a small village. It was a wonder she wasn't run out of town sooner. I heard she went to Bath and into business with an old friend there, running a doss shop for codgers."

He looked up and smiled at Nell's expression. "Yes, I know quite a bit. The lords in the other room aren't the only ones who have hidden resources. They found me, but they didn't know about Ruby. I did. The rest? I had to know exactly who I was coming to meet this evening." He paused. "Why come to

London on your own?" he asked curiously. "Why didn't you go to Bath with your friend Ruby? She's doing well."

"She wouldn't have me," Nell said simply. "She got jealous as a green cow when she lost her looks."

"As well as losing a few expensive souvenirs her old flames gave her—to you, or so she claims." He put the pen back on the inkstand and looked at her directly. "But none of it was just for the money, was it? You didn't live in luxury, but you weren't starving."

She raised her eyes to his. "But I *was* starving— for fun, for excitement, for adventure. There was nothing to do but grow old and die at home. I needed the money to leave."

"And the reason you needed all the men?"

She tilted one shoulder. "For fun."

"You're that enamored of the act?"

"Oh, the act. That's like Ruby said: sometimes fun, sometimes nasty, but always good for an extra coin. It's nice to be wanted too." She stood up. "Are you going to shame me, have them whip me from the house? Or will you let me leave quietly on my own?"

He studied her thoughtfully for a while before he answered. "What would you do if I let you stay on?"

She studied him as intently. "Make a good connection. Then leave. There are men with more money than they can count here in London. I could end up with a fortune."

"And some interesting diseases. Silly slut," he said, "you were running away *to* that brothel you escaped from, weren't you? Found it lower than you thought it would be, did you? And then you found yourself caught by another villain. But you'd have found a way to escape if Eric Ford had bought you or not. He could have saved himself a beating, poor fellow."

She shrugged again.

He shook his head, "What a little fool. With your looks you could marry and very well. You do have that connection with Viscount Baynes, though he'd probably set the dogs on you if you tried to actually own it and visit him. Still, it is a blood connection. Times are changing. Men of station are marrying mill owners' daughters. A woman with beauty and wit can climb high these days, and you have a real connection you could take advantage of. Why settle for being a whore, even a fancy one, when you could marry well and take lovers later if you grew bored?"

"That's playing the whore too," she said.

"Yes, but in acceptable fashion. Those in the *ton* can get away with anything."

Her eyes narrowed. "Why are you telling me this? Why aren't you crying foul and telling them out there? Come to think of it, why didn't you tell them right off?"

"I don't know," he said. He put his hands behind his back and stared into the fire. "It was just a whim that became an idea. An idea that became better with every passing moment. Truth can always be told, after all, and the bad news I had for them was better delivered in person anyway. I didn't want to alienate such powerful people and was curious to meet them. Then tonight, when I did, I had another idea."

He looked at her again. "I pride myself on being a good judge of people. You're not a good woman, cousin, at least not in the moral sense. But now that I've met you, I don't think you're evil. I'd never consider this if I for one moment thought you were. You're selfish, amoral, and incautious, but not cruel or vicious. You might distress your hosts, but you wouldn't harm them."

"Why should I?"

"Exactly."

He considered her and then came to a decision. "I've wealth but no connections," he said. "My side of the family was solid yeoman class until I came along. I'm the first to earn my living without working the land. Still, though my education is a huge thing in my family, to the *ton* a lawyer is nothing but an expensive servant. And I have ambitions. Intelligence isn't enough to get a common man into the highest social circles, not even in these changing times. But if he made an advantageous connection, he could instantly change his status."

"You could change yours by marriage, you mean."

"That would be a good way, yes."

She thought a moment. Her eyes widened. "It's

Camille, isn't it?" She laughed. "You saw her and your heart stopped? Ho! Pull the other one while you're at it. Not that she wouldn't be a good pick for you, mind. She's no beauty, but she's related to half the gentry in England and is friends with the other half. And she doesn't give a hang for titles or convention." She paused. "Aye, very clever, aren't you? She'd be perfect. Not so high in the instep that she wouldn't consider such as you, not half bad to look at actually either. Well-dowered to boot. And you could woo her if you had the excuse of having to watch over me, couldn't you? I don't know if I like that, though. She's nice."

"So am I," he said, showing her a bright smile. "And I wouldn't hurt her. You're right. I've a fancy to court her."

"She fancies Eric Ford."

"And I believe he might fancy you. What could be better?"

"I don't know if I want him or if he wants me."

Now he shrugged. "Then don't take him. I don't care. I only need you to mind your manners and not get into trouble. Remember, I know the truth. But it's your decision. You can go. Or stay, behave, and obey me."

He let her think about that for a moment.

"Why tell me any of this?" she asked, eyeing him steadily. "Why not go on as though you didn't know a thing about me? I wouldn't have guessed."

"I wondered the same myself until this very night. If I assumed ignorance of your past, I could always pretend to be shocked if— when—you betrayed your new friends. But that would present problems, because I've no way of knowing how soon you'd do that. And if you nipped your new friendships in the bud, it would ruin a potentially excellent opportunity for me."

His voice grew cool. "I need you where you are now. I imagine you want that too. But if I'm to keep my silence, you must obey my rules. They are simple enough. No stealing from your hosts or their friends or from anyone while you're under their roof. And keep your skirts down. If not for my sake, consider your own. You don't want to spread ill will in what well may become your new family and circle of friends. Because if you don't make an advantageous connection, I may do it for both of us. Family is family after all. What you do with your body after I'm settled is your own affair.

"And you're never to speak of this conversation," he added, as he saw her thinking. "Because I'll deny it. And I will be believed. Because I have nothing to hide. My only crime is ambition. Yours, I'm afraid, are more tangible—and prosecutable. There's always Newgate or the Antipodes for you if you decide to try to involve me in any of your schemes. I know a lot of magistrates, Cousin Helen."

"Cousin Nell," she said.

"If I'm to remember that, you must forget all I've just said, except for the rules." He cocked his head to the side, waiting for her answer.

She thought a moment and then lifted hers. "I accept."

He offered her his arm. They emerged from the study. The company fell silent and looked at them.

"I'm happy and grateful for your offer on my cousin's behalf, Lord and Lady Pelham," Dana said. "I'll send for her as soon as I can find suitable lodgings and a proper chaperone. But until I can get our affairs straight, I'll be visiting Nell often, if that's all right with you."

He spoke to Miles and Annabelle, but his eyes were on Camille.

"That's fine," Miles said. "You are welcome to our house, Mr. Bartlett, any time."

Dana smiled at Camille.

Camille smiled back at him.

Chapter 8

⁓

Eric's guests were amazed when he opened the doors to his dining parlor and invited them to a light repast. They stopped on the threshold and stared.

Two sideboards on one wall groaned under the weight of the lavish feast that had been set out. There were platters of carved fowl, ham, tongue, and beef. Other dishes held shimmering moulds of galantines decorated with assorted relishes. A serving man lifted the tops off two silver tureens, sending up steamy scents of a meaty ragout and a simmering lobster stew. Across the room, a sideboard held single dishes of custards and jellies. There were trays of little cakes, as well as a cutglass bowl of trifle piled high with cream, a bowl of pudding, and a basket filled with out of season hothouse fruit.

"You," Miles told Eric with wonder, "have prepared a symphony of food."

"No," Eric said, "I couldn't prepare a radish. But I didn't just bring in food from a cook shop the way most bachelors would. Do you know who's in my kitchen right now?"

"A magician," his sister breathed as she inhaled the savory scents.

"Almost," he said. "Louis, the chef from my favorite restaurant in the Strand. I wanted to thank you, Bren and Rafe, for all you did for me."

"But you have," his sister said, bewildered. "Too many times! You sent us a crystal vase filled with hothouse roses, that pair of Venetian candelabras, tortoiseshell combs for me and a set of silver brushes for Rafe. None of which you had to do."

"It wasn't half enough," Eric said seriously and then added, grinning, "But I wanted to thank you all, and this way I can have some fun too. You know how I love to eat. So take a plate and find a seat, if you please."

They heard a moan and turned.

"Ohh," Camille groaned, one hand on her stomach. "Your chef may be French, but I spy Duke of Buckingham Pudding! With sauce. My favorite. I can smell the ginger from here. I had dinner, I'm stuffed. But I'll just have to force myself."

"You mean," her sister-in-law corrected her softly, "I'll just have to take a taste to please you."

"No," Camille sighed. "It's *Buckingham Pudding,* Belle! You take a taste, I'll stuff myself."

Even Belle laughed at that, and then the company descended on the treats laid out before them.

Camille couldn't remember having a better time, and not just because of all the delicious food. She sat at the dining table beside Belle. But it was Eric himself who finally alighted on the empty chair on her other side.

"Having fun?" he asked.

Her mouth was full. Although Camille didn't care a fig for airs and graces, she had manners, so she waited until she swallowed to answer. But she managed a grin.

"What an eloquent smile," he commented, watching her. "Now I know why the Mona Lisa never showed her teeth. She probably had cream cake in her mouth."

"No," she said when she could, "it's damson tart. And it's heaven. I suggest you never let Louis leave your kitchen."

"He actually didn't prepare a thing in there," Eric said. "There isn't enough room. He's only supervising the dispersal of treats. I ordered a ducal feast, but I have merely a bachelor's kitchen."

"Still, it was a glorious surprise," she said, and eyeing Dana Bartlett where he stood by a sideboard talking with Nell. "A surprise on top of a surprise. What do you think of him?"

Eric didn't ask whom she was talking about. He

glanced at Dana too. "He seems a decent fellow. The adventure turned out well, I think."

"For her," Camille said, "but not for you. How is your head?" She glanced away before he could meet her gaze, because she didn't think she could keep her composure or her secret if she did. They were too close, and those hazel eyes of his were too filled with understanding. She was suddenly so stricken with his nearness she felt close to stupid tears.

She could feel the solid warmth of the man. It felt like sitting next to a banked furnace. Her nostrils fluttered. She could detect his scent: verbena, from his shaving soap, she guessed. She looked down and saw his hand holding his wineglass and had to look away again. That hand was so tanned, broad, with such long fingers and well cared for nails, that the sight of it sent shivers down to her stomach and well beyond that.

She was gazing at her plate, struggling for something to say, embarrassed because she always had something to say. He was so close she was sure if she moved a centimeter she'd touch him.

Then she felt a breeze, the slightest breath at the nape of her exposed neck. She froze, excited and thrilled. Was he daring to touch her neck? Here, in public? Or was he merely bending that noble head to whisper something to her? There would be nothing mere about it.

She raised her head.

And almost bumped noses with Dana Bartlett.

He stepped back, looking even more embarrassed than she felt.

"Excuse me," he said at once, "I only meant to ask you a question, Miss Croft, but it's so noisy here I bent to be sure you heard me. I'm sorry I startled you."

"It takes a lot to startle Miss Croft," Eric said. "She was probably afraid you were going to steal her pudding."

Camille froze again, this time in shocked humiliation. It was a jest, she knew that. But it cut her to the quick. Not just because it might mean he thought she was greedy, but because she'd wanted so much more from him.

Dana saw the hurt that sprang to her eyes. "Whatever I might want to steal from Miss Croft," he told Eric, without looking at him but only into Camille's eyes, "however sweet it might be, be sure it wasn't her dessert."

Camille fought a ridiculous impulse to weep. It was so kind of him, and so unkind of Eric, or maybe merely thoughtless of him. But in his case thoughtlessness was as good as a slap in her face, because it wakened her to cruel reality.

"But right now, I was only going to thank you again," Dana told her. "What you did for my cousin was noble. More than that, it was unusual. I've been talking to everyone about you tonight, and they all tell me that both are typical of you. My cousin was very lucky to have met you," he said, bending closer, lowering his voice. "I can only hope that I'll be as lucky in our friendship too."

She felt enormously better; her sense of humor came bubbling up again. "Oh, my!" she said, fanning herself with one hand. "I'm not used to such fulsome praise, Mr. Bartlett! But," she added, grinning at him, "I think I could get used to it."

"I'd sincerely like to see to that," he said.

He was bending over her shoulder because he couldn't sit down next to her, though his words implied that he wanted to. But there was no seat for him. Belle was still engrossed in talking to Miles, and Eric sat at Camille's other side. Dana looked at him in an obvious silent request for his chair. After all, dinner was over, the desserts were demolished, and the guests were beginning to get up and circulate.

Now Camille turned her head to look at Eric too, because Dana's obvious attentions made her more confident.

Eric looked from Camille to Dana and then slowly rose from his chair. As he stood, Dana straightened. Camille looked up and saw the two men take each other's measure, literally. Eric was almost a foot taller than Dana, but oddly, the matter of inches didn't diminish the smaller man. He was strikingly handsome in his own fashion.

Dark to bright, tall and short, the two couldn't be more different, but, Camille thought with a shock, it almost seemed as though they were a pair of stags, measuring themselves before combat—for her. No, not stags, she thought, more like a mighty warhorse and a sturdy pony: one huge, muscled, and combat-scarred, the other prideful, just as strong if half the size, and wily. But these two were men. And what men! They looked like an invading Viking and a defending Roman warrior, squared off to do battle for her.

She wanted to giggle. She wanted to cheer. She wanted one of them to pick her up and carry her off. That, she told herself sharply, as she fanned herself in earnest, is what came from staring at your naked self before you went into company!

It was Miles who broke the tension of the moment. He rose to his feet too. "It's getting late," he told Dana. "We must leave."

"Yes," Dana said. "So it is. Perhaps we could discuss when I could come to visit Nell."

Eric nodded. "A good idea. Since she's staying on with Camille until you straighten out your affairs, we wouldn't want any conflicts of interest. I did promise to show her the town."

Pride, Camille thought as her heart sank, *goeth before a fall.* The greatest pity was that it stayed with her so short a time before she fell.

She hid her hurt, rose, murmured an excuse, and left the table to find someone else to talk with.

But though she spoke animatedly with the earl of Drummond and his lady, Camille eyed Dana as he stood talking with Miles and Eric. Nell's cousin mightn't be in Society or titled, but he was clearly

well educated, and his manners were fine. His
cousin Nell might hang back shyly, but he was neither presumptuous nor timid. He didn't act like a
servant or as an equal, but exactly as he should,
like a man of some means and manners who had
just met them. He looked up from his conversation
about Nell and, seeing Camille across the room, he
smiled at her. It might not have been the smile she
had been longing to see, but she lifted her chin and
smiled back at him.

There was some food left after all. Eric found
half a bowl of trifle under cheesecloth in the kitchen,
obviously meant to be put out if necessary and just
as obviously forgotten by the departed waiters. He
carried it to a table and sat down. He'd said good-
bye to his guests, paid the chef and the waiters he'd
hired for the night, left his man Watkins to fuss
over any remaining clean-up, and was now in his
shirtsleeves, scrounging in his larder for something
to eat. He couldn't sleep.

"Oh, good," a voice drawled. "More food."

Eric looked up. His high-nosed friend, the seemingly languid, always alert earl of Drummond,
stood in the doorway, watching him.

"Watkins let me in," the slender nobleman explained. "He heard you bumbling around down
here, but you didn't hear me at the front door. Too
excited by your party to go to sleep?" he asked, as he
came into the room. "That's just like my Alexan-

dria. She drifts around the house like a bat half the night after we have a soiree. Do you have another spoon?"

Eric hunted through the newly washed silver and handed his friend a soupspoon. Then he sat at the table, his own spoon in hand, but only stared glumly at the trifle. "You didn't come here to eat," he said.

"Indeed, no, but that looks very tempting," Drum said as he took a seat at the table too.

"Cut line," Eric muttered.

"Very well, after some of this." Drum dipped his spoon in the bowl and took a mouthful of trifle. "Excellent," he sighed. "But as for my appearance here now, I wanted to speak with you and hoped you mightn't be asleep yet. Odd, isn't it? If you're a guest at a party, you can go home and fall asleep the minute your head touches the pillow. But hosting changes everything. You replay the event in your head, rating, evaluating, and reliving every moment. Responsibility for something changes one's enjoyment of it. Speaking of which . . . Your party was splendid. I'm not so sure about the reason for it, though. Rafe and I discussed it. Our ladies think we're mad. They're in raptures about the oh-so-suave Mr. Bartlett. In fact, they're almost as taken with him as you are with his cousin Nell."

Eric took a spoonful of trifle, brought it to his lips, and then just stared at it. "Am I?" he asked, as though he was talking to his laden spoon. "You think the party was for her?"

"Wasn't it?"

"I had to call everyone together when I found her cousin. And so I decided to make a party of it."

"Rafe was the one who found Bartlett, actually."

Eric shrugged. "And when I heard about it, I asked him here. Why not? I was the one who first found her."

"Enough," Drum said, laying his spoon down. "Listen. I don't go for midnight rambles anymore. I've a lovely big bed and a lovelier lady waiting for me in it. But I worry about you, my friend. We all do. And we wonder about little Mistress Baynes and her suave cousin. She's charming, but her story is simply too much the stuff of Drury Lane for us. It smacks of melodrama."

Eric looked at him. "So girls don't get abducted off the streets in London? I'm glad to hear it. And every whore in town is happy with her trade and always willing and was from the first?" He shook his head. "A regular Eden we have here."

"No and no," Drum said with a trace of irritation. "And too well we all know it. In fact, when I take my seat in the House of Lords, that's one of the first things I plan to address. London's teeming with fallen women, and the more fool he who thinks a man doesn't fall morally and physically alongside them every time he patronizes one. He endangers his health as well as the welfare of the woman he may profess to love. But that's from a speech for the House of Lords, not this kitchen. It's not what I came here to talk about."

Drum rose and paced the room before he spoke again. "Eric," he said, coming to a standstill beside his friend, "you're a clever fellow, honest and true, unquestionably noble, brave as well." Eric made a face as Drum went on, "You're strong and wise, and we're all proud to call you friend. And yet," he said, holding up one finger, "you're also vulnerable precisely because you are all those things— and maybe lonely now that all your friends are married. This Nell seems too good to be true. At least to us. All I've come to say is that we wish you'd wait on things until you know how true she really is."

Now Eric's expression was as hard as his voice. "I'd think you'd be better off giving that speech to Camille, not me."

"True, she championed the girl from the first. But you're the one who didn't leave Nell's side all night," his friend said blandly. "Camille passed the time with her brother and sister-in-law and us."

"Oh, did she?" Eric asked bitterly. "Then why did she seem to have Nell's cousin grafted to her side? Or didn't you notice? She could hardly wait for supper to be over so she could stand by him."

"Oh," Drum said, and sat down again. He laughed. "Is that what it was all about? Damme, Eric, you've only to ask the girl and she'd be happy to stand by you for all eternity! Everyone knows how she feels about you." He cocked his head to the side. "Could it be that you don't?"

Eric shook his head. "No. I'm not that dull. But I

have a care for her, and so I've been very careful not to claim any more than that." He met his friend's gaze, and Drum's smile faded away.

"Drum," Eric went on seriously, "you have a child now. A son. But you may well have a daughter someday, as dear to you as young Duncan is now. Think about how pleased you'd be if in the prime of her youth, when she first came to Town, before she'd even one Season, she declared her fascination with a man ten years her senior, one who suffered from a recurrent illness no doctor could predict, who moreover was an ex-army man who wasn't rich but merely comfortable. Brave, bold, and wise as he might be, how thrilled would you be if she immediately decided to stand by such a man for the rest of her life?

"Mmm," Eric hummed, watching his friend closely when Drum didn't answer right away. "You're right. Things look different to us when we have responsibility for them, don't they? Whether that thing is a party or a young life."

"But your illness may be passing, and you're much more than comfortable. I know that. I invest along with you. And I know you longer than a season, as does her brother, and we know who you are."

Eric ran a hand over his eyes. "But she doesn't, and she's never had a Season. And though I am well off, I don't have a title or an estate. And most of all, my disease is such that no man can predict its course."

"But in spite of that, you seemed taken with Nell, that's evident."

"Is it? And when I worked with you in Rome, I seemed taken with Signora Colletti, didn't I?"

Drum's heavy-lidded eyes opened wide.

"Yes, I was valuable to you in exposing her as the double agent she was, wasn't I? Gads, Drum, I may look like an ox, but I don't think like one. That was what made me useful to you then. You and Rafe seriously underestimate me if you think I'm always what I appear to be. It was good that my enemies did, but I'm a little annoyed that you do now."

The earl made a gesture of surrender, but Eric waved it off and went on, "I'm not saying Nell Baynes isn't a tempting dish. And when I met her, even I, with all my deficits, would have been a better partner for her than what awaited her in the streets. But I don't know the truth about her either, and how else can I find it but by winning her confidence? And if I win more?" He lowered his gaze to the spoon again and finally slipped it into his mouth.

"Well, yes," he went on as best he could through a mouthful of trifle, "life's been lonely since all my friends waltzed up church aisles with the beauties of their choice. I'm looking forward to being an uncle, but I admit I'd like to be a father one day. I have no hankering to grow old alone—if I'm lucky enough to grow old, that is. But I won't know that soon either," he said bluntly. "So for now I wait and watch and try to deal with life as best I can. You don't trust Nell? I certainly don't trust her cousin. I think we should both wait on things, even simple things, like trying to warn men away from women we believe are evil temptresses."

"Agreed. But as for warning young women away from handsome young gentlemen?" Drum asked, one eyebrow raised. "Do you think that applies to Camille as well?"

"Handsome young *men*," Eric corrected him. "As for whether Mr. Bartlett is a gentleman in deed, if not in name, we don't know that either. But I mean to find out," he promised.

His friends were gone; the trifle was a memory, as was the party. His man was in bed, doubtless sleeping the dreamless sleep of the just. But Eric still paced his bedchamber.

He couldn't get her out of his mind. What he'd told Drum was true, he just hadn't told him everything.

Every time he saw her, it grew worse for him. Now he couldn't stop imagining how good it would have been if she could have stayed when everyone else had left. It was another bitter night. A sharp wind whined around the corners of his house. The only place that was truly warm was here, an inch from the hearth—or in a bed with a warm woman in his arms. Failing that, a fellow could find warmth just sitting beside a woman he cared for. They could sit by the hearth and gossip about the guests who had just left. Or he'd take her in his arms and tell her how much he . . . No.

Eric put a hand on the mantel and stared down into the fire. On such a night, when loneliness and desire goaded him, he knew he wouldn't be saying anything. The moment they were at last alone, he'd take her into his arms and then into his bed and let his lips and his body say it all. He could imagine that, but the pleasure he would find with her would be beyond his imagining. But perhaps, he thought, the greatest pleasure would be after, as they held each other close, warm and sated, heart and body, through the rest of the long cold night.

Eric stared into the dying fire, but it was she that he saw. God, but she tempted him! He couldn't forget the look of her, her face, her breasts, her smooth skin, that mouth. And her scent. Lord! He thought he must be deranged. Some women reeked of gardenia or tuberose. The scent of her was so slight, delicate and floral, as soft and sweet as she was; yet it haunted him. What would it be like to take her into his arms, bury his nose in her neck and breathe in deeply? He could imagine what her naked breasts would feel like against his bare skin as they peaked and pebbled, as he cupped her pretty little rounded bottom and pressed her close and . . .

He picked up a poker and savagely poked at a ruddy log, shattering it, exposing its rosy heart and making it crumble to fiery pieces. He turned all his attention to the fire in the hearth to keep his mind off the one in his body. It might not just be the nearness of her this evening that was driving him mad. It could merely be that he needed a woman. After all, it had been a while. But he knew he needed a lover even more.

Men of his class and condition took mistresses for as long as the women pleased them. For too long a time now, none had pleased him. As he grew older, he realized he didn't like the thought of sex as commerce, however it was done. He'd never enjoyed the idea of buying a female for an hour or a night. He'd tried it in his youth and not since. It was an empty transaction, making what should be pleasure into pound dealing, like buying a sausage . . . or paying someone to accept one, he thought wryly. Paying a woman to receive his body for weeks rather than hours wasn't so different. Sex, at least for him, was about more than his member.

That didn't mean he'd been celibate. Finding sex was easier than finding love. His lovers had always been women who couldn't or wouldn't marry for one reason or another, and so their lovemaking had been something shared, not negotiated. Now he wanted to share more. No, he realized, as he stepped from the hearth and prepared to go to his lonely bed, he needed more.

He stripped off his robe. After years in the army, never knowing when he had to leap from his bed and into danger, sleeping naked was a luxury. He went to turn down the lamp and paused, gazing at the reflection of his body in the long glass over his bureau. *Not bad,* he thought, automatically sucking in his stomach. He looked at the scars on his leg and flexed it. He'd been lucky. He crooked an arm and stared. He still had muscles, the sickness he suffered from hadn't depleted them. He didn't look half as old or worn as he felt tonight. But the crux of the problem was that he wasn't at all sure he would live to get much older. Doctors guessed, he prayed, yet nothing but time would tell him.

He turned away from himself. No sense in posturing before a mirror like a damned dandy before a ball. Who better than he to know how deceptive appearances were?

So he couldn't yet offer for his little heroine, even though every part of his heart and body ached for her. But he could watch over her, he vowed, as he swept back his coverlets and got into bed, as long as he kept even stricter watch on himself.

Chapter 9

"So what do you think of your newfound cousin?" Camille asked Nell early the next morning.

They were sitting in the salon, waiting for Belle to join them so they could go for their usual early walk through the park. But time was marching on, and Camille wasn't, so she was fidgeting. Her dogs had to stay in the stables until she came to get them, which was the only bad thing she'd found about staying here in London with her brother and sister-in-law. At home, the dogs would have shared Camille's bed, not just her bedchamber, but they weren't allowed into Lady Annabelle's town house.

Camille couldn't really blame Belle for that. Rags and Muffin were her favorite dogs, but though they were her best behaved, that only meant that they didn't bite people or bark all night.

Friendly as they were, Camille's pets hadn't much idea of how to behave in polite company. Rags would steal a biscuit out from under a person's nose. Muffin would not only steal one from a person's mouth if he could, but if he didn't like the taste of the biscuit, he'd bury it under a rug or try to dig up the floor if there was no rug. Though they had charming names, even Camille had to admit they were a boisterous pair of lighthearted setters, more suitable to the fields of home than the manicured parks and sedate town houses of London. That was one of the reasons she insisted on walking them herself if she could. She also liked the exercise. And she would have hated for her brother's footmen to quit his service, as they sometimes threatened to do when they had to deal with the dogs too often.

Now Nell smiled at Camille's question about her newfound cousin. "Dana? I like him very well." Then, casting a sly look at Camille, she added, "How do you like him?"

"He seemed very nice."

"More than that, I'd say," Nell said.

"Oh," Camille said in surprise. "You like him that much? My word! Your future may be settled in more ways than one, then."

"What?" Nell asked, frowning.

"Well, I mean, if you're that taken with him, you might become more than just his ward." Seeing

Nell's confusion, Camille added, "He could be more than your guardian. Bother!" she said when Nell continued to frown in puzzlement. "Nell, you could end up marrying him, and that would solve all your problems, wouldn't it?

Nell laughed. "Oh, no! I like him, but I wouldn't want to marry him. He's handsome and smart, but he's only a solicitor. That is," she said hastily, remembering whom she was talking to, "I've heard marrying your cousin isn't good for your babies. It makes them weak-minded."

"Oh, bosh," Camille said, "half the *ton* and most of the royal family are married to their cousins." She giggled. "Well, you may be right about that!"

Nell didn't see the humor in Camille's joke. Camille didn't mind; she'd realized that her guest was literal-minded and often didn't get a joke.

"No, he's not for me," Nell went on. "Actually, I was wondering if he might be for you." Seeing Camille's eyes widen, she added, "He was very taken with you, anyone could see that. And he is very handsome and smart as can be. You should think about it. After all, you are past the age for your come-out, and yet here you are, out in London, and I don't see that many offers coming your way. . . . I didn't mean to hurt your feelings!" she cried when she saw the shock on Camille's face, her own eyes suddenly filling with tears. "Please don't be angry with me. Sometimes I just say what I'm thinking before I can think better of it. Oh, please don't be mad!"

"I'm not," Camille said, because she wasn't. She was just hurt. "I have had offers," she added, raising her head. "I imagine the reason you don't know that is because I don't make a fuss about them and manage to stay friends with a fellow even if I don't want to marry him."

But her spirits did sink. Although she'd had offers and masculine attention, it was true that they weren't like what other girls got. Her sitting room had never been filled with flowers after a night of dancing, and no one had ever written poetry to her. Her disappointment was her secret, because though she knew it was all nonsense, she did love flowers and poetry.

"My cousin admires you very much," Nell said in a little voice. "He told me so last night."

"Well, that was quick," Camille said. She forced a smile. "Don't look so woebegone. I don't think less of him for saying it anymore than I do of you for wondering if I'm going to wind up on the shelf. Anyway, I think Dana only meant that he liked me for helping you. How could it be anything else? We hardly know each other. And, as you pointed out, gentlemen don't swoon when they first see me. I grow on them," she added glumly, in spite of herself. "Like moss." She gave a little chuckle at her own sad joke. "Which isn't so bad," she said before Nell could look sorry for her again. "After all, that's what marriage is all about, isn't it? Two people growing on each other over the long term?"

She was glad that she heard Belle finally coming

down the stairs. She was dressed in blue, which usually suited her perfectly, but she looked washed out this morning. No wonder she looked tired, Camille thought, they were up late last night, and she was a lady who usually slept until noon, like the other Fashionables in London. She was rising earlier because of Camille, even though Camille often told her she didn't mind walking through the park with only a maid or a footman in tow or, as now, with Nell. Still, Belle didn't want to change the habit they'd grown into at home, claiming the early exercise was good for her. Miles sometimes went too, but he'd stopped since Nell came to stay.

Camille hoped Belle's exercise really did help her, because she looked so wan this morning. But when she put on a cherry-red cape trimmed with fox, her face took on delicate color and she looked wonderful again.

Nell looked lovely, as usual, in a white gown and fresh as springtime when she put on the long green cloak Camille had lent her.

Camille was the one who actually handled the dogs, so she dressed accordingly. She wore a warm woolen gown, a dark, heavy cloak, and a pair of her most comfortable half boots, broken in nicely after dozens of such expeditions in the fields at home.

Belle looked at her and frowned.

"My gown's clean," Camille said defensively. "There was sleet last night and it's thawing. The ground will be spongy, so I wore old boots. The cloak's short, I know, but it won't trail in the mud if I have to go off the path chasing after one of the lads. And it doesn't matter if my hems get muddy, because my clothes are so old I don't care."

Belle rolled her eyes. "But the gown is saffron and the cloak is olive—or was when it was new, which might have been when you were fifteen, and neither color does you a bit of good. And the boots look like the gardeners'."

"But who's going to see me?"

Belle hesitated and then sighed. "True. Most sane people are sleeping. And the gentlemen reeling home after a night on the town are probably not seeing too clearly anyhow. But we have to get you some attractive ensembles to walk in. Sturdy can be pretty, you know."

"Like you yourself, Camille," Nell said softly.

Both Belle and Camille looked at her, but Nell seemed oblivious to her implied insult. She'd intended a compliment, Camille realized. It couldn't be helped that it could also be taken another way.

Dana Bartlett thought Camille looked just fine. At least, his dark expressive eyes said so when he met her in the park a half-hour later.

"Miss Croft!" he said, sweeping off his high beaver hat, his eyes taking her in as though he beheld the sun rising though the gray morning's mists. "Cousin," he added with a nod to Nell, and "My lady," he said, making his bow to Belle. "How good to see you!"

"How odd, too," Belle said, raising her brows. "I'd no idea you lived nearby or fancied such early excursions."

"I don't," he said with a disarming smile. "Not usually. But last night, when Nell mentioned her habit of going for an early walk, I remembered how the air used to smell at dawn at home. I'm from Sussex originally and have memories of fine country mornings. So I decided to kill two birds with one stone. I came out in the hope of meeting up with you."

He took a long, deep breath, closed his eyes, and smiled. "Yes, exactly. This is delicious, isn't it? The way the air smells before sun heats the smoke from all the city's coal fires." He opened his eyes. "May I join you? I've some questions to ask Nell. Last night it occurred to me that since I'm going to be looking for new lodgings, it would only be fair to get her opinion about what she would like in her new home. Your opinions would be welcome too. Well, what do I know about what a young woman needs or wants in respect to number of rooms, their sizes and colors and that sort of thing?"

Belle inclined her head, considering. It was kind and generous of him to take Nell's feelings into account. Too many men wouldn't even think about asking a woman what she wanted. Still, she'd noticed that the fellow kept his eyes on her sister-in-law the whole time. Camille could do better for herself than a mere solicitor. But a walk in the park wasn't a proposal of marriage, and anyway, there was no way she could politely say no. "We'd be pleased with your company," she said.

Camille let out her breath, surprised to discover that she'd been holding it, waiting for Belle's answer.

They walked on in pairs. There was one awkward moment before Dana took up position beside Belle, because she was the senior lady. Camille had to go ahead of them, because Rags and Muffin didn't like to follow. Nell came with her. Camille thought she would have a permanent crick in her neck from trying to hear everything said behind her back.

"So," Dana finally summed it up, as they strolled on toward the lake, "I see what we need. A town house would be perfect. I'm not a Midas, but renting one for the rest of this Season would be possible. I don't doubt Nell will have found her own place by next season—at the side of a man she can call her own, of course. Now, my lady, please tell me which district I should be looking in."

He bent his dark head to hear Belle's opinion. Camille didn't. It had been hard enough trying to hear everything said about rooms. A discussion of neighborhoods wasn't worth the effort. She was free to look around again.

There was a lot to look at this morning. The wait for Belle had delayed them, and so they were in the park later than usual. London was waking up now, and the park was filling up with more than maidservants and nannies walking their charges—lapdogs

and babies. Since their little party was walking
along the side of a broad avenue that went through
the park, they could see the traffic increasing. Dashing high phaetons with ruddy-cheeked gentlemen
guiding them went by, as well as heavy carriages,
knots of horsemen, and strollers on either side of
the road. All seemed to be enjoying a little respite
from the busy London streets on this clear, bright,
not too cold winter's day.

Belle nodded to some people as she kept talking
with Dana Bartlett. Nell gawked at everyone.
Camille told her who they were seeing, hoping that
it was still too early for any courtesans to be on display. Belle would not appreciate Nell's awe of
them, and heaven knew what Dana would think of
his cousin's odd opinion of the demimonde.
Camille would hate for Nell to lose her one good
chance at a fine new life. It wasn't all charity on her
part. Charming as Nell's cousin Dana was, Camille
still wanted Nell herself to move out of her life as
soon as possible.

"And that's Lord and Lady North," Camille told
Nell as she gave a bright smile to a handsome couple on the opposite side of the roadway. "Top of
the trees, the pair of them, and as nice as they are
good-looking. She's lovely, but did you ever see
such a handsome man? And faithful to her as the
sea is to the shore," she added quickly. "Oh, and
there, with the infant in the pram? Lady Kidd, a really decent sort. She didn't mind when Muffin
licked her baby's nose last week, and you know

how some ladies would have carried on." Camille paused to try to tug Muffin back into line, because it looked as if he wanted another taste of the baby.

"And that's the man Lady Annabelle said we shouldn't speak to, isn't it?" Nell whispered, pointing toward a dark gentleman on a showy black horse who was riding down the middle of the road toward them.

Camille frowned. "Yes," she said, hastily dropping her gaze lest the dark-eyed lord should catch her staring at him. "Don't point! Dearborne's worse than a rake. He's debauched through and through, the worst kind of sneaking coward too. Many of our friends have had run-ins with him. His father disowned him, but here he is again and on a fine mount too. I suppose he got back into his family's good graces. Good heavens!" Camille said, looking up to see Nell staring at Dearborne, who was staring back at her with interest. "I said don't look at him! Now you've done it," she grumbled, peeping up from under her lashes, "he's looking at us."

Camille stared at her dogs' tails and so couldn't see if Lord Dearborne was still studying Nell with the bold, insolent look of appraisal that he'd been surveying her with a second before. But she peeked at Nell and saw her still looking back at him, a strange smile growing on her lips.

"Nell!" she hissed. "I meant it. Stop. Belle will murder you, and rightly so." She couldn't see if Nell obeyed, because she kept staring at her dogs as

Lord Dearborne came near and didn't move her head until she heard the approaching hoofbeats go on by, as the dark horse and rider rode on. Then she looked up again. Dearborne was gone, and Nell was simply looking into the distance ahead.

Belle spoke up. "Why was that wretched fellow looking at you?" she demanded of Camille.

"Who was that? Was he distressing you?" Dana immediately asked.

Belle cast a blank look at Dana. Nothing could have sunk him more in her eyes, though he couldn't know that. Camille did and felt embarrassed for him and a little wistful too. Because Dana had just reminded them how distant he was from their world. Anyone in Society, or familiar with it, would have known who Dearborne was.

"Who knows why he was staring?" Camille said and then, looking at Dana, added, "He's just a bad man, one we want nothing to do with."

Camille decided on the spot that later, when they were alone, she'd tell her sister-in-law about Nell's obvious interest in Dearborne. There was a limit to how much she was willing to protect the girl, and a few words from Lady Annabelle on her highest ropes were better than any lecture Camille could give to Nell. Still, Camille realized with a trace of sadness, there was absolutely no point in telling Dana more. He wasn't going to be part of her life after all. And by the time his cousin went to live with him, the matter would be moot.

Something flickered in Dana's dark eyes as he

watched Camille's changing expressions before he turned his attention back to Belle. "You were saying, my lady?" he asked her. "About where I could find a likely chaperone for my cousin?"

He'd need one, Camille thought on a stifled sigh as she turned back to see Nell staring at a richly dressed young fop in his high-perch curricle.

"That's Lord Breckinridge," Camille told Nell under her breath. "He isn't an out and out cad, only one of the most stupid men in Town. And yes," she added before Nell could ask, "he's rich. Also married."

Nell didn't stop smiling. But Camille did when she realized that what she said hadn't blunted Nell's interest in the idiotic Lord Breckinridge in the least.

So when Eric came riding up, he saw Nell look up at him with a charming smile as she walked along beside a grim and thunderous-looking Camille.

"Down, Rags! Muffin, stop that!" Camille shouted, scowling even more as her dogs tried to get to Eric, even though their efforts made his horse dance dangerously in place.

Eric laughed, reached into his pocket, and tossed something to the dogs, causing them to scramble at Camille's feet and not at his horse's.

"If you didn't carry dried sausage for them in your pocket, they'd leave you alone," Camille panted as she struggled to keep her pets in check.

Eric put a hand on his heart. "You wound me! You mean they don't love me for my own sake? But you do, don't you, my lady?" he asked Belle. "Good morning, Bartlett," he said with a nod to Dana. "And how are you this morning, Nell?"

Eric looked grand, Camille thought. He was dressed all in brown, and from the glow on his face to the smile in his eyes, there was no way anyone could tell he'd ever been sick a day in his life.

"We'll do," she said before anyone could answer him. "But no need to ask about you. You're in fine fettle, aren't you?"

"Better now that I've met up with you," he said.

She had to grin. "Much luck it will do you. You're riding, we're walking."

He slipped down from the saddle. "I can walk as well as ride. Might as well take a weight off Thunder's back." Taking the reins in one hand, he ambled to their side, leading his horse behind him.

Belle's smile was real and warm. "Yes, come stroll with us, Eric. We're going to walk until Cammie's rambunctious beasts get tired."

"Oh, an all-day affair," Eric said. "Fine."

And so it was, for Camille—until Rags saw a squirrel and tried to take off, with Muffin eager to join him. By the time Camille got their leads sorted out, it was Nell who was walking beside Eric, favoring him with the same rapt attention she'd given Dearborne and Breckinridge. And he didn't seem to mind at all.

"My cousin," a voice said at Camille's ear, "is a handful, is she not?"

Camille looked up and into Dana's concerned

eyes. He wasn't so much taller than she, and it made his gaze seem more intimate.

"You'll have to watch her," she said honestly. "She doesn't . . . That is, she's new to Town," she concluded weakly, because she didn't want to seem to be disparaging his cousin.

She didn't have to. "But she's obviously not new to the world," he murmured in worried tones. His dark eyes searched Camille's so deeply and with such intensity she felt as stirred by his attention as she did embarrassed. But she couldn't look away.

"It's a great deal to ask," he said as he gazed at her. "But will you help me with her, at least until I can take her under my own wing? So that she doesn't ruin her chances for the future?"

Camille felt as let down as relieved that his request had to do with Nell and not herself. "I will," she promised.

She was so confused by her own reactions that she was glad to look away and at Eric.

Until she saw he was too busy chatting with Nell to notice.

Chapter 10

Eric paced in the parlor. He'd arrived too early, and that surprised him. Camille was always ready ten minutes before an appointment, much to her fashionably late sister-in-law's perennial disgust. Maybe Belle was having some influence on Camille after all, he thought. He smiled. Not likely. It was much more probable that Camille was still in the stables, fretting over a sick horse or supervising the delivery of a litter of kittens. Miles and Belle were probably dealing with some last minute catastrophe of their own, a snag in Miles's neckcloth or a tear in Belle's gown. Or maybe even a last minute of lovemaking. They'd only been married for a year, after all.

He looked up as someone slipped into the room.

"Good evening," he said, bowing. "You look lovely, Nell."

That was the usual thing to tell a young woman on her way to a ball, but in this case it was only true. The girl looked exquisite. They were going to a costume ball, and she wore an antique gown with a laced waist and a sweeping bell of a skirt, her neckline low enough to show the tops of her pretty little breasts. Her hair was done up in inky ringlets, her blue eyes sparkled with excitement. Even from where he stood, he could scent her sweet perfume. She'd have been a sensation tonight even if the dramatic tale of her rescue hadn't gotten out.

"Thank you," she said, curtsying low enough to show him even more of those lovely apple-shaped breasts.

He cleared his throat and raised his gaze to her face. "But since no one else is here yet, you'd better go find them. It isn't proper for you to be alone with me. Not that I'd presume," he added quickly. "But those are Society's rules."

Instead of retreating, she came further into the room, only stopping when she stood in front of him, and then only because she couldn't get closer for the bell of her skirts. She looked up into his eyes and then lowered her own gaze, starry black lashes shadowing her petal-smooth cheeks. He backed a step and felt as foolish as confused when she took a step closer.

"But I've something in my eye," she said plaintively. "It stabs at me, and there's no one else around. Can you help?"

The scent of gardenias was strong. She put her head back and bent toward him, her eyes closed. They were so close he could feel her soft breath on his face. Her rose-colored lips parted. The room was very still.

He heard voices somewhere in the outer hall and quickly stepped back. "I've hands like hams," he said gruffly. "I'd do more harm than good. You'd best go find someone with defter fingers. Tell you what," he said, moving away toward the door, "stay here. I'll see who I can find."

He left the room. She might or might not know the rules of Society, but he did, and they were nothing to trifle with. A speck in her eye might have earned him an instant wife or at least the contempt of his friends. Being found alone with an unmarried female, touching her face or staring into her eyes, would have been damning, however innocent his motivations. So he was delighted to look up and see his friend Miles coming down the stair.

"Belle's slow this evening," Miles reported. "Cammie's no better. You'd think we were going to the palace instead of just another ball. And one held in public rooms, at that."

"Women," Eric said, "are mysterious creatures. You ought to know that by now, especially since you are married. By the way, Miss Baynes is in the salon complaining of something in her eye, and I wondered . . ."

"Oh!" Nell said gaily, as she stepped out of the salon and into the hall, "no need to worry! I blinked, and it's out."

Miles smiled, looking at her as approvingly as any healthy male would.

"Excellent," Eric said, looking at her with new speculation.

"Sound the trumpets!" Camille sang from the top of the stairs. "Here we are!"

Eric looked up and went still. "Well worth the wait," he said gallantly.

"See?" Camille laughed. "He knows what's good for him."

She took Belle's arm and came down the stair, merry as she could be, because she knew she looked well, if not wonderful, and as that was the most she could hope for, she was content.

Camille's contentment didn't last the night. She was as panicked as she'd be if Muffins or Rags ran away from her straight into traffic. Because it was nearly midnight, the ball was in full swing, and Nell had vanished.

Nell had disappeared from a crowded ballroom and been gone nearly a half-hour that Camille knew of. It might have been longer. While taking a breath after a rowdy country romp, she'd realized Nell hadn't joined her as she was supposed to do after each dance. So Camille refused her next partner and started looking. Nell was nowhere to be seen either inside the ballroom or in the ladies withdrawing room.

It was too cold for her to be outside, but that wasn't what worried Camille. She was more upset at the thought that Nell could be somewhere inside, either in one of the private rooms in the massive opera house or in some convenient dark niche, closet, or hallway. That was where secret lovers had their trysts. She'd seen plenty of them squirming in each other's arms in the shadows as she'd hunted for Nell. That was why she hadn't told Miles, Belle, or even Dana Bartlett about his cousin's disappearance.

Nell's life could have been in danger, though Camille doubted it. There were few murderers in the *ton*. But there were plenty of seducers. And it seemed to Camille that Nell had returned the salacious smiles of every one of them before she disappeared into that last dance from which she hadn't returned. More likely Nell's reputation rather than her life was at stake. That was why Camille hadn't raised an alarm yet. If Nell was caught at her own foolishness, as Camille suspected might be the case, it could cast a shadow of scandal on Miles, Belle, and herself. It would definitely ruin Nell. She was not, after all, a member of the society she found herself in.

No matter what was preached on Sunday, Camille knew that a woman of birth and means could disgrace herself with a man and yet survive it. Of course, she'd be taken out of London into the country, where an arranged marriage would quietly be made for her.

But Nell didn't have a noble background, and who could say if her newfound cousin Dana would take her in if he found her carrying on? Unless, of course, Camille thought, whatever man Nell had disappeared with was willing to marry her and save her name by changing it to his.

Camille was very worried about that.

Because Eric was gone too.

And Camille knew it might all be her own fault. She'd been the one to insist that Nell come to the ball. After all, they'd discussed the invitation in front of her.

"Young Lord Ragland and his dewy bride are giving a ball," Belle had said. She often read out invitations to the family at breakfast to see who was interested in them. "But they haven't the house-room for one yet."

"No," Miles said absently, his nose still in the newspaper as he lifted his coffee cup. "They can't have ours. Ragland's an ass."

"They don't want ours," Belle went on. "They also say," she read from the card she was holding, "they want to 'share the joy they found in Venice on their honeymoon.'"

"Should have stayed there, then," Miles muttered.

Camille giggled.

"And so they've rented the opera house and sent

invitations for a grand ball." Belle said, ignoring him. "The theme of which, of course, is to be Venice. What fun!"

"Can we go?" Camille asked.

"Can we?" Belle asked Miles.

He peered out from the side of his newspaper. "Can I survive if we don't?"

"I don't think so," Belle said seriously.

They all laughed, even Nell, who had been sitting, as usual, mute as a mouse. It was only when everyone was done laughing that she asked, in her soft, small voice, "Am I to come too?"

Camille felt terrible and shot an agonized look at her sister-in-law, because Belle usually didn't seem to be aware of her guest. It would be cruel to say no after saying how grand it would be, Camille thought, holding her breath. Belle might sometimes be unaware of people she considered beneath her, but she was seldom cruel.

Belle glanced at Camille, pursed her lips, and sighed. "Yes, you may, of course," she told Nell. "We'll ask your cousin too, if you like."

"Thank you. I'd like that very much, and so would he. I know he would," Nell said. But it was Camille she smiled at as she said it.

When they arrived at the opera house, Camille saw why Belle wanted to be there. Their hosts had dreamed up an inspired notion. Where else could a sumptuous canvas backdrop depicting St. Mark's Square support the merry illusion that they were actually in Venice? There were other theatrical devices to add to the effect: artificial waves made of wood marked off the dance floor, false gondola poles stood at the sides of the room, servants pretended to row stage set half gondolas. Musicians and serving men were all in Venetian costume. Even so, they didn't catch the eye as much as the guests did.

Each guest seemed determined to outshine the others. They were dressed in stunning representations of the Italian Renaissance, perhaps even gaudier than the original had been, certainly more outrageous.

Belle had gone to the trunks in her mama's attics and come up with perfect costumes for them all. She herself wore a blue gown with wide panniers. Nell had been lent one that was striped bright pink and white. Camille was ecstatic with the gown she'd been given. It was daringly low at the breast, permissible to wear because its antiquity made its boldness acceptable. She refused to wear the heavy wire cage fashioned to hold up its skirts—the petticoats that came with it were enough for that. The gown also had froths of ivory lace sleeves and hem. That, as well as age, cooled the brilliant gold of the fabric. And it fitted as though made for her.

When she looked at herself in the spotted mirror up in the attics, Camille was only sorry she hadn't been born a century or two earlier, when fashion flattered figures like hers. Wide at the skirt as it was low at the breast; it nipped in her waist to make it look tiny. The whalebone stays were merciless, and breathing was hard. But it was only for one night. And what was being short of breath to looking like a princess?

Now Camille stood at the sidelines of the room and squinted against the dazzling light, searching for a glimpse of Nell's gown. It was hard to find, because many guests were dressed in such brilliant colors and other women also wore period costumes. Some of the men wore shirts of many colors with puffed, slashed sleeves, and their form-fitting tights had ribbons tied on their legs. Some ladies wore eyemasks, some men had on commedia dell'arte masks with enormous noses and jutting chins.

Other guests chose standard formal wear instead, as Eric and Miles had done. When they got to the opera, they'd paused on the stair and surveyed the room in amazement.

"Thank God," Camille heard Eric murmur to Miles, "none of those fops decided to wear a codpiece for authenticity. I don't think I could deal with that."

She'd been about to say, "I don't think *you'd* have a problem," but just in time remembered she was a lady and this wasn't a stable.

He looked wonderful to her as he was in his dark jacket, white linen shirt, satin breeches, and white stockings, and she thought it would have been a pity if he'd worn a mask to hide that wonderful face. They'd had one dance, then he'd disappeared. She'd danced the rest of the time away with other partners. Even now, a few hours into the ball, everyone was still clearly having a grand time.

But Camille wasn't, because soon supper would be served and there'd be no way to conceal Nell's absence. Camille felt hurt and betrayed.

"Cammie? What's the matter?" Eric asked. Camille looked up to see him smiling down at her.

Her hand flew to her breast. She couldn't answer right away. She was surprised by his sudden appearance at her side and not sure what she should say. "Where have you been?" sounded presumptuous. And she wasn't sure she wanted to hear his answer if she asked, "Where's Nell?"

She started to blurt, "I can't find Nell," but couldn't. The words died on her lips—because she looked at his.

His lips were firm and shapely, but they were also red. And they looked smudged with rouge.

She tried not to show the pain she felt and tried to think what to say.

He saw the direction of her gaze and frowned. He took a handkerchief from his pocket, touched it to his lips, and then looked at it. "Lord, like a boy at a jam pot," he said, with a chuckle. "You'd think I'd have learned to be more fastidious."

Camille thought her heart would crack.

"Have you tried that punch?" he asked as he dabbed at his mouth again. "Too sweet, I know, but I'm partial to strawberries, and I'd had too much wine, so I was really thirsty. The punch only made me thirstier. . . . What's the matter?"

The handkerchief showed red smudges; his mouth no longer did.

"Nell's gone!" she blurted, so suffused with relief there was no room for tact.

"I know," he said with a frown.

She stared.

"I've been looking for her," he said. "I saw her in a set with Copley almost an hour ago and remembered I'd promised her a dance. But when the music stopped, she was gone and so was he. I didn't want to raise a hue and cry for her sake. But I don't trust Copley, and she is new to Town. That was a while ago. I was just going to ask you where she was."

"I don't know," she said. "When I saw her last, about a half-hour past, she was with Osborne, though."

Eric raised an eyebrow. "Osborne's a fool, not a cad, though he does keep bad company too often for my taste. Come, let's dance. It's so crowded that's the only way to see the whole dance floor. She's such a little slip of a thing, for all we know she may have been dancing all this time."

Camille took his hand.

So I get to dance with him so he can search for her, she thought as she stepped into the dance with him. *And though "thing" is not the most lover-like description, still, I'd never be called a little slip of anything.*

But she could not regret the dance for any reason.

A ball was like a lottery. Partners had to dance to whatever music was playing when their time came round. Camille rejoiced, for she and Eric stepped into a waltz. He put up his big hand and she placed hers in it and moved in close to him. She felt his arm go about her. They barely touched. But she had never been so aware of a man's body. He was so large, so strong, a wall of warm male flesh. Still, he held her so gently, as though she was treasured, as though she were fragile. Prudes might say a waltz was shockingly familiar, but it wasn't half enough so for Camille. She wanted to burrow into his arms, not just stand inside his clasp. But she was close enough to feel the heat of the man, near enough to revel in his clean scent and feel his warm breath on her ear as he spoke to her. He spoke pleasantries. She heard rhapsodies. She was in Eric's arms, and they moved together.

He was an accomplished dancer, and though he said he'd look for Nell, every time Camille looked at him she saw his smiling eyes bent on her. She couldn't look into those eyes, she didn't dare. But neither could she look away from them for long. When she did, she studied his face. She could see how closely he had shaved. She could see the fine grain of his skin and notice the bracket that formed at the side of his mouth when he smiled down at her, and he did that often, as though he knew no greater pleasure than to hold her.

She'd have paid the musicians her whole dowry

if they would only have kept playing; but too soon the dance was done. She turned to Eric, her eyes alight.

He was looking over her head. "There she is," he said.

Camille turned to see that Nell was with her cousin Dana. They'd just stepped out of the dance together and were a pretty pair to watch, both dark, fine boned, and even featured. They turned as one and came directly to Eric and Camille.

"There you are," Dana said to Camille. "May I have this next dance?"

"You could, but not with me," Camille said. "We've had two dances already. If we have one more, they'll have us leg-shackled."

"What a sweet fate," he said, smiling at her.

Nell looked up at Eric, her question clear in her eyes.

Eric nodded. "But we haven't even had one, have we?" he asked Nell. "Shall we?" He offered her his arm.

Camille's heart sank when she saw the sort of smile Nell gave him as they danced off together. The difference in their sizes would have looked ridiculous if they hadn't looked so well together. Eric, so tall and broad and fair, Nell so slight, lithesome, and dark. Eric's hand almost covered the whole of her narrow waist; her head was thrown back to show the smooth line of her throat as she looked up at him. He was so much bigger than she was that he had to bend over her so that they could speak quietly. He looked so attentive, their closeness seemed so intimate, that Camille caught her breath. They stood the proper distance apart, and when they danced, moved only to the music. But they seemed absorbed in each other, and he frequently laughed, and Nell's smile was much older than she was.

Camille's stomach hurt.

"My cousin," Dana said slowly, "is perhaps a bit too free with her smiles. Or is it the nature of them that worries me?"

"You don't have to worry about Eric," Camille said. "He's a perfect gentleman."

"It's not Lieutenant Ford I worry about," he said, turning his attention to Camille. His dark eyes were steady and searching. "I must ask you, has my cousin been . . . circumspect? I mean to say, I've been watching her this evening. Her reactions are too candid. I worry they may be misinterpreted. For example, I wonder if her smile of greeting is a shade too welcoming. Or am I wrong?"

"It's not her smiles," Camille said bluntly. She made a decision. "Thing is," she said slowly, "I was worried too, and not just because of smiles. I didn't see her for the longest time tonight. I looked for a half-hour, and she was nowhere to be found. It would be a disaster if she went off with someone on her own."

Dana's face went still. Then he nodded. "Oh, that, yes," he said. "I've kept my eye on her all night too, but I didn't see her for a few minutes either, and I got worried as well. But I found her in the hall outside by herself, trying to look like part of a potted palm. It took me a full half-hour to talk her back into the ball. She was overwhelmed. She was so popular, so many gentlemen had asked her to dance, that she had an attack of shyness. She said she couldn't find you or me, and so she was waiting to get her courage back. She never realized that by so doing she might endanger her reputation. I'm glad I found her when I did."

"So am I!" Camille said with relief. Her heart felt considerably lighter, even though Eric was dancing with Nell. But she still wished the music would stop.

"Nell isn't the only one who has trouble with parties," Dana said suddenly. "I do, or rather, now I do too. Society rings us round with taboos. I'm very glad your brother invited me to come with Nell this evening, but it frustrates me as well. I know I can't have more than two dances with you in one night, but the truth is I want to spend time with you." He took a breath. "So," he said quickly, "since I'm new to your world too, forgive me if I make a disastrous mistake. But I must know. I'd like to see you, Miss Croft. I'd like to go riding, walking, dancing, whatever you please, with you. Would my attentions be unwelcome?"

Camille blinked. She didn't know what to say.

He smiled. "Don't worry. I'm not making you an offer—though it is an offer of friendship that might

one day lead to more. But I don't know how high
the barriers are in your world. I'm only a man-at-
law. You're a lady. So I have to ask: would you,
could you, consider seeing more of me in order to
know if you would like to see more of me? That's
all I meant. If the answer's no, I would still always
be grateful to you for how you took Nell in."

He waited.

"But the thing is, I . . ." Camille found herself in
a tangle of words she tried to sort through. Dana
was a very nice man, but she didn't feel *that* way
about him. She didn't dislike him either, and she
never wanted to be thought of as a snob. She
sought the right thing to say, lifted her eyes, and
saw his cousin and Eric gliding past, looking like a
couple made of sugar on a wedding cake.

Camille tossed up her head. "The thing is," she
finally said, "that it would be fine to go for a walk,
or take tea, or dance with me. So long as you know
I'm not very serious about it, at least, not right
now. A gentleman doesn't have to declare his intentions for things like that in my world. It's only
when he wants to 'declare his intentions' that . . ."
She laughed. "But we don't know each other
enough for anything like that."

"I hope to remedy that," he said, looking deep
into her eyes.

Flirtation was something she understood. She
might be too overwhelmed by Eric to get up to
much of it with him, but this was different. She
knew how to defuse a flirtation too. Camille snapped

open the fan she wore at her waist. "Now I see why this was part of the costume," she said, fanning herself vigorously.

He joined her in laughter. She looked up to see Eric's head turn to look at them. And then she really felt like laughing.

But not for long.

The pleasure went out of the evening for Camille after that. She couldn't dance with Eric again, and she certainly couldn't bear watching him dance with other women. Nor did she want to encourage Dana. She'd danced her fill, and it was a while until supper would be served. Until then, there was nothing she really cared to do. No other men interested her, and the silly gabble of most of the fashionable young women always bored her to bits.

"Besides," she commented grumpily to Belle's suggestion that she chat with someone more her age, "this is not the best place to strike up a conversation with anyone. I don't know how they expect girls to pick husbands in this sort of situation," she went on, warming to her subject. "You can't really hear, much less get to know anyone, at these monstrous parties. It's all shouting quips, giggling, and posing."

"Don't get on your favorite hobbyhorse with me," Belle said. "I agree. But do go dance or flirt or at least try to look happy to be here."

Camille decided she'd go for a breath of fresh air. The ballroom was crowded, and the mingled smells of hot candle wax, burning lamp oil, and perfumes was making her dizzy. When she'd searched for Nell, she'd noticed someone slipping out of a door down at the end of one of the many corridors that led from the ballroom and had felt a fresh breeze against her face as the door closed again.

"Very well, I'm off," she said lightly, left Belle, and wove through the crowd in the ballroom in search of the exit she'd seen.

The opera was like a rabbit warren, with many exits and entrances, so it wasn't easy to find the one she sought. There was one door that seemed quite popular with the gentlemen who were going out to blow a cloud, or so it seemed from the scent of tobacco that wafted in every time the door opened or closed. That certainly wasn't her door.

It took some time before she found the right corridor. It was a long one, and at last, she came to a heavy green door. It took some pushing, but Camille wasn't a weakling, and soon she had it open. She felt a cool breeze, pushed harder, and looked outside. The door opened on a dark, cluttered alley—and the cold, breezy night. There was no one there. Camille smiled, and stepped outside.

She walked a few paces, breathing in the fresh air, congratulating herself on her cleverness. But the refreshing air quickly felt chill on her bare shoulders, and the brick floor icy against her thin slippers. She looked around and decided that a silent, empty, dark alley wasn't the most comfortable place to find herself. Ominous shadows seemed to be lurking in the shadows. She decided to return to the ball.

She had taken only three steps back before she gasped in pain.

Camille hopped wildly on one foot and tried to grasp the other in her hand so she could see what she'd stepped on. Whatever it was, it had pierced her slipper and hurt like the blazes.

She could see nothing because of her wide and wildly swaying skirts. She looked around for a place to sit and decided against hopping into further darkness to find one. So it was either sit on the floor, among who knew what filth, or try to make her way back into the opera house. Camille hopped to the door and pulled—but she couldn't get purchase standing on one foot, and the door remained closed, no matter how hard she tugged.

Weeping wouldn't help, so she refused to cry and was ashamed of the whimpering she heard coming from her own throat. But her foot felt on fire and she was very worried. Could she hop all the way to the front of the alley? But what direction was that? She tasted tears on her lips and hated her own weakness.

And then the door swung open.

"Cammie!" Eric said. "What the devil are you doing here?"

"Hurting!" she cried, and hopped toward him.

He caught her in his arms. "What the devil . . . ?" he muttered.

"The devil this, the devil that," she said from between clenched teeth, "I stepped on something
sharp and I can't put my foot down again."

He picked her up in his arms as though she
weighed a feather and strode back into the opera
house with her. It was beyond wonderful to be
caught up in his arms, held close to that hard body,
and actually feel the words as they rumbled in his
chest.

"You were gone so long Belle got worried and
sent Miles and me to look for you," he said. "I
asked around and discovered your direction. I tried
the door because there was nothing else to see
down that corridor. Lord, Cammie, where was
your head? A stabbed foot is the least of what
could have happened to you out there in the dark
by yourself. Let's have a look," he said as he strode
toward a bench under a flaring gaslight high on the
wall.

He sat with her on his lap, pushed her skirts to
the side, and picked up her foot. She bent her leg so
he could see it, but was hesitant to look at her
wound herself. Instead, she watched his face to see
if she could discover the extent of her injury by his
expression.

He frowned and grunted, "Blast. There's blood.
But I can see what it is. Ah! You're lucky, it's a piece
of glass. Much worse if it had been a nail. Hold
still, lass. This may hurt."

It did. But Camille put her face in the crook of
his neck and bit back her cry of pain.

"Sorry," he murmured, holding up a wicked-looking shard of glass. "But there it is. Looks like from a broken bottle. Luckily it's dark green. We can see if there's any more in there. I'll just ease your slipper off and see. There. Doesn't look like there's any left. Feel that? No? Or that? Good. It's all out, I think. Cammie? Are you all right?"

She sniffed. "No, it hurts."

His mouth ticked up in a little smile. "Well, yes, slicing up your foot will do that. But it was a clean cut. You may not be dancing any more tonight, but you'll dance again, I think. With me next time, if you will."

"I'm not a child," she said haughtily. "You don't have to promise me treats to get me to stop crying."

She wanted to vanish when she heard what she said and ducked her head again. He sat silent for a moment. She stayed unmoving, feeling his warm body beneath her, knowing she should move away from him, knowing she could not.

She felt his fingers on her cheek as he lightly touched the wetness of her tears. Then he silently handed her his handkerchief, picked her up in his arms, and strode back to the ball. Neither of them spoke again.

Eric paid the hackney driver, stepped out of the coach, and stood on the pavement in front of his house, breathing deep. It was sleeting, but he needed ice on his overheated flesh. He wasn't sick again. Lust was the only fever he suffered from tonight, and he knew it wouldn't kill him. Not right away, at least.

Tonight had been hell. He'd only held two women in his arms. One had nearly broken his heart, while the other was a temptress. One only served to point up the fact that only the other mattered. Why had he thought he could hold her, touch her, and remain unmoved? She'd interested him from the moment he'd seen her again. But he'd deceived himself, hiding his desires in a welter of rationalizations.

He'd told himself he wanted to see her because he enjoyed her company, felt rested and at home in her presence. Nonsense. He enjoyed many women's company.

He reacted to her the way he did because it had been a long time since he'd had a woman? Idiot that he was. He'd never known a woman like her.

He always preferred dark beauties? That was his biggest self-deception. What she had went beyond any other woman's beauty.

When he'd seen her tonight in that gown from another century, it had all come clear to him at last.

There she'd stood silent, smiling, reveling in her new finery. He'd taken her hand and instantly felt the shock of her touch. The rightness of it equaled the excitement of it. And when she stepped into the dance with him, she'd seemed to him to be the eternal woman, exotic and unknowable but familiar as his next breath. It was as if she'd come to him from another time and place, but she felt just right in his arms.

No more deception, he told himself. He had to have her. It was as simple as that. His flesh knew it, even if his high-flown principles had not. He shook his head. The sleet collecting on his high beaver hat flew off in a tinkling shower. He didn't notice. He was too busy thinking of the reason for his awakening.

He'd danced with her once too often. Her gown had been so low that when he'd looked down, he'd fallen—at least all his fine resolves had. He'd wanted to breathe the scent of that valley of shadowed skin between those high, arching breasts. He'd needed to taste that silken flesh so badly it was all he could do to remember that they were only dancing, that he couldn't drag her closer and devour her.

She felt slight in his arms, but any woman would, compared to him. But she wasn't so fragile that she made him feel like a clumsy, oversized lout, as many women did. She was fully grown, deliciously curved, and woman enough for him. Her eyes, her scent, the way she moved—he ached for her. He'd mocked the men in codpieces tonight, but he'd have been better off with one if he'd worn Renaissance finery. Good thing he hadn't. Skintight hose wouldn't have let him keep his secret unless he had worn such antique foppery. And he'd thought himself a master of control!

It wasn't just the sexual attraction. He was not such a fool. It was everything she was and what she meant to him. He'd reined himself in and knew that from now on he'd have to keep doing so, if he kept seeing her. And he had to keep seeing her, if only for just a little longer.

He bargained with himself.

A few more months, only a few more. If he could get through this winter without another attack, he would ask her to be his wife in spite of the difference in their age and experience. If he got sick again, he'd leave as soon as he could, go abroad, and stay there until she found a younger, healthier man. She would. She was so enticing she hadn't missed a dance all night, except for that little while when she was missing from the ballroom. He'd gone in search of her, beside himself with fear. *He*, who had faced enemies at rifle's end and saber's edge and never quaked. Because she was, for all her cleverness, only a young woman.

He'd planned to go home, he'd promised his parents he'd be there at Christmas. He'd write to tell them not to expect him soon. He wanted to bring her to them as his fiancée, whatever time of year that might be, if it could be at all. She'd have him, he knew it. He also knew it wouldn't be fair to ask her now.

It wasn't just the need for her body, though that need was overwhelming. It was the spirit that lived in that lovely body that had overmastered him at last. The charm of her, the uniqueness of her, had finally undone him. He smiled just thinking of her bravery, honesty, her constant excitement with the world around her, her belief and reliance on the goodness of mankind. And best of all and most remarkable of all, her candid and obvious interest in one lucky man: himself

Eric smiled at last. Such a little heroine she was, such a joy, such a love. His love. His wonderful, beautiful Camille.

Chapter 11

❝A❞nother engagement!" Miles groaned.

Belle looked up at her husband from her dressing table, her powder puff poised in her hand.

"I know," she said sympathetically. "We've been trotting hard. I used to love going out, but I'd like to stay home of a night with you and toast our toes before the fire. But we can't," she said with more energy. "We have to get Camille settled. Her foot is healed, she can dance, and she must. We can't sit back and hope her future husband's coach breaks down in front of our house. We have to get her out there so she can find him."

He bent and kissed the top of her head. "My little general. I know. But anytime you want to sit home with me, tell me, and we will. I have a feeling she'll do well enough on her own."

"We may one day," she said absently, staring at herself in the glass. "But for now we have to try. We have to attend this ball. Cammie's so looking forward to it. Eric will be expecting us there as well. Go on down. I'll join you in a moment."

Miles went down the stair, suppressing a yawn. He wished he could sit with his wife before a fire now or lie down with her before one or . . .

"Oh!" a soft voice exclaimed in pain.

He looked up. His houseguest, Nell Baynes, was standing at the foot of the stair holding on to the newel post. She had her leg raised high enough for him to see her shapely calf and was twisting around, trying to look at the bottom of her foot. She saw him and guiltily lowered her leg. "I stepped on something," she said haltingly, her color rising. "It must be catching. First poor Camille, now me. It's a tack, a nail, I don't know, but it hurts." She bent her leg and raised it again, unsuccessfully trying to keep her skirts down, unable to because she was crooking her leg to the side, trying to see her sole.

Miles saw more than her calf this time.

"Here," he said, and went to her, about to take that little slippered foot in his hand to see what was hurting her. He wouldn't kneel at her feet, so he put his arm around her slender waist to support her before he lifted her foot high enough to see. He lowered his head and smelled the wild hot gardenia scent of her and felt her supple body grow breathlessly still. . . . .

And then he got a glimpse of a fleeting look in her eyes. It was a flash of triumph. He dropped his hand and stepped back as though her slipper were a hot iron.

"Here," he said smoothly, recovering his poise, "hang on to the banister. I'll get a footman to carry you up to your rooms, and we'll send for the housekeeper to tend to it."

She gave him a strange look, gone too soon for him to measure. Then she bent and plucked off her slipper in one smooth motion. She shook it and exclaimed, "Oh, that was all it was! A pebble. It's out! I'm fine. I'm sorry, my lord, it's just that my skin is so sensitive."

She'd have been sorrier if Belle had come down before he stepped away, Miles thought. Because she'd have been turned out into the streets again, no matter what Cammie said. And he'd have applauded. He heard no pebble rattle on the floor when Nell shook out her slipper. The only thing that would have bothered him about tossing the chit out on her rump was the thought that Belle might have been hurt, even for a minute. He resolved to tell her about this incident the first chance he got—and get Nell Baynes out of his house the very next one.

But for now, he had a party to go to. And he devoutly hoped his sister wouldn't be the only unwed girl to find a future husband there.

* * *

"Where have you been?" Eric said when he finally saw Camille, as she entered the ballroom. "Not out looking for broken glass. I thought you'd given that up."

She made a face at him.

He grinned, unapologetic. "This is our dance, isn't it?"

"She's gone again," Camille said gloomily. "I've been looking. I haven't seen Nell in a long time, have you?"

He frowned. "No. I'll go look then," he said, turning from her.

"No," she said quickly, grabbing his sleeve. She dropped her hand, blushing, as he turned back to look at her in puzzlement. "I didn't mean that you should go now. I mean, I'm worried. But"—she hesitated, lifted her chin, and said—"It *is* our dance, isn't it? I came back just for it. Nell may be gone, but I don't think she's in dire straits. Maybe she's just feeling shy again. She'll come round, she did last time, didn't she? Even if she doesn't, we can find her after, can't we? What I mean is—how many more waltzes will they play tonight?"

She fell still, feeling flushed and bothered, staring down at her slippers, wondering if she'd sounded as petty, jealous, and selfish as she felt.

"You're right," he said, offering her his hand. "She's safe enough in this house, wherever she is. Since you can dance again, we'll do that now. Seize the day—or the night, as the case may be."

She nodded, and gladly moved into his arms.

The musicians were playing a popular tune. Camille hoped she wouldn't tread on Eric's feet, because she couldn't pay attention to music, not when she was in his arms. She closed her eyes and concentrated on the hard strength of his arm around her, the motion of his long, strong body with all its fascinating alien contours. Her breasts tingled when they lightly grazed his chest, and she moved closer. She wanted to feel more, to curl into him, to . . .

He moved slightly away.

He stepped only a fraction back, making the space between them no more than an inch apart, but she felt as though he'd left the room. She opened her eyes and stared up into his.

He looked . . . embarrassed?

Camille almost stumbled, forgetting the music and the rhythm of the waltz.

"I'm glad I finally have a chance to make good on my promise," he said quickly, "but I wish I were a better dancer. Have I trodden on your foot?"

"No," she said, and couldn't think of what else to say.

The waltz was held to be a scandalous thing when it debuted in England. But there wasn't a puritanical soul at that ball who could say that the way Eric Ford danced the waltz with Miss Camille Croft wasn't as unexceptional and proper as a minuet.

And all the while he silently agonized—because

it was torture to be so close to her warm and yielding body and keep himself so far away. Because even an inch of width between them was almost too much to bear. But he could not, would not tempt himself or her. Not now, not yet. The fever in his blood was caused by her merest touch. But he couldn't be sure that his malarial fever wouldn't return an hour from now. And until he was sure, he'd remain her friend and no more than that, whatever the cost to him because of his balked desire.

"I'll go look for her now," he said the second the music stopped.

"I will too," Camille said.

They went off in opposite directions, neither thinking about the truant Nell.

"I'm worried about you," Camille said.

Nell stopped stroking the brush through her hair and looked at her with a wide surprised stare. It was obviously not what she'd expected her hostess to say. It wasn't what Camille had planned to say either. But once she had, she knew it was right.

They sat in Camille's bedchamber and talked in whispers. The rest of the household was asleep, but Camille was too keyed up after her night out and Nell had said she was too. After her maid left, Camille had crept down to the pantry to get a late night feast of whatever she could forage from the kitchens. She returned with leftovers, fruit, cheese, and bread. Now she and Nell settled in for a chat.

"Look," Camille went on, sounding harassed,

"it isn't my business—Dash it all, it is!" She put down the apple she'd taken a bite from and looked hard at Nell, who sat watching her with a carefully blank expression.

"You seem to me to be playing with fire, my girl," Camille said brusquely. "Don't tell me you're not, because I won't believe it. I don't know what you did this evening, but I'll wager my back teeth it wasn't hiding behind a potted palm, as Dana said you did at the Venetian Ball. You've done it too often since. And besides, you don't have a shy bone in your body," she scoffed. "No one who looks at men the way you do could."

When Nell didn't answer, Camille nodded. "Look, I know how you feel about your old friend from home, the Covent Garden nun who struck gold. Are you thinking of setting up something like that for yourself here? I mean, be plain with me. Are you looking for a protector or only to snare a chap in parson's mousetrap? Well, the first's a thing I won't hold with. And the second won't work. The gents you're toying with have all the money and power on their side. I promise you, you won't get one of them to the altar, whatever rig you run. Unless he falls madly in love with you, which odds are, he won't. Or if one does," she added conscientiously, "his family will have something to say to that!"

She put up a hand. "I know," she said, though Nell hadn't said a word. "The Gunning girls didn't have money, family, or reputation either, and they married into the gentry. But that was generations ago, and it was a scandal even then. Rich old doddering barons who marry tavern wenches these days may make the newssheets, but that's because they're rare as hen's teeth. Even if a wellborn fellow isn't looking for a titled wife, money marries money.

"Now, the truth, if you please," she went on impatiently. "Because you owe it to me. And because what you do reflects on my family as well as me. I won't cry rope on you, but keep it up and I won't have to. You'll hang yourself. If that's what you want, fine. But I won't have Belle and Miles dragged into it. So. What's happening here?"

Nell cocked her head to the side. She looked so innocent and puzzled that Camille felt stricken.

And then Nell laughed. "Well, why not?" she said, starting to brush her hair again. "I'm tired of all the nonsense. And you've been good to me, Cammie, I'll say that for you. All right then, the truth. I won't embarrass you or your family. But I was meeting with a gent. I'm looking for the best I can do for myself, which means I'll be getting myself a rich fellow to pay my bills soon as may be. Then I'll be out of here before you know it. I'm discreet, so no one will know anything until I turn up dressed to the nines in a gold carriage pulled by white horses. By then I'll have taken another name. So don't worry, no one will make the connection to you."

She laid down the brush and put her head to the

side again. "But maybe a black carriage with black horses, to go with my hair? I have to make a name for myself, and a rig like that ought to draw attention, don't you think?"

"But you have a chance to make a good life for yourself now!" Camille gasped. "You have a kind cousin and a chance to meet nice men—"

"Oh, Dana is kind," Nell said quickly, "and handsome and smart, and he has money and a fine position too. He's got manners and breeding as good as any man, and better than most. He'd be a catch for any girl, duchess or doxy," she went on, sliding a glance at Camille. "But not me, because he's my own cousin. And not me, because to tell the truth, as you said I should, even if he was a prince, I don't want to marry at all."

"You want to be a . . . kept woman instead of a married one?" Camille asked in disbelief, "even if you have a choice?"

Nell picked up an apple and took a bite with a snap of her white teeth. "Yes," she said as she crunched it, "because what's a married woman but a kept one who can't change partners when she gets bored?" She chuckled at Camille's expression. "Close your mouth, Cammie, or you'll draw flies. It's simple. I'd rather keep having my pick and choice instead of just one chance to get it right. That way, if a fellow disappoints me or starts nagging or pinching at me—the way men do when things go wrong for them even if it doesn't have a thing to do with their women—why, then, I can just cut loose, go on my way, and find someone better. And I tell you," she said, shaking her apple at Camille, "I'll be picking up a grand sum of money along that way too."

"But what about love?" Camille started to say.

"Oh, be sure I'll have that too!" Nell laughed. "As much as I like, and good love too. Because you know, even that can get boring with the same fellow all the time."

Camille closed her mouth. She was shaken. Nell had said a great many shocking things that almost made sense. But that last did not. Camille wasn't very religious or a Puritan. If anything, she'd discovered, her mind could stretch too much. But she believed in love.

"I'm talking about love," Camille said, "not sex."

"So am I," Nell said simply, taking another bite of apple. "One's the same as the other. I wouldn't love a fellow I couldn't swive." She giggled. "Swive: do a push, make ends meet, have a bit of buttock. You're a country girl, you know what I mean: mate."

Camille found herself beyond shock in a new place filled with confusion and curiosity. "But you've never been in love," she argued rather desperately.

"Of course I have."

"But you've never mate . . . made love, have you?"

"Of course I have." Nell said, finishing up her apple and nibbling on the core.

Camille swallowed hard. "But maybe he just wasn't the right man for you," she said, knowing she was out of her depth but fascinated in spite of herself.

"He?" Nell smiled. "I wouldn't be planning what I am if it were just he. I've done the deed often enough. I know what I'm about."

Camille sat quietly. Belle was right, she thought sadly. She never should have offered her home to a stranger. This girl wasn't just a stranger, she was almost an alien. And now that she had obviously decided to be completely honest with Camille, Nell's personality had changed too. She was at once slyer and more open in her speech, vulgar and yet friendlier. Camille was disturbed and alarmed at this new familiarity. But at the same time she was acutely aware that Nell knew things most girls Camille was acquainted with did not and spoke of things no women Camille knew would ever discuss.

And there were some things, Camille suddenly discovered, that she just had to know. "You've done it—often?" Camille whispered.

Nell nodded as she chewed the apple core.

"It's that good?" Camille asked, wide-eyed.

"Glory! No!" Nell laughed so hard, Camille shushed her and looked nervously toward the bedroom door.

"Look," Nell said, sobering, "maybe I'm not like most girls, I'll grant you that. And you're a well brought up girl, so I shouldn't say this. But since you are, the more reason why I should, I suppose. You've been plain with me, and I owe you something, don't I? I've had it off with my share of lads, and I have to tell you it isn't that much. They make it sound like the sun and the moon, of course, to get you. But it's nothing, really, when you come down to it. Oh, it's nice enough sometimes. But mostly it's a bore, and it can be nasty."

"And you do it anyway?" Camille gasped.

"Why not? It's usually over so quick it hardly matters. Less than the time it takes to boil an egg if you've primed them right. It's a great thing to men, but it doesn't have to be for us. They have to be excited to do it. We don't. That's where the gold is in it for us. It's always good for them or they can't do it. We can while we're thinking about something else. And we can always tell when they're done and if they've had a good time, but they never really know with us. The truth is they never have to know how you feel if you don't want them to."

"The most important thing," Nell said, as she licked apple juice from her fingers, "is that though men say some women are better than others, because this one was so beautiful or that one moved right, it's really all about how she made them feel about themselves. Every fellow thinks he's a dab hand at it, but he's never really sure. So if you tell him it's wonderful he thinks you've given him the moon. Even if you have to think of someone else while he's at it, so as not to push him off before he's through with you."

"Oh," was all Camille could say, because she certainly wasn't going to tell Nell what her sister-in-law had told her about marital relations. They'd been speaking of Camille's future one soft summer evening when they'd been alone together. Belle hadn't said anything graphic, of course, and all she did say about the act of love was couched in terms of suns and exploding stars, to be sure. But she hadn't had to give details, because Camille had raised horses. And the look in Belle's eyes as she'd spoken had told Camille even more and made love-making sound like the most rapturous experience a woman could have.

"But what about children?" Camille persisted. "I am a country girl, and sure as check, I know one thing follows another."

"With cows maybe. There are ways people can stop it from happening. That much, trust me, I know. And those that take up the trade don't have children often," Nell mused. "That's strange, but that is so."

"And you'd pass up the chance for love entirely?" Camille asked.

"No," Nell said. "Who knows what may come along in time? But for now? Why should I be some fellow's unpaid bedmate, servant, and whipping girl? I want more for myself. I want more fun and money than any one man can give me. Even if I were to marry a rich man, I wouldn't get his money, you know. If he died—and all men do in time, especially the older ones who have the most money—all his property, even jewels he might have given me that came from his own mother, would be taken from me to go to his sons, if he had any. And if he didn't, it would all go to his nearest male nephew or cousin or such, whether he liked the lucky fellow or had even met him."

Nell's expression grew cold. "Then I'd have to count on the charity of a stranger. A woman's a fool to count on any man's charity. It depends on how she looks when she needs it, and you can't be young forever. Do you think even a noble fellow like Lieutenant Ford would have fought for me that night I was shoved at him if I'd been a scrawny old besom?

"And not only men," she said when Camille opened her mouth to defend Eric's honor. "Would you have offered houseroom to an old woman that night? You're a nice girl, Camille, but I can't see you offering your time and company to an old crone. Even if you had, your brother and sister-in-law would have thought you'd run mad—madder than they did when you invited me into your home," she corrected herself with a twisted smile.

"No, even if I married the Golden Ball, by the time he died and his fortune went to his next of male kin, I could be too old to find a better arrangement for myself. And then where would I be?"

Camille sat still. What could she say? That much was true, and it wasn't fair. It was just that until now she'd never questioned it herself, any more than she'd question the fact that this was England or that it was the right of the king to rule her or the right of the sun to warm the sky.

"As for love itself," Nell laughed. "Look, all men have the same thing to offer, and they all offer it readily enough. Any clever girl can make her fortune if she takes what's offered. You don't even have to be pretty. Although," she said, tossing back her head, "I know what I have to give in return is what they want."

"Surely there are no ugly courtesans!" Camille said, watching Nell's long black hair slithering in a stream down her slender back as she tossed her head. If she shook her own head until morning, Camille thought bitterly, all she'd get would be a bird's nest tangle and be dizzy as a bat at noon, to boot.

"Harriette Wilson had beady eyes, hardly any breasts, and was thin as a rail," Nell reported. "Altogether she looked like nothing spread on toast. Yet she had her pick of the *ton* in her time. Everyone from Wellington to Ponsonby to the Prince, they say. There's many another like her. A successful courtesan has to know men, that's all. Why, there are beauties who have to throw up their skirts in alleys in order to buy supper and hags that get diamonds big as pigeon eggs for their favors. It's all in the attitude, that's what Ruby told me, and so I've seen for myself."

This whole conversation was beyond improper, Camille knew that. It went past common and coarse and turned into offensive. If she were truly well bred, if she had a grain of sensibility, she'd clap her hands over her ears and run out of the room. But she was awestruck. And besides, she might never get another such chance to learn what she most wanted to know.

"So," she said slowly, trying not to sound as interested as she was, "how do they do it? I mean, how does an ugly woman become so famous a demimondaine? Courtesan," she explained to Nell's puzzled look.

"You're not ugly!" Nell said.

Camille wondered if she would actually die of embarrassment. She'd underestimated Nell, and she suspected many people did. The girl wasn't bright, but she was very clever. And now Camille knew there was no sense in denying her interest in what Nell was talking about. They'd gone past every propriety anyway.

"I'm not beautiful," Camille said.

Nell cocked her head to the side again and looked at her as though measuring her up. "Not in the common way, no," she said. "But men like you, and there's many another who'd be taken with you if you knew how to show him what you've got. You've a good, firm body, nice breasts and rump. They like that. And you have a merry laugh. They like a woman who makes them feel good about themselves."

"I thought you were going to say something about my hair or the way I dress," Camille said, amazed to find she'd stopped blushing. The preachers were right. One did become inured to sin. Now this discussion was more interesting than embarrassing to her.

"Oh, no," Nell said, reaching out and tousling Camille's unruly curls. "Your hair is very nice indeed. It's pretty and soft. It reminds a fellow of a haystack or of being in one with you. And he wouldn't be afraid of messing it up. It makes you ever so much more . . . accessible," she said, smiling because she'd found the proper word. "That and your way of laughing. Men like a lass with merry heart. I told you, your appearance is the least of it."

"But you never laugh much," Camille said. "You just smile. That does seem to fascinate men. I've seen it."

"Well, that's because I don't have that lively a sense of humor. My smile tells them I know what men are thinking and that I approve," Nell said on a yawn. She rolled over on her back and spoke to the ceiling as she continued, "It's the way you look *at* them, really, even more than the way you look *to* them. A girl can't just sit like a flower waiting to be plucked. She has to let them know she's ripe for plucking. Little things matter. Your set, the ladies," she said scornfully, "they think it's all a matter of fluttering fans and batting eyelashes. But it's more."

Camille's voice came slow and low. "What little things?"

Nell giggled. "Not for you to know or do, my lady."

"Why not?"

"Because you're a lady."

"And if I weren't?"

"Well," Nell said, stretching her arms upward and staring at her linked fingers, "looking in a fellow's eyes is very fine, but looking at his crotch is better."

She giggled again at Camille's audible gasp.

"They want you to," Nell said imperturbably. "Why else do they wear such tight breeches and have their jackets cut long in back but high in front so that it all shows clear? And why wear all those glittering fobs and chains and such to draw your eyes right there? Every man thinks his is amazing, and they think we do too. But still, they worry that the other fellow's is bigger. Though why they should think we find ballocks a treat I'll never know," she mused. "So if you look there, they know you're interested, and if you keep looking, they're sure you're fascinated. And then, maiden or whore, you've got them. The truth is that any man wants any woman who wants him."

"They're different sizes?" Camille murmured almost to herself, because the thought had never occurred to her.

Nell chortled. "Oh, lord love you, of course they are. Like feet or noses. A big fellow can have a little one, and just the opposite too. There's no predicting by how big or tall he is, and it makes no sense that they should care so much, but there you are. Some chaps even pad themselves out! Though, truth to tell, one's the same as another to me."

She sat up. "Now I know I've said too much. You're red as a beet. Listen, Cammie, you're a nice person, but a good girl, never the kind to follow my lead. Find yourself a good fellow, marry him, and settle down, and you'll be happy—happier, I suppose, for not knowing how he measures up!" She flopped back on her back again.

Camille sat still, thinking. Nell's words rang true in many ways. She raised a grave gaze to her guest, studying her. Nell wore a thin night rail and was utterly relaxed. Now Camille could see that her guest hadn't that much to offer a man after all. She was slight, with small, apple-sized breasts. Her legs and arms were thin and pale. Her features were fine and even, but now that her eyes were closed, Camille could see she was so even-featured that she actually was plain. All her attraction was in her animation when a man appeared, in the little things, as Nell herself had said.

What struck Camille more than that now was the fact that Nell would never have been so bold or forthcoming if she meant to stay on. Even though she might think her hostess was a rough and ready, hurly-burly sort of girl, she had to know what she'd said was low, vulgar, and even if momentarily diverting, would eventually give any gently bred young woman a distaste for her. That meant she already had plans to leave and soon. Which relieved Camille wonderfully. She herself wouldn't have to look like a jealous cow by telling Belle and Miles how uncomfortable Nell made her and why.

"So," she asked Nell, "when are you going to leave us?"

Nell lay still but opened her eyes. "Soon as I find a gent I want to go with, and that won't take long." Her expression was unreadable as she angled her head so she could search Camille's face. "What do you think of Eric Ford?"

Camille's sudden loss of color was her answer.

Nell shrugged. "I'm not saying he's the one I'll choose. There are others I have in mind as well. I've been talking to some of them when we're out at balls and such. My cousin found out too," she added. "He's smart. He realized it right off when we were at that Venetian Ball and tried to protect me by saying I was shy. You're right, that's a cawker, isn't it? Don't blame him. He's a decent man and a kind-hearted one. He didn't want to see me blot my copybook. He wants me to have a future. And he doesn't know I kept at it after, or he'd murder me! A fine lecture he read at me, I can tell you. I hung my head, like a nice girl should. But I was seeing what my possibilities were, and I still am."

"You've . . . met . . . with Eric then?" Camille managed to say.

"No, but I'm not done interviewing," Nell said. She sat up abruptly. "Look, that's all I do. I give a taste. I show a sample to a few chaps, nothing more. I told you, I'm not destined for Haymarket ware. A girl who throws up her skirts right away is a slut, and she'll never make a decent living, much less her fortune, that way. You have to tempt and lure, make yourself seem scarce and rare, if you want to succeed.

"Because," she said, leaning toward Nell for emphasis, "a woman's worth in bed is what she makes it. It's like men and their sizes, it doesn't really matter that much. Most of it is in the mind and the method, not what you were born with. You make a fellow think that he's done wonders, and you are one yourself, at least to him."

"And the pleasure in it for yourself?" Camille asked, though she thought she already knew what Nell would say.

"The pleasure is in the success," Nell said. "Are you going to eat those grapes?"

Chapter 12

❦

After last night's talk with Nell, Camille couldn't look at any man now, because she didn't know where to look. When Dana Bartlett arrived to take Camille and Nell for a carriage ride, she'd had to keep her eyes firmly fixed on his. She didn't want to look down, and because she knew she shouldn't, she had an overwhelming urge to do just that. She couldn't imagine Dana wanting her to look there either. He wasn't the kind of man whose presence led to such thoughts.

Now sitting beside him in a carriage, Cammie felt much better as he continued to point out sights while their coach rolled on. "There, on the right, coming up, is Blackfriars Bridge. In the fourteenth century it was considered . . ."

Camille hardly listened. Neither did his cousin, who seemed to be sleeping with her eyes open. He'd been showing them the sights of London for a half-hour now. If Camille could have gotten up and walked through the places he was talking about, she might have been interested. But not only was it a cold and windy day, he said some of the places were too dangerous for women to see on foot. Since Nell couldn't ride, the only way they could go was by coach. So they sat in a coach with hot bricks at their feet and gazed out the breath-fogged windows while Dana told them about everything they couldn't see close or clearly.

And so instead of gazing at London, Camille was covertly studying her host. Her study verified everything she'd been thinking about him since the night they'd met. Or rather, since after that night, because that first time he'd seemed attractive, interesting, even mysterious. But not anymore. Not after several walks in the park, a few interminable teas and polite conversations and dances at the few parties they'd been at together.

There was nothing wrong with him. It was just that there wasn't anything particularly outstanding either. When they'd met, his dark good looks had seemed seductive, at least by lamplight. Sunlight showed that he did have clear skin and shining black hair, and his eyes were just as dark as they looked by night. But the lack of shadows made them and him much less magnetic. In fact, the whole man seemed diminished. He even seemed smaller than he did by night. Now Camille noticed how small and neat his gloved hands were, as were the feet in his tidy brown boots. Or maybe, she admitted, it had nothing to do with moonlight or sunlight or his size. It was just that a big man who dominated the scene in any light had permanently dazzled her eyes.

Dana Bartlett was attentive, polite, and seemed interested in her, Camille concluded sadly. But she just wasn't attracted to him. It would have been nice to have a beau instead of just her dreams of Eric. Certainly Dana was one man who wouldn't want any woman to look at him as Nell suggested. It was hard to think of him even possessing a . . .

Camille's eyes flew to the window, and she fixed her gaze on a distant church steeple. How ridiculous! She had dozens of men friends and had never had to worry about such a thing before. Male fashion did emphasize a fellow's front, but it also showed off his backside and legs. Of course, a woman noticed things, she just didn't dwell on them the way Nell suggested. After all, you could hardly help noticing—Nell was right about that, at least. But Camille had never stared at the fall on a fellow's trousers, or ogled anything under his unmentionables. *Lord!* Calling them unmentionables ought to give a girl a clue to where she wasn't supposed to look. Nell's advice was wrong, for a decent woman at least. But it had definitely changed Camille's outlook on life—literally.

She hoped she could forget Nell's advice and fast. Because she was seeing Eric this afternoon for tea, when she got back home. He'd think she'd run mad if she kept squinting at his . . .

Bother! Camille thought, squirming in her seat. Unless, of course, Nell was right. And if she followed her advice, would Eric finally see her differently? As a woman at last? And maybe . . .

"Miss Croft?" Dana asked. Camille spun her head to look at him, feeling as guilty as embarrassed because she hadn't been paying attention. "You're a Londoner now," he went on gently, "so perhaps this tour is a little too elementary for you."

"Oh, no," she said honestly, "I'm a country girl and haven't been here very long. I go to parties and balls, but there are lots of things I haven't seen yet. Why, I never saw that tavern you just pointed out. It was very interesting," she lied.

"I'm sorry I couldn't take you two into it. It's built where Shakespeare's Mermaid Tavern was, but I think it's not quite the thing for young ladies. Now, where we're going next is the seat of justice. Excuse me." He rapped on the front window, and a second later the coachman he'd hired pulled back the leather curtain that covered the window and opened it.

"Yes, sir?" the coachman asked.

"Why are we stopping here?"

"Ah, well, y'see, the crowd's too thick in front for us to go on ahead just now. It be a Monday, sir, there's a topping to see, and every soul in Lunnon wants to be there too, same as you."

"A Monday? Good Lord!" Dana said, looking aghast. "It's hanging day at Tyburn tree!"

"Yes, sir, it be that. I hears there's six set to dangle this morning, but never ye fear, I'll have you there in a trice, and where you can see most of it, if not all."

"A topping?" Camille asked with dawning horror.

"A hanging," Dana said angrily. "I never realized it was a Monday or I wouldn't have planned to take you to see Old Bailey, but it's right next to Newgate. I didn't think about that, though I should have," he added in chagrin.

"A hanging?" Nell asked, sitting up, suddenly more animated than she'd been for an hour. "Oh, good! I so wanted to see one. And only think, there'll be six! Can you get us a broadsheet, cousin? I hear the condemned write all sorts of funny things you can read as you watch them being hanged. And chestnuts too. My friend Rub— A friend told me the chestnuts and meat pies sold on topping days are the freshest and best." She giggled. "Maybe because no one wants to sell bad stuff that close to the gallows. But she said to watch for pickpockets, because they find their best business in the crowds then, no matter the risk. And risk there will be, because the Runners are there to see the hanging's done right."

"But we won't be," Dana said curtly. "Turn

around," he told the coachman. "Find another route. We'll skip Old Bailey."

"Thank you," Camille breathed.

"Why can't we go?" Nell protested.

"Some of us don't find hangings entertaining," Dana said, noting how pale Camille had grown.

"If you dance you must pay the piper," Nell said on a shrug. "Even if it's a dance on air. They're only getting what they deserve. It's great fun, my friend says," she went on in wheedling tones, looking at Dana hopefully. "There are folks from all parts of Town, the richest and the poorest together, shoulder to shoulder. It's a fine show, for some go up to the gibbet bold as brass, and some wail and weep like babes, and you never know from just looking at them which will be which when the time comes."

"They hang children," Camille said dully, "and old women."

"Well, there's a pity, I suppose," Nell said. "And many a sad ballad we'll hear sung about it if there are any of those to be topped this morning. But if they did wrong, they deserve it."

"Indeed?" Dana said silkily. "And so you believe a person must tread the line or else suffer the consequence, do you, cousin?"

Nell, ever responsive to a tone of voice, caught the ironic tone in his. She went still and watched him warily. Camille looked at him oddly too, because this sounded more like the man who'd intrigued her by lamplight.

"You believe that a man who takes a man's wallet should hang from the same gibbet as one who took another man's life?" Dana persisted. "And that a boy who stole a cheese ought to be hanged alongside a man who sold his country's secrets? And that a woman who sold herself to a man should be punished the same way as one who stole his wallet?"

"Well, there you're out, cousin!" Nell laughed. "They don't hang whores—I mean, harlots."

"No, I suppose they don't," he said, his face a mask of civility, though his eyes seemed to burn into hers. "But there are hundreds of them in Bridewell, where they are beaten soundly and suffer other indignities I'll not mention here. Hundreds more languish at Magdalene House, where they aren't physically abused but their spirits are beaten into submission. Others are transported. Many more find their way to Newgate, because their way of life leads to crime as surely as a river runs to the sea.

"Speaking of which," he said, as if on a sudden thought. He knocked on the window again, and again the coachman popped back the curtain. "Take us along the river," he said. "Find us a place where we can get a good view of the river."

He turned to his guests again. "Forgive me," he told Camille. "It will only take a moment, but there's something I want my cousin to see. I hate to lose an argument," he explained with a tight smile that never reached his eyes. "One of the problems with being a man-at-law, I suppose."

Camille could only nod. She was surprised by his barely suppressed anger until she remembered that Nell had said that he knew what she'd done at the Venetian Ball. So he had to have guessed something about her plans for her future. His lecture, Camille realized, must have been so he could show Nell the error of her ways. Her opinion of him rose again. Bless the man. Maybe he could talk some sense into the girl. Camille didn't want to throw her out immediately, for fear of looking jealous or spiteful, at least to Eric. But she didn't want her staying on either.

They all sat quietly, wrapped in their own thoughts, as the carriage rattled over cobbles as it headed toward the Thames. When it finally stopped, the coachman called, "Will this do?"

Dana nodded in approval. "Yes, fine. We'll get out. Wait for us. We won't be long."

They were in a warehouse district near the wharves on a street across from an unoccupied dock, so they could see the river clearly. The Thames was wide here, slate-gray today, rippling with choppy, rushing, white-fringed waves. Small fishing trawlers and packet boats looked like miniatures as they sailed by the great-bellied, spire-masted ships at anchor.

"Come," Dana said. "It's safe enough here by day, and this is a thing you should see, even you, Miss Croft, because it is interesting."

They alighted and walked out on the empty dock. It was quiet except for the sounds of water lapping at the pilings of the pier and the laughter of gulls riding on wind currents high overhead. The cold breeze snatched at Camille's hood, trying to tug it free. The smell of the sea was brackish but invigorating, and she took a deep breath. She felt her spirits rise. She loved the out of doors and especially rivers and the sea.

"Look downriver," Dana said to Nell as they walked to the end of the dock. "What do you see?"

"Nothing much," she said. "Ships, land on the other side. What am I supposed to be seeing?"

"That ship to the north."

"What, that enormous one?" she asked. "I can't see it, just the outline. It's a big old hulk, isn't it?"

"Yes," he said. "Exactly. It's an old man-of-war, here on the Thames before it goes to its final berth at Woolwich, where it will lie at anchor with others of its kind. That one is the *Euryalus,* some are more famous."

Nell relaxed and started to smile. Camille sighed. She'd been wrong; this was just another bit of sightseeing from afar.

"But I think all would rather you forgot their names," Dana went on. "Those on board them are forgotten too."

Both women turned their puzzled expressions to him. But he only looked at Nell. "Oh, yes," he told her. "They're the hulks, you see, dear cousin. Prison ships for the overflow from London's prisons. There's not enough room in Newgate or in Bridewell or any of His Majesty's prisons. They hang them six at a time these days, as you saw—or almost did—and even so there aren't enough hangings to reduce the number of prisoners or enough transports to take them all to Botany Bay.

"So now we have the hulks too. They go nowhere, nor does their wretched cargo. Way stations for transport to Australia and Botany Bay. Now they're as good as permanent—permanent enough for many poor souls who board them, because few live to walk off them."

He stared at Nell, the look in his eyes now cold as the wind that whipped around them. "Believe me, cousin, I know this too well: all the other prisons, even with their jail fevers and corruption, are luxury hotels compared to the hulks. And I promise you, every man, woman and child on those ships once believed they were too clever to ever end up there."

Nell stood silent. Then she met his eyes, tossing back her head in a pert gesture. Her hood fell back, and the wind whipped her inky hair round her face. "Thank you, cousin," she said with a little twisted smile. "It's ever so nice of you to show us how you earn your living."

Dana's lips thinned, and he shot a glance at Camille.

Camille didn't know what to say. Nell had aimed her barb well. Nothing could have shown the disparities in their rank more clearly. Nell had pointed out that unlike most of the men Camille knew,

Dana had to earn his living. In fact, it elevated him in Camille's eyes, but she knew he wouldn't think so, any more than her own sister-in-law would.

"Are there no ways to prevent this?" Camille asked, trying to let him think she hadn't understood the meaning of Nell's thrust.

"Prevent crime?" Dana asked. "No. Maybe we can prevent the things that cause it and perhaps reduce the number of reasons for imprisoning people. But we can at least," he said, looking at his cousin, "impress upon people the need for caution and wisdom and make them realize the folly of unlawful dealings."

Nell stood with her head high.

Camille fidgeted.

"Well," Dana said, pulling out his watch. "Time to go, I think, or your family will have *me* clapped in irons."

When they returned to her brother's house, it wasn't Camille's family they found pacing in front of the door but Eric.

"Where have you been?" he demanded the minute Dana stepped down from the carriage. "You were supposed to be here an hour ago!"

Dana gave his hand to Camille, then to Nell, and didn't answer until he had helped both women down the few steps to the pavement. "We were delayed by the crowds," he finally told Eric.

"Crowds?" Eric asked. "In the park?"

"We didn't go to the park," Nell said brightly, giving Eric a warm smile. "My cousin took us on a tour. We went to Newgate—that's where the crowds were—for the hangings. But there was such a throng we couldn't get through! So then he showed us the hulks instead. At least there was no one on the docks to trouble us there."

Eric's hands fisted at his sides, his mouth grew tight, and his eyes blazed with light. Camille suddenly saw it might not be just a joke when his friends laughingly referred to him as a Viking.

"You took them on a tour of the prisons?" Eric asked incredulously, staring at Dana.

Dana stood poised and stared back at Eric. "They were never in any danger. I thought," he said slowly, "it would be edifying."

"It was!" Camille broke in, looking from Dana's wary posture to the outraged giant in front of him. It would be disastrous if the men fought. It would be worse if she tried to explain Dana's motives. At least she could tell some of the truth.

"That's not all we saw," Camille said quickly. "We also saw where the Mermaid Tavern used to be. But from afar, because it wasn't the thing for us to go in, Dana said. But just think, Shakespeare's favorite tavern! We passed Doctor Johnson's house too and Blackfriars Bridge—and so much more," she added, running out of inspiration. "The only reason we met crowds was because Newgate is so close to the Old Bailey, where Dana was going to take us next. But he wouldn't hear of us going near Tyburn. And standing by the river was so exhilarating, Eric! I love the sea, and we're so hemmed in by buildings here it's easy to forget England is an island. The air was delicious and the view was extraordinary. Thank you," she said, turning to Dana. "I had a lovely time."

He took her hand. "No. Thank you," he said gravely. The look in his eyes told her he understood and was both amused and pleased by her defense of him.

"We're just going to take tea," she said impulsively. "Would you care to join us?"

"Thank you, but I can't. I must be back at work. I do work, you know," he added, absorbing the insult Nell had implied and making it a point of honor.

Camille was impressed.

"Another time I'd be pleased to join you, so please remember me. Good afternoon, cousin," he said to Nell. "Lieutenant," he said with a curt nod to Eric. He stepped into the carriage and drove on, leaving Camille smiling, Nell watching thoughtfully, and Eric looking balked.

"The fellow's clever as he can hold together," Eric said bitterly an hour later. "Then what must he do but make me look like an idle lout? 'I must be back at work,' he says, as though he's the only man in London who does anything worthwhile."

He'd met his friend Drum on the street after he'd left Camille, and now, in the style of gentlemen, they were ambling along together as though it were a balmy morning instead of wintry twilight.

"But a gentleman doesn't work," Drum said reasonably.

"I do," Eric said gruffly, still smarting, "when I'm at home. I work training horses, helping my father and his tenants at all sorts of things, moving lumber if I must, raising roofs, farm work too," he said, aggrieved. "Real work, not just pushing papers. Though I do that too. You know I handle my own investments."

"Oh, I do," his friend said mildly. "But the point you're making is that the ladies concerned don't know that, isn't it?"

Eric scowled. "The point is that the fellow used what might be considered disadvantage to his advantage. He's sly, Drum, shifty too, I'd swear it."

"Well, he is a lawyer," Drum mused.

"That's not what I mean. Why show them prisons and the hulks, for God's sake? And don't tell me it was an accident. That one's too smooth to do anything by accident."

"But do you know women as well?" Drum said mildly. "I agree, doubtless he had a reason. Did you ask Camille what it might be?"

Eric snorted. "I didn't have to. She told me all about it. Constantly, all through tea. It seems, Drum, that the sun rises on Dana Bartlett's right shoulder and sets on his left one."

"And the little heroine, Mistress Nell, she defended him too?"

"He's her cousin," Eric said on a shrug, "so of course she wouldn't say anything against him. The girl doesn't have much to say for herself anyway."

Now interest sprang into Drum's eyes. He turned his head to look at his friend. "And you find that . . . disappointing?"

"Why should I?" Eric asked, honestly surprised.

Drum smiled and seemed to relax. "No reason at all," he said with pleasure. "I find her a dead bore myself. The only interesting thing the chit ever had to say for herself was 'Help.'"

Eric laughed, then sobered. "That's true. But you know, I'm not sure she's the best company for Camille. At first, I thought there'd be no harm, but now . . . The girl is—I don't know—too quiet. It begins to appear to be slyness rather than reticence. Just like that cousin of hers. Though I hate to think I'm letting that influence my perception of her. No. I can't trust her somehow. And Camille won't cut her loose until Bartlett provides a home for her. It can't come soon enough. Not that I begrudge Nell a safe haven," he added quickly. "But while she stays, he has an excuse to hang around. Do you think Camille has a *tendre* for him?"

"Who can say? Camille has a tender heart for everyone. But this I can tell you. If she did care for him, Belle would be hiring assassins right now. She does not favor that match."

Eric's smile was more thoughtful than amused.

"Still, Camille should have the right to decide her future."

"Wait until you have a daughter before you say such a revolutionary thing. So. Since we're expecting you for dinner tonight, this was a fortunate meeting. Why don't you come home with me now, and we'll raise a glass or two before we eat. Alexandria would love extra time with you. You're one of her favorite people."

"And she's one of mine, you lucky dog. But I have to go home and change my clothes first."

Drum stopped and looked at his friend from head to toe. Eric's massive frame was impeccably clad, as usual. He wore his military-style long coat open even on the coldest days, and so his brown jacket, spotless linen, and form-fitting ivory breeches could be seen. They all looked pristine.

"Lord! We're not giving a ball, just a small supper. You look fine."

Eric glanced down at himself. "So I thought," he said with a frown, remembering Camille's strange, constant, hastily concealed glances all through tea this afternoon. "But I think I'd better change these trousers. That's why I left Miles's house early. There must be a spot or a stain on them that can't be seen in this light. I turn here. See you at seven," he said, and strode away.

Drum went on his way, deciding that Eric was bedeviled and not thinking very clearly. But if it was Camille who had addled his wits and not the girl he'd rescued, Drum was glad. Because that meant Nell Baynes would be out of his life when she left Camille. That was all to the good. Drum considered himself a good judge of people too.

Chapter 13

⟡

"**W**hat's the matter, Cammie?" Eric asked with such gentle concern that it almost broke her heart. "Have I offended you?"

He'd found a moment alone with her when they'd returned from their morning ride and were standing in the stables in back of Miles's house. There was no groom around. Eric had sent him on an errand to be sure he had a moment to talk to Camille without anyone hearing or watching. And now there was no dignified escape for Camille. She had to answer him.

Eric stood in the hay-lined aisle and absently stroked her horse's outstretched neck as he waited for her answer. Camille suddenly found herself wishing she were that fortunate creature. For one thing, Eric's touch would be so welcome, and for another, she wouldn't have to talk.

"No, of course you haven't offended me," she said.

He stood silhouetted by the light of the open stable door, his face in shadow, his honey-colored hair a nimbus of golden light. She couldn't see his expression and was glad of it. Bad enough that she heard the warmth in his voice. She didn't have to see it in his glowing hazel eyes as he looked down at her. She couldn't have withstood that, and it was important for her pride that she should resist it—as well as the almost overwhelming desire to cast herself into his arms and tell him all her troubles. But he'd stepped away from her in the dance the last time they'd met, and she didn't think she could bear his retreating from her again.

"So what's the matter, then?" he asked. "Is something troubling you?"

"No," she said, looking down at her toes.

"No?" he echoed, a world of sorrow in his voice. "That's not an answer I'd expect from you. It's too short, it's too curt, and it's not true."

Her head shot up. No one called her a liar! Then her shoulders slumped. She couldn't argue.

He nodded. "You're right. I've no right to question you. However much I've thought of you as your brother's little sister, you're not a child anymore. If you don't want to speak to a fellow, you don't have to, whatever his claims of family friendship. Forgive me for pestering you."

"You're not!" she exclaimed. "And I do like talking to you."

"Really? Then why haven't you been? You were mute as a mime yesterday at tea. I kept looking at you to see if you'd give me a hint of what was wrong, but you kept looking away from me. And just now, we rode through the park without speaking, and that's something you've never done. Is it because I was angry with Bartlett for keeping you out too long yesterday? I shouldn't have said anything, but I was worried. Still, it wasn't my place, and so please accept my apologies. If you'd like, I'll apologize to him when and if I see him again. It's just that Miles wasn't home, and I suppose I thought I had to stand in for him."

Camille bit her lip. She turned her head aside and began to stroke her horse's silken nose, because she didn't know what else to do. He'd come right out and said it. He thought of her as his sister. "I'm sorry you were worried," she said in a small voice, because she had to say something.

"Camille, we used to have good times together, or so I thought," he said softly. "You never had any trouble talking to me. In fact, those rides we had were enlivened for me because of the way you used to ask me sixteen questions a minute, answering half of them yourself. But you couldn't or wouldn't even look at me yesterday. You kept glancing away as though the sight of me hurt your eyes. What am I supposed to think?"

She felt the blood rush to her head. It was true. She'd been so stricken with lust by seeing the contrast of that fragile teacup in those big, tanned hands of his that she'd lost her breath along with her wits. She couldn't even look at him as Nell suggested, because she could hardly bear to look at him at all, and yet every time she glanced at him, she remembered what Nell had said.

She knew she was so passionate in her enthusiasms that it was a family joke. But this wasn't funny. Suddenly, it was as if she'd caught Eric's own dreaded malady—at least, the symptoms seemed the same. Just looking at him sent shivers up and down her back. If he happened to meet her eyes, she'd flush with heat and then freeze with embarrassment. Her hunger for him affected her like a mortal illness, because now she really believed that if he ever left England or married another, she might very well die of it.

It wasn't first love or calf love or a simple case of hero worship. She knew very well he wasn't perfect. She didn't think she'd have liked him if he were. She knew about infatuation, because she'd had a few. But she'd known them for what they were after a short time. Men she'd worshipped from afar had been ones she really hadn't wanted to get too near when the opportunity came. The others had been flirtations that never amounted to more because she'd only enjoyed the teasing and never wanted them to grow to anything else.

This was different and permanent.

For all her enthusiasms, she wasn't fickle; in fact, she was too constant for her own good. Her word, once given, was never taken back. Her heart, once lost, would never be wholly her own again. And she'd given her heart wholly to him.

She didn't know what to do. It was clear he wasn't in love with her. So if he guessed how she felt, he'd be as stricken as she was—but with guilt. How could she tell him he was the problem she was having, without him leaving her? So she said nothing.

He gave her horse a final pat and dropped his hand. His shoulders rose and fell in a shrug. "Well, then. If I can't tempt you to tell me, I suppose there's nothing more to say. I'll leave you, then, and wish you well. If you ever feel you can confide in me, know that whatever it is, I'd keep your confidence to myself. And if you don't . . . I'm sorry if I offended, and I won't bother you again."

He felt sick. Something had happened. It might only be that she'd grown up and out of her infatuation with him. That would be a good thing for her, but he felt as though he'd been struck to the heart. There was nothing more he could say.

He bowed and turned.

And she couldn't bear it anymore.

"No!" she cried, catching onto his sleeve, dancing around him and twisting so she could see his face. "Don't go! It's not you, it's me, it's all me. I can't look at your eyes because I don't want you to know how I feel about you, and I can't look at you anywhere else because of what Nell said, but you didn't do anything. Oh, what a mess I'm making of it, but the truth is, Eric, that I love . . . I . . . Oh, Eric, I care for you so *damned* much I can't bear it!"

He looked as if she'd hit him. He caught the hand plucking at his sleeve. He looked down at her, amazed.

"What?" he asked, dumbfounded.

But she wasn't able to speak again because she was ashamed and upset and afraid that if one more word escaped her lips she wouldn't have a secret left to her name.

"Cammie," he said, looking down into her eyes, "you're saying you *love* me?"

She nodded.

She felt his hand tighten on hers. He shook his head. "I'm older than you are."

"What?"

"I said, I'm older than you. By over a decade."

"Well, so what?" she was able to answer, because she couldn't stand the sorrow in his voice, and she'd defend him against anyone, even himself. "You're not ancient. And I'm not a child."

"You haven't had a chance to meet other men," he said a little desperately.

"I have nothing but men friends!" she retorted angrily.

"Yes, but they don't have malarial fever." His voice grew grim even as his grip gentled. He stroked the back of her hand with his thumb as he sought the right words. "Look, Cammie, I've been to physicians, I've read all the books about it. I thought I was over it and I wasn't. The sum of it is that I may recover and I may not. My future's uncertain."

"Who's future is certain?" she demanded. She tugged her hand from his. "Oh, bother! No more excuses. They aren't necessary." She drew herself up. "I understand. Let's just drop this, shall we? How embarrassing," she said in tones that unconsciously mimicked her sister-in-law at her most acid. Now that she'd actually found rejection she also found she wasn't going to cry. She supposed a person didn't cry when they were first shot, the shock and pain probably being too profound. Tears would come later. It seemed that Camille Croft was once again a good fellow, a fine companion, but no man's idea of a lover, and especially not Eric's.

She couldn't read his expression. But his continued silence was eloquent.

She lifted her chin higher. "Don't worry. I do not pursue where I am not wanted. I will not trouble you again. We can still be friends, I hope. Pretend I never said anything, please."

"*Damned* if I will," he finally said with a growl, and pulled her into his arms.

He'd meant to let her leave. He'd resolved to ignore her declaration. It had been stunning, but to take her up on it still would be wrong. Yet in the end it was the way she stood there, proud and strong, filled with hurt pride, unshed tears making her brown eyes shimmer. It finally broke him. But it was the way her lips met his that swept every last resolution away.

Her fashionable little hat went flying as he cupped the back of her head in one big hand so she could meet his kiss. For one second, as their lips met, she seemed stunned. In the next, she was meeting him, joining him, welcoming him. Her mouth was softer and even sweeter than he'd imagined, her enthusiasm devastating. She didn't kiss like a shy virgin or a skilled temptress. She kissed with her whole heart, and that disarmed him completely.

She flung her arms around his neck, pulled his head down, kissing him measure for measure, wriggling closer until she was pressed tight against him. It was like nothing he'd ever known. It was exactly right. She wasn't some fragile creature he was afraid of hurting. She was, as she claimed, fully a woman, responsive and warm. Her body was curved and ripe. When his tongue met hers, she sighed with pleasure. He lifted her with one arm so that he could feel her breasts against his chest. He needed the other hand to stroke her as they kissed.

She twined her arms around his neck, rested completely against him, and kissed him until he ran out of breath. He found he'd rather kiss her than breathe.

For Camille, it was exactly what she wanted and so much more. He was impassioned yet gentle. She could feel his barely restrained urgency. It made her lose all her control, but that was good too, because she ceded it all to him. She trusted him completely.

But for all his passion, he was experienced, and slowly began to realize their exposed position. He remembered they were in a stable. Anyone could walk in. The groom should have been back before this, which might mean he was somewhere near, waiting for a chance to decently interrupt them. Eric realized that if they continued there wouldn't be a shred of decency left to them.

So too soon for both of them, he raised his head. He slowly lowered her, setting her down so her feet touched the floor again.

"Lord," he said. His smile was wry as he looked down into her flushed face. He touched her rumpled curls. Then he took a deep breath. "All right. Don't say I didn't warn you. I still think you're too young for me. I still believe I may yet be too sick to be thinking of marriage. But I can't deny what just happened. If you're willing to throw your life away, I'm grateful and eager to catch it. Let's go in and talk with Miles."

She'd been trying to collect herself, straightening her riding costume, but she paused when he spoke. She looked up at him.

"What?"

"I said it's time for me to talk to your brother. It's customary, you know, as you have no father."

She waited to hear what else he'd say. He only stood there, smiling fondly at her.

She didn't smile back at him. He hadn't said a

word of love. She'd given him her heart but she'd
be damned if she'd take his for the sake of propriety. That might be worse than not having him at
all, because she'd always know he'd been forced to
what she yearned for. She thought she might bear
that. But it just wasn't fair.

"You think that because you kissed me we have
to be married?"

His smile faded as he saw her expression.

"What nonsense!" she fumed. "Why, if every
man who kissed a girl had to marry her, there
wouldn't be a single man in England!"

"I'm not every man and you're not every
woman."

"No, indeed. And so I will not let you be cocrced
into a lifelong commitment because of one moment
of . . ."

He took her hand. "You don't want me?" he
asked, his eyes searching hers. "It was only one
moment for you?"

"I didn't say that," she said, flustered. "I just
think it's not fair for you to feel trapped, because I
swear I'd never have kissed you if I thought I was
obligating you."

"I want to marry you, Camille. I've wanted to
for a very long time, but I knew my shortcomings. I
should," he said on a gruff laugh, "they're the only
short things about me. Seriously, look at my situation from my viewpoint. I'm as old as your brother
is, and though that's not ancient, it can't be dis-

counted. Aside from that, I have a treacherous ailment. Though I have reason to hope, I don't know if or when I'll be completely well.

"Did you think I was indifferent to you?" he asked. "Do you know how hard it was for me to pretend? But I kept asking myself what sort of a husband a man with my problems could be for a young woman like you, so I kept close watch on myself whenever you were around. Still, I wanted to be around, if only to be near you for as long I could. That's why I was concerned about how you were ignoring me. Then you said you cared for me, and my good intentions crumbled. Are you saying otherwise now?"

"Well, no, but you're not saying anything about how you feel about me!" she cried in frustration. "I mean, *why* you want me . . . and such."

He checked. Then he laughed. She tried to pull her hand away, but he held it tight. "How I feel about you? I feel you're beautiful," he began, and couldn't go on when he saw her freeze.

"Don't mock me," she cried, tears spilling down her checks.

"I'm not. Why should you think I am? You're beautiful. Has no one ever told you that?"

She ducked her head and fumbled in a pocket. Not finding a handkerchief, she swiped at her eyes with the back of her sleeve. He quickly handed her his handkerchief. "No," she managed to say as she buried her face in the sail-sized handkerchief, "no one ever has, because I'm not."

"That's absurd! Why, of course, you're beautiful. I'm not a poetic fellow, but anyone can see you've got the most wonderful eyes, so big and brown. And curls—I love your hair. And you have the most amazing figure. It really is . . . damme, but I wish I had the words."

She slowly lowered the handkerchief. He saw her pink nose, reddened eyes, and newborn smile, and thought she looked adorable.

"Wonderful?" she asked, believing his doting expression more than his words, "and amazing? Well, it isn't a patch on some of the poetry I've heard spouted to other girls, but it will do for a start. Do you really mean it?"

"I don't say things I don't mean."

"No, you don't," she said with rising joy.

"So let's go see Miles."

"No." She shook her head. "I'd never feel good about it if you did that right now. Give it time, a few days or more, and then if you still feel the same way, fine. No, better than fine, because I do love you, Eric. But I believe in fair play, and I'd never be happy if I ever thought your hand had been forced into mine."

She'd said it gruffly, the way a well brought up young man might if he felt he'd compromised a young woman.

Eric grinned. That was part of her charm, her uniqueness, that absolute sense of integrity. He nodded. "A few days? Three's a lucky number. Will that be enough to suit you?"

"If that's enough for you."

"Oh, I don't need three minutes, but fair enough. And maybe by then I can even come up with some proper, or even improper, poetry for you. Let's see. There was a young girl named Camille, whose manner was far from genteel."

She giggled.

"I'll work on it," he promised. "For now, it is time to go in. If you don't worry about your reputation, I do about mine."

She picked up the hem of her skirt and took his arm. Just feeling that strong, hard arm under hers thrilled her. She didn't know how she'd be able to keep his declaration a secret. She wanted to share her news with the world. But she had to give him a chance to change his mind. Then if he came to her and asked her to be his wife, her celebration would know no end. She eyed him and felt her senses bubbling again. He'd be hers! She'd sleep next to his big body every night, she'd be able to kiss him whenever she felt like it, and she'd . . .

"There's one thing I still don't understand," he said as they strolled down the alley to the front of the house. "Why did you say you couldn't look at me after what Nell said?"

Camille stumbled and was glad of the strong arm that held her upright. "It was nothing, really," she said quickly, feeling her cheeks growing hot again.

He paused. "You know, another reason I love you is . . ."

"You love me," she cried, clutching his arm hard.

"Well, of course I do. Why else . . . ? Oh, the words. Yes, I ought to have said them." He took her back in his arms and smiled down at her. "I love you," he whispered, and kissed her.

Too soon for them both, and with both of them breathing hard, he reluctantly released her. He took her arm again. He cleared his throat. "As I was saying," he said as they began walking again, "another reason I love you is that you're the worst liar I ever met. Which is not to say that you lie all the time, but that you do it so badly. What did Nell say? I regret the day I found her. I don't think she's the right sort of companion for you. As for that, when's her cousin coming to take her away? As for *that,* how do you feel about him?"

"He's a charming man," she said, tugging at him to get him walking again, "and I'm grateful if you're at all jealous."

It was like tugging a boulder. "What was it Nell said?" he persisted.

Camille looked at the toes of her riding boots. "What does it matter?"

"It mattered enough to keep you from looking at me. Come, keeping secrets? You wouldn't like it if I did the same."

"You're right," she sighed. And told him.

It took him a long time to stop laughing. She had to give him his handkerchief back so he could wipe his eyes. But when he finally sobered, he was very sober indeed.

"Stare at a man's trousers instead of into his eyes if you want to win his heart? That's outrageous," he said, "but for all I know it may be true. For other fellows, that is. As for me, you may look all you like. I'd be flattered. Though I'd be more puzzled than thrilled if it was anyone else goggling at me." He frowned. "That's not the point. She doesn't belong in your house. The girl's hell-bent on becoming a Cyprian, and that's her affair. But I don't want her influencing you."

"Afraid I'll take up the trade?" she joked.

He didn't smile.

"Actually," she added with a saucy grin, "some of the things she told me can be helpful to you."

"I'm not a prude and neither are you or we wouldn't have so much to laugh about together," he said seriously. "And I trust your good sense. But she's headed for danger, and I don't want her involving you in it."

"How could she?" Camille said blithely.

"Oh, love," he said, "never tempt the fates by saying such things."

So she tempted him by grinning up at him, and it was a while before they could walk on.

Chapter 14

Camille didn't know how she could keep her feelings to herself now, and she didn't want to. She wanted to keep holding Eric's hand, she wanted to kiss him again, she wanted to simply lean against the warm, solid strength of the man. But she said she'd give him more time and so was determined to do the impossible. She walked back into the house with him, fighting to keep her expression impassive and her hands off him. But she couldn't and wouldn't even try to stop the incredible joy she felt suffusing her.

She had Eric's love! She didn't need anything else—except the restraint to keep it to herself for just a few more days.

"I see you had a good ride, Cammie," Miles

commented, looking up as they entered the salon. "Did you meet anyone we know?"

She hadn't seen anyone. She hadn't even seen Eric when they were riding this morning, because she'd been so busy trying to avoid his eyes and so concentrated on avoiding looking at any other part of him that she'd kept her head down. She'd memorized every hair on her horse's neck, but she wouldn't have noticed anyone in the park even if she'd run into—or over—the king himself.

"The usual crowd of park saunterers," Eric said smoothly, saving Camille the necessity of speaking. "But we were too busy galloping to stop and chat with anyone. It was cold, just right for riding. The sun was bright. You should have joined us."

"So I should have," Miles said, looking at Camille curiously. "You must have had quite a gallop. My sister's glowing and, come to think of it, so are you. Maybe I'll join you tomorrow."

"Maybe you will not," his wife said quickly, looking from Camille to Eric. "You promised to take me to Madame Celeste so I could have my last fitting for the new gown I'll be wearing at our soiree. Did you forget? We're hosting a party on Saturday, and I have to look superb."

"I confess, I forgot," Miles said, taking her hand. "Possibly because I can't see how anything could make you look better."

She beamed at him; he stared at her. They stood gazing at each other until Eric cleared his throat.

"I must be going," Eric said, "I'll see you again soon."

"I'll walk you to the door," Camille said, and left her brother and sister-in-law and went into the front hall with Eric.

"Then, until tonight?" Eric asked her when they stood by the door.

She frowned. "Tonight?"

"The Shipleys' dinner party. I thought everyone was going."

"Oh," Camille said in frustration. "No. I promised Belle we'd go to the theater tonight."

Now Eric frowned. "I'm promised to the Shipleys. I thought you'd be there. There's no way I can politely get out of it. Still, we'll ride tomorrow morning as usual? And tomorrow night you'll be at the concert?"

Camille nodded. "But I promised Dana I'd go there with him and Nell. Miles and Annabelle have to be home to take care of last minute details to do with their party."

Eric frowned.

"It's only a concert," she said, laughing. "And I'll see you there. I'll only be with him for the ride to and fro."

"A fellow can get up to a lot in a carriage," he said.

"How interesting. Really?" she asked, grinning. "You must tell me about it one day."

"I'd be happy to do more," he whispered, bowing.

"You don't have to see me every minute," she told him as softly, when he took her hand.

"Of course, I do," he said, taking her hand to his lips.

She wished he could take more than her hand. But a footman stood at the door. "I mean," she said quietly, so they wouldn't be overheard, "you must have some distance so you can make up your mind fairly and dispassionately."

"*I* mean I have to see you, plain and simple," he said, "and there's nothing fair about not being able to. And believe me, there's not one thing I feel that's the least dispassionate. Take care. I'll see you in the morning."

Camille stood at the open door, watching him leave. She wore a silly smile until the footman coughed to remind her how cold it was getting in the hall. She reluctantly let him shut the door. If she hurried, she could get upstairs in time to watch Eric ride away. She fairly flew up the stairs, but when she got there, all she could see was his broad back as he and his horse disappeared up the street. He was gone, and she wouldn't see him again until tomorrow.

Her first impulse was to go to her room, jump back into bed, and sleep until the next morning, when she'd see him again. She consoled herself by thinking that there was just one more afternoon then one more night to get through. Then her world would be right again—if he didn't change his mind, she warned herself.

But even though she earnestly tried to keep her

hopes down, when she skipped down the stair to go back to her brother and sister-in-law, it was very hard to stop smiling.

"Oh, good," Camille said as Nell slid into the seat beside hers in the theater. "You're back. You were gone so long, I thought you might miss the pantomime. That's always your favorite."

"The ladies convenience was so crowded," Nell whispered, "I thought I might miss it too."

No whisper was too low for Belle's ears. She glanced at Nell. "I didn't see you there."

"I wasn't in the one for the ladies," Nell said softly. "I used the one for the servants."

"Oh, but there was no need of that!" Camille said.

"But the other was too crowded," Nell said, casting her gaze down. "Have I made a mistake?"

"No, you were clever," Camille said in chagrin. "I had to wait forever."

"One goes," Belle said in awful tones, "where one is expected to."

Camille giggled until Belle had to smile at her inadvertent pun.

"And where's your cousin?" Miles asked Nell, looking at the empty seat Dana had occupied until the intermission.

"Yes," Camille said, "I'd hate for him to miss the pantomime."

"Why, thank you," Dana said, as he parted the curtain and came into the box. "Thank you for your concern. It's just that there was such a crush in the hallway. You know," he said to Nell, "I saw you there."

Nell sat up straighter. "Did you?"

Dana took his seat. "Of course," he said softly. "Remember, I watch over you."

She turned her head and stared straight ahead, although if anyone had been watching, they would have seen she paid little attention to what was happening on the stage. But no one noticed. The pantomime was hilarious, and everyone else in the party seemed in a good mood when it was over and they got up to leave the theater.

"That was fun," Camille declared, though her heart wasn't in it. The pantomime, funny as it was, had seemed never-ending. Or was it just that she couldn't wait for the night to be over? Nothing could be amusing to her tonight. She kept thinking about Eric. She hoped he was having a good time at his dinner party—no, she didn't. She wanted him to find the food tasteless and the company flat because she wasn't there. It wasn't very loverlike to wish that on him, she knew. But she couldn't help smiling at the thought.

"That gown looks very well on you," Belle remarked as they waited for the crowds to thin so they could make their way down to the lobby and their waiting carriage. She eyed her sister-in-law critically. "I wasn't sure salmon was your color, but you look radiant in it."

"Thank you," Camille said with a grin, because

she did feel as if she was glowing, but it had nothing to do with her gown.

They said good night to Dana in the lobby. He said a brief private good-bye to Nell and then bowed to Miles and Belle. Then, while Miles and Belle were occupied with a friend they'd met, he took Camille's hand.

He held it a second longer than was proper. "Until tomorrow night," he said.

"Tomorrow night?" Camille asked absently.

"Why, yes. The concert. Nell asked me to come get her, and you said you'd ride there with us. You forgot?"

"Oh," Camille said in a small voice, "I suppose I did." She had, she realized, because she really didn't want to go anywhere with him. He'd been bland company before, bordering on boring, but now she wouldn't have been able to pay attention to him even if he'd been fascinating. Not with Eric on her mind and in her heart. But Dana looked so hurt and surprised that she added, "But I am looking forward to it."

He smiled, and she was relieved. Except, she thought, as she watched him walk off into the night, she'd have felt a lot better if she hadn't made the appointment in the first place. Although it had been fun to tease Eric about it, she keenly regretted missing any opportunity to be with him, even for a few minutes in a carriage. Still, it was true that Eric couldn't monopolize her company unless he wanted everyone to know they'd reached an understanding.

But they had, hadn't they? That thought made Camille feel as though she'd just downed three of the many champagne toasts that would soon be made to her. Because wouldn't Miles and Belle be happy? And Drum? And Rafe and all her friends? Most of them were also Eric's friends. They'd all want to celebrate. Camille wanted to turn cartwheels.

She knew it as though Eric were there at her side, telling her. He'd declare for her the minute the three days she'd asked him to take were up. Saturday night. It was the perfect time and perfect place: at the party Miles and Belle were giving. With their friends there, what better time for such a declaration?

She clasped her hands together in her fur muff and hugged it to her breast, trying to keep her happiness inside. Eric Ford, big, handsome, capable, entirely lovable Eric Ford, *her* Eric, was going to be her husband!

"Are you feeling all right?" Belle asked her, eyeing her curiously.

"Oh. Yes, better than all right," Camille sang.

Belle glanced at Dana's retreating back. Her eyes narrowed. "Has anything happened that I should know about, or rather, that your brother and I should know?"

"Oh, no, believe me, when that something happens, you'll be the first to know!" Camille said with a secret and growing smile.

Belle's eyes widened.

The house was dark, the hour was late, but Camille wasn't sleeping. She'd come home from the concert full of glee, but once she'd gone to bed all her doubts assailed her and murdered any thought of sleep. She was too fearful and too joyful and wished she could catch hold of one emotion long enough to study it.

Eric might change his mind. He might not.

She could picture him bringing her a single rose on Saturday night and whispering, "Can I tempt you to be my bride?"

No. He was not so modest.

She could almost hear him saying, "You are mine."

She pounded her pillow and turned it over yet again. What would he say? She could hardly wait to hear it.

Camille sat up and stared into the darkness. Oh, why had she given him three days to make up his mind? That wasn't what feminine, confident, intelligent women did. That alone might make him reconsider his offer!

She just wouldn't sleep until Saturday, then, she decided glumly as she rose from bed. She lit a lamp, but there was nothing she wanted to read or write. She was heartily tired of herself, so she rose and went to the window. This was a fashionable district near the park, well lit by the new gaslights, so there was always something to see, even at night. She might spy a troop of young bloods staggering home after a night on the town or the old watchman making his solemn patrol down the street or carriages bringing travelers, physicians, or partygoers to and fro. Anything would be better than her own tedious company.

She moved back the curtain and looked out.

There was a man standing directly opposite beneath the gaslight. He was looking up at her window. He must have seen the light bloom in her room when she lit her lamp. She couldn't see his face from this distance, but there was no mistaking that monumental figure.

Camille gasped. She ran back into the room, threw on her dressing gown, and started to race to the door. She stopped. She glanced at herself in the looking glass. It was such a ratty old dressing gown, one of those that Belle despaired of, and with good reason. But she couldn't wake Belle to borrow another. And she certainly couldn't wait a moment more.

She ran to her door, went out into the hall, and tiptoed down the stairs, wincing at every creak of the wood under her feet. Her bare feet, she realized, as the cold floor registered under her toes. There was no time to turn back to get slippers. She flew to the wardrobe in the hall, pulled out a long velvet cape, and permitted herself a satisfied grin as she threw it over her shoulders. This was more fitting for a heroine's midnight meeting.

Her grin slipped as she fumbled with the door latch. This might be the beginning of the worst moment of her life. Something clearly had to be amiss if he was pacing under her window at midnight, and he not even knowing if she was awake!

At least, she thought, heart racing as she opened the door, he wasn't ill. He wouldn't be here if he was sick, would he?

She threw open the door.

Eric caught her up in his arms and kissed her so thoroughly that she staggered when he released her at last. He was breathless too. She might have been surprised, but she'd have had to be dead not to return his kiss as completely as he'd given it.

They stood looking at each other in the flickering light of the lantern over the door. She licked her lips, as though trying to taste his kiss again.

Eric took her hand, his eyes fastened on her lips. His expression was grave and pained. "You must marry me," he said. "I cannot be such a fool as to wait a moment more." He bent his head and kissed her again, his mouth and his tongue saying everything she'd ever wanted to hear from him without his saying a word. But when he did speak again, it was everything else she'd wanted to hear. "Not just because of that," he breathed against her hair, "though God knows that's a fine reason. For more than that, though I don't know how I can live without that for much longer."

He leaned back and met her eyes, his own stark and sincere. "You asked me to think, to consider. You asked too much. I have thought. I wouldn't have proposed if I had not. I know my mind and my heart. How could I go to a dinner party and think of you somewhere else? You ruined my dinner, little wretch. As you'd ruin my life if you didn't spend yours with me. I think I must have willed you awake. I couldn't sleep until we spoke. We must marry, and that is that—and everything else."

"Oh, yes!" she said.

He smiled. "Now go to bed," he said and stepped away. "I will too, because now at least I can sleep again. I'll see you in the morning. Oh, for God's sake," he said, "get upstairs, because one moment more and I'll haul you up there and will not be responsible for what happens next."

"Oh, good," she said with a grin.

He hesitated, then smiled, bowed, turned, and went off into the night again. She didn't go upstairs until she could no longer see him. Though she discovered that she still did, even when she at last closed her eyes and went to sleep with a smile on her lips at the sight.

It was so cold that their boots made squeaking sounds on the snow as they walked along the side of the bridle path. He took her hand and led her behind a snow-laden fir tree. There, in the blue and white shadows, he stopped and looked down at her. Then he lowered his head and feathered a kiss on her upturned lips.

His mouth was warm, and her blood ran hot, so Camille opened her mouth against his and held on to Eric's shoulders to make sure he didn't let her go.

He caught his breath, raised his head, and looked into her eyes. "I'm going to ask Miles for his permission when we return to the house."

"He's out," she said breathlessly, "and will be until late. I want to be there when you tell him. I know! Ask him on Saturday before the party. That will be such a good surprise."

He smiled and kissed her again. "If he says no, be at your window at midnight," he eventually said in a hoarse voice against her ear, as he rocked her in his arms. "I'll be below with two horses and a road map. We'll be in Scotland and in our marriage bed by dawn."

She laughed and kissed him again. When she had to stop at last to take a breath, she complained. "I can't feel your skin! Your neckcloth's too high. You're wearing gloves and a greatcoat. It's like making love to a woolen stocking!"

He put her at arm's length and stared down at her, his eyes dancing with light. "I'm supposed to say that."

She actually blushed. He was charmed. "But I don't mind you saying it," he added, drawing her back into his arms.

"I say what I mean," she said seriously, gazing

up at him. "I've no patience for girlish games. So if that's what you want, you'll have to find another woman. I know I'm not in the common way, and I suppose . . ."

He kissed her until she forgot what she was going to say or suppose, as well as the cold, the park, and the fact that they were both dressed to the ears.

But he couldn't forget where they were, not with the feelings her hot little tongue kindled in him. When it became too frustrating, he pulled away again and looked down into her flushed face. "You are exactly what I've always wanted. Never forget it. So. Saturday night we become officially engaged and marry as soon as decently possible?"

She nodded.

"Then let's celebrate prematurely tonight," he said. "But we have to move on now. We can't stand here like erotic statues all day. That would be fine in India—I must show you a book I have of them— after we're married of course—but it's not the thing here in Regent's Park. There are others foolish enough to go riding on such a frigid day, ardent lovers and ardent horsemen. It wouldn't do for us to be discovered yet."

She didn't move, only stood staring up at him.

"It would ruin our surprise," he said, touching a gloved finger to the tip of her nose.

She only gazed up at him, smiling.

He returned her smile. "Your groom's being polite, but the poor fellow's probably freezing. And the horses can't stand until they look like statues."

"Oh! My poor Hermes!" she cried, stepping back. "I forgot, of course. Let's ride on."

He was amused at how concern for her horse could supercede all her other desires, even ones for him. But his smile faded at what she said next.

"But we can't celebrate tonight," she said as they hurried to where the groom was waiting with their horses. "There's that concert I promised to go to with Dana Bartlett. No one will know about our engagement until Saturday night, and I can't disappoint him—at least, no more than I must when he hears our news, I suppose. I think he's been wooing me."

"Well, so long as it's only something you think," he said, "then I suppose I can be generous and let him live."

She stopped and turned a rosy face up to his. "It's true, isn't it?"

He didn't have to ask what she meant. He smiled at her tenderly. "I keep asking myself that too. But it is. We're going to marry, you and I, and as soon as I can arrange it. Never doubt it, or me."

"It seems too good to be true," she said with a worried look.

"It's true and nothing can stop . . ."

She clapped a gloved hand over his mouth. "Never say it!" she whispered, horrified.

"So," he said, taking her hand in his, "you don't have a missish bone in your whole beautiful body, but you have a lot of superstitious ones?"

She nodded, wide-eyed.

"I don't," he said, "but I won't upset you."

"Eric," she said, her eyes searching his, "please. Never say that nothing can stop us getting married. At least not until after you say 'I do.' To me," she added fastidiously.

He considered her a moment, and then, remembering the damned disease that had almost leveled him, his own expression grew grave. He nodded. "I promise. But don't doubt me. I'll never go back on my word."

"I know," she said. "I wish that was all that mattered." She wasn't thinking of his malarial fever. That was a thing she would deal with if and when it ever recurred. She was thinking of all the things that might change his mind about her, from his finally realizing she was not beautiful to his meeting the real woman of his dreams.

He began to speak again and closed his lips. He couldn't know her thoughts, but he knew his own too well. There was nothing he could say to reassure her. Or himself.

Chapter 15

Dana's expression changed so drastically Camille became alarmed. His eyes went flat, his mouth thinned. His dark complexion grew pale, looking sallow in the light of the lantern set at the side of the coach. She hadn't meant to tell anyone about her plans before Eric made the announcement, but it wouldn't have been fair to let what Dana had just said go unanswered.

"So," she went on nervously, twisting her hands in her lap, "though I'm both flattered and grateful for the honor you do me, I must respectfully decline your kind offer."

They were alone in the carriage after their night at the concert, waiting for Nell. At the last minute she'd said she had to visit the convenience and had hurriedly left the coach at the curb and dashed back into the concert hall. Camille hadn't known if it was the girl's overactive bladder or whatever gentleman she had eyed during the concert that made her leave so suddenly, but now she suspected Nell had gone because she knew what her cousin wanted to say and was giving him the privacy in which to do it.

The moment they were alone, Dana had seized her hand and made his offer of marriage. Camille was startled and saddened by it. She'd turned down other men's proposals, but few had made her feel so bad. He was not only shocked and unhappy. He seemed angry.

"Dana, you're a good man and a fine catch for any girl," she said earnestly. "But not for me, because I've already found my future husband. He is Eric Ford," she said, unable to hide her smile as she said the name. "I didn't cancel tonight's outing, although I suppose I ought to have. But I didn't know what you intended and I didn't know my future for certain until this very morning. The announcement won't be made until tomorrow night at our party.

"In fact, you're the first one who knows it, so please don't tell anyone else yet. But I thought it was only fair to tell you," she went on, "because I didn't want you to think it was any fault in you that made me refuse you. I hope you'll still come tomorrow too. Nell's expecting you, and you know I'll always consider you a friend."

"That is not quite what I wanted," he said stiffly. Then, as though realizing he was being churlish, he added, "But I wish you well. If ever you change your mind, please believe I will continue to be at your service."

They sat in awkward silence for a few more minutes that seemed like ages. Then Nell came into the carriage, rosy-cheeked and breathless. She was smiling until she saw her cousin's expression. Then her smile vanished, and she sidled into her seat and sat as silent as they were all the way back home.

They stayed silent until Dana walked them to the front door. "If I may have a few words with my cousin?" he asked when they got there.

"Of course, come in," Camille said.

"Oh, I think here is as good a place as any," he said.

"But it's cold out tonight," Camille said, noticing that their words came out like puffs of white smoke in the frigid air. She looked from one of them to the other. Neither looked happy.

"It won't take but a moment," he said brusquely.

Camille nodded, said good night, and went in, the footman shutting the door behind her.

"You knew of this?" Dana asked Nell the moment they were alone.

"She turned you down? How could I know that?"

"She turned me down because she's going to marry Eric Ford."

Nell cocked her head. "Is she? Or is she just saying so? If wishes were horses, beggars would be riding all round the town."

"They're announcing it tomorrow night."

"That I didn't know," she said in amazement. "She's a slyboots after all. She fooled me."

"She's no more sly than a puppy. She said he just asked, and of course, she hopped at the chance to have him."

She shrugged. "He's her brother's friend. It could be an old promise he has to keep. That explains why he didn't respond to me. I was being careful not to get Camille's nose out of joint, but he's a man. A capon could have seen what I was offering, and he's far from that."

"You can't see past your mirror," he said furiously. "Every male who doesn't want to lift your skirts isn't denying himself. It wasn't only her social position that made me decide upon her. She's a desirable woman. Ford has the taste to see that too."

Her expression showed she didn't believe him, but she was shivering in the cold. "So what are you going to do?" Nell asked, shifting from foot to foot.

"Remains to be seen," he said thoughtfully. "There's many a slip twixt the cup and the lip, and the ring and the altar too. I'll be here Saturday night."

He turned and left her abruptly without so much as a farewell. She shrugged again, then raised the doorknocker to get back into the house, to hear more of Camille's news.

But Camille had gone straight up to bed after bidding her brother and sister-in-law good night.

* * *

"Your sister's got a secret," Belle told Miles as she settled into bed beside him that night. She made an angry huffing sound and pounded her pillow before she flung her head down on it. "She ran upstairs like a scalded cat tonight, not even bothering to stop and gossip with me. And she was smiling to herself."

"I know," Miles said, looking as troubled as his wife was. "That's not like her. She's been dreamy all day and was worse tonight. Do you think it's something to do with Dana Bartlett? He's not a bad fellow, but I confess, I'd hopes . . ."

"*She* had hopes," Belle said angrily. "Very different ones too."

"I know." Miles sighed. "Who does not? She's clear as running water. Her dreams are there to see in her eyes. But it's better that she doesn't end up with Eric if his heart isn't involved. You know, I confess I had a secret fear he might offer simply out of friendship for us. That wouldn't do, not for someone as passionate as our Cammie."

"My only hope is that she hasn't given up on him completely," his wife said darkly. "Because whatever Dana Bartlett is or is not, he's clever. If he realized where her heart was fixed and then saw she was getting discouraged because she felt Eric would never see her as a possible wife, he might use it. Bartlett may be using that to persuade her to look at him more seriously. That would never do. It wouldn't be the first time a woman saved her vanity by taking another man when she couldn't get the one she wanted."

Miles didn't answer. He lay very still.

"Oh," she cried. She sat up and turned to him. "Oh, no! Oh, never, my love! We've been through that so many times. Miles, I did marry you for all the wrong reasons, but before God, you ought to know by now that it turned out to be for every good reason I didn't even know enough to hope for. I do love you to distraction, and the only reason I don't tell you about it all the time is that I don't want you getting too complaisant, because that would change who you are and why I love you and . . ."

She had to finish her comment against his lips. He pulled her close and kissed her until she had nothing to say but murmurs of desire.

"I know," he finally said, looking into her dazzled eyes. "I do know." He smiled. "But how could I get you so romantically inclined tonight if I didn't pretend not to know? You seemed so wide awake and eager to do nothing but gossip. But you look so beautiful tonight that I couldn't help trying to make you feel just a little apologetic and eager to please. Ouch!" He laughed as she swatted him with a pillow.

He retaliated in a different way. And then they found nothing to laugh about but much to sigh about. Camille's secret could wait. They had more vital things to do.

* * *

Miles slapped Eric's broad back and then shook his hand vigorously.

"I couldn't be happier!" Miles said again. "So that's why she's been smiling like a little cat that got into the cream. You're going to be my brother-in-law! I could not be happier for you both—and myself and my Annabelle. She'll be so pleased, Eric, this is such good news!"

"Well, then, you could stop punching me," Eric said, rubbing a shoulder that Miles had just buffeted.

"I could drop a piano on you, and you wouldn't notice. Lord! But this is happy news. We thought it might be Bartlett who had her smiling so much last night and this morning."

Eric stopped rubbing his shoulder. "Well, that's a relief. I thought you were just eager to get her off your hands. Seriously, you didn't think she wanted Dana Bartlett?"

"*He* certainly wants her, you can see it in his eyes, and he's been haunting the place since he met her. He said he'd provide a home for Nell, but he's been mighty slow to find one. It was obvious he was using the delay to court Camille, because so far as I can see, there's little affection between the cousins. Speaking of which, now that I know *you* were haunting the place because of Cammie, I can tell you that's an odd bit of goods you landed on us."

Eric frowned. "Nell? Aye, she is that. The sooner she's gone the better. And I wasn't the one to land her on you, that was Cammie's doing. Your good wife invited her, but I suspect Camille had much to do with it. We'll have a houseful of strays, I think. But at least I can hope she'll take my advice on which ones to take in."

"Good luck with that," Miles murmured. "But come, we have to tell Belle."

"I think all you have to do is open the door," Eric said with a smile.

"No, he does not!" Belle said, as she threw open the door and marched in, wreathed in smiles. "I wondered why you would ask for a private interview with Miles. Why should you be so formal after all these years? So I asked Cammie."

"And I told her!" Camille sang out from the doorway "Because I didn't think Miles would turn you down."

"Well, I don't know," Miles said. "It was a close thing. Having Eric for a brother-in law will certainly cost us. We're close, so you'll be visiting all the time, and just think of the grocer's bill."

They laughed a great deal, and amidst all the hugging and kissing, Miles called for a bottle of the best.

They drank a toast to the newly engaged pair.

Then Belle set her glass down firmly. "No more. You may get drunk as a pair of sows tonight, gentlemen, but as for now, we have to make ready for the party. Now it will have to be a grander affair." She waved a hand to still Camille's protests. "I'll have to send to the florists and the baker and—

well, never mind. This will be an unforgettable night. Too bad your mama won't be here," she added. Miles and Camille exchanged grins. "But my mama, as ever, will be thrilled to take her place. Now, who's going to make the announcement? It should be at midnight."

"I leave that decision to you," Eric said, sketching a bow, though keeping his arm around Camille. "I've already made mine."

"Then midnight it is," Belle said. "Miles will call for silence and make the announcement and raise a toast. Then you can toast Camille."

Eric looked down at Camille. "Gladly. And then we can be married."

"If only it were as easy as that," Belle started to say. "There are plans to be made and—"

"We want to be married with as little delay as is socially permissible. Don't we?" he asked Camille.

"I wouldn't even bother with the socially permissible," she said thoughtfully.

Eric's arm tightened around her waist as Miles laughed.

Belle smiled. "That's a discussion for another day. Now we have a gala to prepare for! One that will be memorable."

"I think they already know," Eric whispered to Camille.

She looked around her brother's crowded grand salon and saw many of the guests, most of them old friends, smiling back at her. "Well, they look happy enough. I'm sorry, I didn't tell anyone—well, except for Dana, and only because I had to. I suppose he told Nell, but I don't think she knows anyone here. I didn't want to ruin the surprise. But I think they guess. I just can't stop grinning—or looking at you."

"Neither can I—I mean grinning and looking at you. Lord! But you look lovely tonight."

She preened, holding out a fold of her skirt. Her gown was a long, silvery green column of silk, artfully draped beneath the breasts to give her figure definition. "Isn't this a lovely gown? But I look good because I'm glowing, and the radiance is because of you. And don't you look fine! Oh, Eric," she said softly, "you are just the most handsome man!"

She sighed with pleasure as she gazed at him. He looked superb in formal evening dress. He didn't wear the fobs and fripperies of the dandy set but was commanding in black and white, the only color the slate-blue pattern in his waistcoat, the gleam in his golden-brown and green eyes, and the glow of his honey-hued hair.

"Now I know we have to get your eyes examined—after we marry," he said, taking her hand. "But if you think so, it makes all the effort worth it. Do you know how hard my poor valet worked tonight? This neckcloth is so full of starch I could drop dead and still hold my head high. And if my jacket were any tighter, my hands would be numb. I suffer for you. It's worth it if you like the effect. But you're not supposed to tell me so, even if

I looked like an Adonis instead of a mammoth tarted up to look like a gentleman. You're only supposed to giggle, remember? And then bat me with your fan—or eyelashes."

"Actually," she said, "I prefer you in your riding clothes." Actually, she thought, she'd rather have seen him without a high neckcloth, so she could have seen the strong column of his powerful neck. In fact, she dreamed of seeing him with his collar opened, his shirt opened, his . . .

"The joy of having a girl with a tattletale complexion," he murmured, bending so he could speak in her ear, "is that a fellow knows when she's having wicked thoughts. Now you've gone from a glow to a blush. I wonder what I can do to raise it to a fever?"

They laughed.

Their company stole glances at them, and most of them smiled.

Some, of course, did not.

Dana watched the proceedings with no expression at all. Because he was Nell's cousin he had to be invited. To have done otherwise would have been to add insult to injury. He had come, but he was not happy about it.

Nell glided through the room wearing her usual serene expression. A trail of love-struck young men followed her. She wasn't eligible, they all knew that. But she was a heroine, and so damned lovely that they wished they could afford her, however she could be maintained.

"I don't care for that one," an exquisite blond woman muttered to her host and hostess as she watched Nell narrowly.

"She's the current heroine," Belle told her. "Haven't you heard the story of her rescue?"

"I heard the story and I like her even less," the blonde woman said. "And I've just spoken to her, and I tell you, Belle, I don't trust her one bit."

"Because she made eyes at Damon?" Miles laughed. "Come, Gilly, he's used to that, and besides, we all know your husband doesn't see anyone but you. He doesn't dare."

"Aye. He values his eyes, that's why," she said, to make everyone laugh, including her husband. "But that one . . . She's up to no good. I'd swear to it."

No one laughed at that. Their friend Gillian Ryder might be considered a lady now, but she'd come from low beginnings and was an astute judge of the kind of characters few of the nobility got to know.

"We watch her," Miles said seriously. "But she'll be gone soon. Her cousin, Dana Bartlett, the dark fellow brooding so Byronically over there by the window, will be taking her to live with him as soon as he finds a place that's suitable."

"Newgate would be suitable, I think," Gilly said, studying the man in question. "I wouldn't trust him either."

"You," her husband told her, "need to dance the glooms out. Too much time in the nursery and not enough in the ballroom. I told you so."

"No dancing tonight, I'm sorry to say," Belle said. "There's not enough room. Everyone who was asked has come. Such a crush," she said happily, because that was the hallmark of a hostess's wild success.

Gillian Ryder wasn't the only guest at the party from humble beginnings. Eric Ford was a popular man, unusual in that he had friends of both noble birth and low origins: men who were politicians and landowners, scholars and athletes, women of wit, style and charm, from many classes. His old school and army friends were there, along with the extended family of close friends he'd made over the years, all also friends of Miles and Belle. It was as much a reunion as a party, and the word had gone out that there'd be something else to celebrate before the night was over too.

Camille was as much hostess tonight as Belle, so she had to circulate amongst all the guests. She and Eric drifted apart. Though they tried to keep each other in sight, it was almost impossible. There were new arrivals to greet, introductions to be made, and news to be brought up to date. The sound of voices and laughter grew louder as the hour grew later. Wine and punch were served. Waiters passed through the rooms with trays of food. A feast would come after midnight, which was not far off. The guests were enjoying themselves too much to mind the crowding, but even though the windows had been thrown open to the chilly night the room was growing hot.

Eric felt himself beginning to grow much too hot. His heart picked up its pace. He tried to fight off panic.

God, no! Not now, not again, please!

He excused himself from the people he was speaking with and went to a far corner of the room to try to suck in some cooler air near the windows. He ran a finger beneath his cravat. His neckcloth had been annoying, but now it felt as though it was cutting off his breath. He shivered, and his heart, so high a moment before, began to sink.

"There you are!" Miles said when he found Eric leaning against a wall by an opened window. "There's no escape for you, lad. Your time's almost up. Getting cold feet? There's still time to run, you know."

He laughed, but Eric didn't.

"Come, big fellow," Miles went on sympathetically, "this will be much easier than riding to war, although I suppose the results can be just as lethal. Still, courage, it will be over before you know it. Now, ready? I'm going to tap a glass and call for silence soon. Are you prepared, or do you want another minute?"

Eric didn't smile. He didn't respond at all, he only stood very still, frowning, as though listening to something no one else could hear.

"Eric," Miles asked, suddenly serious, "are you all right? Are you unwell? Is it the fever again? Tell me. Oh, damnation," he said as he noticed how sallow Eric was. His own color fled. He turned to some nearby guests. "See if Harry Selfridge is still here, someone. Or any other doctor. I think Eric's fever's returned."

Eric shook his head and grimaced with pain of doing it. "No!" he rasped with effort. "Not fever. It's not the fever." An expression of surprise crossed his face, and he grabbed onto Miles's shoulder. "Damme, it's not the fever," he groaned as he crumpled to the floor.

Miles knelt and loosened Eric's cravat.

"Too much wine?" a guest asked.

"Probably the fever," Miles said through tightened lips.

"No," Eric said. His eyes were closed, his lips were white, but he managed to say, "Stomach, head. Too fast, feels differen'. Hard to talk. Ton-tongue's numb . . ."

"We'll get you to bed," Miles muttered, kneeling beside him.

"No," Eric moaned, before his eyes rolled up. "Don't. Need soap."

"You should have come to us before this," Miles said, rising to one knee. "He's delirious. I'll get him into bed," he told Drum, who had come running. "Tell the others."

A hand gripped his sleeve. Eric clutched hard, dragging Miles down so he could speak to him.

"No," Eric whispered with effort. "*Soap.* Get soap. 'S poison. I've been poisoned."

Guests began gathering around Eric's fallen figure and those gentlemen kneeling by his side.

"Too much to drink," one of them said wisely. "Jug-bitten. Dammed fool thing to do at a party such as this. Surprised, I thought the big fellow was a knowing one."

"Get a pail," Miles called as he and Rafe pulled an ashen Eric to his feet. "Fill it with warm water and soap. We need soapsuds."

"Soapsuds?" a matron said, wide-eyed, "But that's for purging."

"Aye." An older gentleman shook his head. "That will make the poor lad cast up his accounts. He'll cascade for hours."

"But soapsuds are a specific for—Oh! Was it the lobster patties?" the matron asked frantically, clutching her fan to her stomach like a shield. "They tasted a bit off."

Belle came running, a little blond whirlwind of a woman helping her force her way through the crowd. Gillian snatched up the glass of wine Eric had put down. She held it to the lamplight and then sniffed at the red wine in it. She dipped in her finger, brought it to the tip of her tongue, and scowled horribly. "Faugh! Thought so! No one will get sick on any food here unless they stuff themselves like pigs. Someone's slipped something into his drink. They tried to croak him."

"Hush," her husband said. "No need to assume the worst. It might just be a headache powder. He suffers from them when the fever is on him."

"Aye, this stuff would cure it," she said bitterly,

"for good. There's enough whore's eyewash to choke a horse in that glass. Belladonna," she explained, as those near her gasped. "Demireps put it in their eyes to make them bright as stars. It also blinds them for a spell. Those that get tired of the game drink it because it's kinder than a rope. You have to get it out of him fast," she told Miles as he and his friends lifted Eric.

"Bring the pail and a doctor to the blue bedroom," Miles told a footman, as they carried Eric from the room.

Chapter 16

Eric woke at dawn. He remembered the tingling and numbness on his tongue that made him set down his glass. The clumsiness of his tongue made it hard for him to speak, then the rapid onset of heat, fever, and chills made it impossible. He remembered his sudden panic, then falling. He winced as he remembered waking to thinking he was drowning, as vile liquids were forced down his throat. He wished he could forget the bouts of vomiting that followed, his friends' voices in his ears, urging him to hang on. So, he thought, looking around the all too familiar room in which he'd spent his last recuperation, he had survived—though there'd been times when he hadn't wanted to.

He swallowed and felt how raw his throat was,

how dry his mouth. And then he sighed with gratitude to whichever deity was watching over him.
He'd been very sick. But it had not been with
malarial fever, he'd realized that soon enough, and
even poison was preferable to that. It could have
been a bit of lobster gone bad, an antique clam in
one of those tasty patties he'd popped into his
mouth. Whatever it was, he'd recover from it. The
important thing was that he wouldn't have to re-
nounce his engagement to Camille.

But he hadn't gotten a chance to announce that
engagement! She must feel terrible about that. He
certainly did. He had to talk to her immediately.
He raised his head and felt a stab of pain but managed to swing himself up into a sitting position in
spite of it.

"Are you mad?" a tired voice asked. "Lie down."

"Do lay back, sir," he heard his valet urge him.
"You've been very ill."

"But not with the fever," he croaked. "And you
got to me in time. Thank you." He refused to lie
down again, but he did hang his head; it felt too
heavy to lift. "Hello, Miles," he said wearily. "I
was that sick that you're still here by my side?"

"That sick," Miles agreed.

There was something in his voice that made Eric
raise his head and look at him. "What is it?" Eric
said quickly. "What else happened? Where's Cammie?" he asked on a sudden wild surmise.

"She's missing," Miles said helplessly. "She vanished last night. And so did Nell."

Eric stared at him.

"Their wraps are still here, and there are no notes left behind," Miles said, anticipating his question. "She'd have told someone if she meant to leave for more than a moment. No one saw them leave either. With so many people coming and going, that's no wonder. When we got over our surprise and horror and saw you weren't going to die—at least not right away—we wondered why she hadn't come to see how you were doing, and so we sent for her. She'd disappeared. When did you last see her? Can you remember?" he asked urgently.

"I kept her in the corner of my eye all night," Eric said in bewilderment. "That is, up until I began to feel sick. Then I deliberately went to the back of the room because I didn't want to worry her. But it wasn't my fever, after all, just bad luck with the catering, I suppose."

"No," Miles said heavily. "There was belladonna in your wine. Gilly spotted it. The doctor said it's used often enough in other potions, but not in such a large amount, and not in wine. Lucky for you that you didn't down the whole glass. You were deliberately poisoned."

"To get me out of the way," Eric said, thinking with difficulty because of shock and an aching head. "To get me to stop watching Cammie." He looked up. "But you said she left no note. Have you received a ransom note?"

Miles shook his head. "Nothing. That's what's

so strange. Why would anyone go to all that trouble, take her, and not try to profit from it?"

Eric's eyes widened. "Dana Bartlett! What did he say?"

"Well, that's just it," his friend Drum, who had been sitting quietly in a chair by the window, said. "He's disappeared too."

Eric leapt from the bed.

It took both his friends and his valet to get him back into bed after they picked him up from the floor. Then it took the three of them to hold him down.

"Softly, softly now," Miles panted, as he strained to quiet his friend. "If running out into the streets would help, we'd be there. We're looking as best we can. We've got the word out all over town. Not just the Runners, and the best are already on the case, believe me, but all our friends as well. We're lucky. We had so many old friends who used to be in the game here last night. They're already on the trail: Rafe, Ewen Sinclair, Leigh, and Talwin. We got word that Wycoff is on his way here to help us too."

"And as Gilly knows the worst of London intimately," Drum said, "she's put out the word in places we don't even know about."

"The doctor says you have to rest and drink lots of fluids," Miles said, as he felt his friend stop struggling. "Do that, and you'll be able to join us in the hunt. Get up now, and you'll be of no use to Cammie at all."

Eric watched his friends' relief as they stepped back and studied him. He would have thrown them off, if he could, but he hadn't the strength. He felt a seething mixture of fury and helplessness. "If he thinks he can abduct her and force her to marry him, he's wrong," he growled. "He doesn't know her or me."

"That's true enough," Miles said. "So rest easy."

Eric eyed his friends' weary, unshaven faces. "As easy as you are? Certainly." He closed his eyes, and when he opened them again, he looked grimly determined. "Bring me the blasted liquids. I'll drink gallons. I'll be right in no time. And then I'll bring her home."

"Of course I'm getting dressed," Eric snarled at the two men who entered his room a few hours later.

His friends were taken aback. This wasn't the man they knew. A huge man with formidable strength, Eric had obviously been taught to control his temper years before. He was always the most patient, steady man they knew, even in the most difficult situations. Both Miles and Rafe had worked with him on matters of life and death and had seen him upset. But never like this. Even his valet, usually so passive, stood at his master's side looking wretched. Eric's teeth were clenched, his eyes were wild, and he was dragging on his clothes as fast as he could.

"I got up as soon as I knew I could without

falling down," Eric said, as he hurriedly tucked his shirt into his breeches. He stood in his shirtsleeves and stocking feet, his shirt still unbuttoned.

When he saw his friends' expressions, his changed. "If I lie in bed, I think," he explained, looking at them with entreaty. "I think of what could have happened to her, what could be happening to her. She's as brave as any man I ever met, resourceful, high-spirited, and clever. But she's very young and so *damned* beautiful . . ."

Rafe blinked at that. In spite of the dire situation, Miles had to smile. Any doubts he had about his friend's true feelings for his sister vanished.

Eric passed a hand over his eyes. "I can deal with any situation I can get my hands on, but I can't deal with my imagination. I can't accept my helplessness as well as thinking about how helpless she may be. It destroys me. But I wouldn't be standing if I thought I'd fall down again. I'm not a fool, that wouldn't help anyone. Trust me. I can do this. I'm big as an ox and strong as one, and I know my limits, both physical and mental. So don't argue, please. I *must* be up and about so I can find her or at least get on her trail."

"But not quite so fast, my friend," Drum said from the door. "We have a present for you."

Drum and another tall, dark gentleman, his cousin, Ewen, Viscount Sinclair, stood in the doorway. They had a man between them. They wore grim smiles. The man did not.

Dana Bartlett looked as haggard as Eric felt. He

was still in his evening clothes, but they looked much the worse for wear. His hair, usually carefully brushed, was unkempt. He had a recent bruise on his forehead and one swelling on his cheek as well. His eyes were red, and he was unshaven. Being so dark, it looked as though he hadn't shaved in days. He bore the stale scents of liquor and perfume. Most notably, to Eric's eyes, he looked both afraid and defiant.

Drum prodded him into the room. Belle was at their heels.

"We found him coming home an hour ago, when the sun was well up," Drum said. "He claims that he didn't know Camille was gone and doesn't know where she or his cousin may be."

"And be sure," the Viscount Sinclair said through thinned lips, "we asked him thoroughly."

"I spoke only the truth," Dana said bitterly.

"Oh, yes," Eric retorted, striding over to him. "And since you're a lawyer we certainly should believe you, is that it?" His face was gray with fatigue and worry, but his hands were fisted and his jaw was clenched as he confronted Dana. "Cut line," he growled. "Your cousin was a bad influence on Camille. You knew that but didn't tell anyone. What's your game now?"

"I thought I could keep Nell in line," Dana said sadly. His eyes darkened, and he stood straighter, staring Eric in the eyes. "If you knew she was a bad influence, why did you let her stay?" He nodded and added in the momentary silence that followed his remark, "I don't know what happened last night. I didn't even know Camille was missing until this morning, when your friends told me. Nell might be involved, but I am not. By God!" he exclaimed when he saw a vein beating wildly in Eric's neck as he clenched his teeth hard. "Why should I harm her? I aspired to her hand. I wanted to marry her. If that's a crime, if you think a man shouldn't dare reach beyond his social position, then yes, that I am guilty of. But nothing more."

"And if you aspire so high you forget your manners so easily?" Belle asked incredulously.

He looked at her.

"You left last night without saying good night to your hosts," she said, "and you expect us to believe you couldn't be found until now because you're completely innocent?"

Dana spread his hands. "I left last night before midnight and yes, without saying good-bye. Because I knew what was coming at midnight. Camille herself told me and asked me not to tell anyone else. She had to tell me, you see, because I offered for her the night before. I came to the party because I'd said I would, but I didn't want to stay for the announcement or the celebration because I'd no reason to celebrate her choosing someone else. I'm not a very good actor and I didn't want sympathy or pity. So I felt it best that I leave quickly and quietly before the festivities."

He turned to Eric, his eyes dark, flat, and cold. "I'm a poor loser. But not a stupid one. What would it profit me to take her away without her permission? Camille is a woman of spirit. She'd have torn me apart if I'd tried," he said with a peculiarly reminiscent smile. "That's part of her attraction. She's an uncommon woman in so many ways." He saw the look in Eric's eyes and went on, "I didn't want to go home either. So I went out, drank too much, and . . . visited too many unsavory places. I was trying to get through a difficult night, trying to forget. I didn't come home until morning, when I found your friends waiting on my doorstep."

"And I suppose you can't tell us all those places?" Eric asked.

"No," Dana said on a bitter smile, "I can, every one. It seems I couldn't manage to forget anything, whatever I did."

"And Nell?"

"Ah, Nell," Dana said wryly. "Find her, and I believe we'll find Camille." Eric scowled at the word "we" as Dana went on, "There must be a reason they're both missing, and I think Nell knows it. My cousin is warped, gentlemen. She is both devious and sly. I believed it was a thing she'd grow out of, because it might have something to do with her mother: Martha Baynes is a woman of little humor and less compassion."

"She is?" Eric said, seizing on the word. "Rather say 'was.' She told us her mother was mad."

"Mad, yes. As in furious with her daughter, not insane," Dana said. "I didn't tell anyone about it, and for that I am sorry. I was honestly trying to help Nell. If I had told you she was lying, none of you would have wanted a thing to do with her, and I knew she'd lose a chance to advance in the world. She was young. I hoped she'd change with good influences to guide her. I offered her a home and a chance for a decent life." He shrugged. "She was never interested. She had her own plans, and they were to become a famous courtesan. I thought it was nonsense. Her mother had written to mine complaining that a debased female who had followed that profession had inherited a house in their town and that Nell was dazzled by her. I lectured Nell, thinking she was merely a foolish young woman. But I slowly became aware that she was, instead, an utterly immoral one."

"Nice of you to tell us that now," Belle muttered.

"But if I had told you that before, I'd have been tarred with the same brush, wouldn't I?" Dana asked her. "Who among us has no difficult relatives? Would you want people to judge you by a distant cousin? Your friends, at least, all know each other's lineage as well as your own. But you didn't know my family."

"And what did Nell offer you in return for your generosity?" Eric demanded.

Dana's head came up. "Not herself, if that's what you're thinking. Nor would I have been interested. What she offered that I did want was a window into Camille's feelings." He saw the pure murder in Eric's eyes and added, "There was nothing indecent about that. Nell said she'd keep telling Camille about my virtues in order to promote my suit. She also promised to keep me informed of my courtship's progress. She lied, of course. She can't do anything else. I see that now."

Dana gazed at Eric steadily. "One thing I can tell you that perhaps you don't know. Nell was meeting men on the sly at every party and every ball, at the theater, and late at night when the household was asleep. She was looking for one to set her up as his mistress in extravagant style."

Belle gasped. "How dared you not tell us about that?"

"I would have, if I had felt there was a need, but she told me she'd be leaving you in a matter of days. I believed her decision had been made and she'd trouble you—and me—no more."

"Names," Rafe said tersely.

"I'll tell you all that I know. But believe me, I don't know them all. Nell is as secretive as she is devious, and that's saying a lot. Look you, gentlemen," Dana said harshly, "whether you believe me or not, I tell you I'm as upset as you are at the thought of harm coming to Camille. She's the true innocent in all this. And remember please, I wasn't the one who inflicted my cousin on her in the first place."

A muscle leapt in Eric's clenched jaw.

"Nor," Dana went on, "did I ever mean Camille the least harm. Now, whatever you think of me, also remember that I am a man-at-law and a good one. I've dealt with criminals and have learned how their minds work. Most want only easy money. Making off with a lady of quality is not easy money. So I tell you this too: you're looking at it from the wrong angle. If you want to find her," he said slowly, as he gazed at each of them in turn, "look to your own enemies and not at anyone who loves Camille."

"Nell doesn't love her," Belle protested.

"No," Dana said. "But she doesn't hate her either."

"True," Eric said slowly, thoughtfully, "a woman like that doesn't love or hate anyone unless they can either help them or stand in their way." He looked at his friends. "The man is right. Camille is missing because she is important to Nell for one reason or another." He began buttoning his collar. "Let's get Bartlett's list of men Nell was involved with and make our list too to see if any names crop up twice. We have to think of who has reason to want to harm us. By abducting Camille, they strike at me, of course, as well as Miles, but given our friendship, they'd have to know they would involve all of you too."

Miles and his friends looked back at him with matching grim expressions. They were men who had fought in the wars and in their time had worked as spies for their king and country. Since peace had come, they had tried to work for a better England, lobbying in Parliament and the House of Lords.

That meant they could think of too many people

with reason to want to harm them. And far too many of them were people they didn't want to speak of in the same breath as Camille, much less think of in the same room with her.

Chapter 17

She came awake all at once but lay still, because she was dazed and she was remembering. She'd been snatched from her home. And struck on the head. Nell—Nell had to have betrayed her, she realized.

Camille didn't know where she was, but knew it wasn't a place she wanted to be. She was remembering enough to know that.

She had been waiting for midnight, for her chance to tell the world about herself and Eric. Jittery and excited, she'd kept watching the tall case clock in the corner and, raising herself on her toes, trying to see where Eric was. He was her touchstone and compass throughout the seemingly endless party. She'd been polite, sociable as she could be while her mind was on nothing but him, but it was difficult.

Still, Belle wanted the midnight announcement to come as a grand surprise and had decided that if Camille hung on Eric's arm all night it would ruin all the drama of the moment. Camille didn't care about drama but she did care about Belle. So she had tried to keep her mind on the other guests until a glance at the clock showed that in a matter of minutes their moment would come, and she'd decided she didn't have to wait any longer. She didn't think she could anyway.

But she couldn't find Eric. He wasn't where he'd been only moments before. He'd been chatting with old friends, joking, seemingly involved with them. But they'd exchanged glances all night. She wondered where he'd got to.

She'd got a glimpse of someone who might have been him. But why would Eric suddenly be alone all the way across the room, standing by a wall? A pair of gentlemen walked past, obscuring her view. Camille stepped forward to go to him and felt a small, cold hand on her arm.

"Cammie?" Nell had said breathlessly. "Come with me—you have to see this!"

"What?" Camille remembered saying absently, craning her neck, trying to look past the men, "What is it?"

"Something you have to see. Come."

"Not right now. Have you seen Eric anywhere?"

There was a silence. Then Nell had whispered

urgently. "Yes, that's it. That's what I have to tell you. He's not here. He needs you and he sent me to get you."

Camille had swung around, suddenly terrified. "Is he sick again?"

Nell nodded.

"Let's get Miles," Camille had choked, spinning around on her heel.

"Oh, no! Not that kind of sick," Nell had said quickly, grabbing Camille's arm to stop her. She'd laughed weakly. "Not like last time. Not at all, actually. Oh, I hate to ruin the surprise, but it's something else, and he specifically said he didn't want anyone but you."

"A surprise?" Camille had laughed, both charmed and vexed with Eric. "A quarter-hour to go and he's plotting a surprise?" Amusement had won out. "What fun. Fine, let's go, lead on, where is he?"

"Come," Nell had said, tugging her by the arm, leading her through the crowd by taking her along the margins of the room, hugging the wall.

They'd headed along the long hall toward the kitchens but passed them by and went to the servants' entrance in back.

Camille remembered feeling her first twinge of hesitation then. "Outside?" she'd asked. "It's freezing out. I have to get a wrap."

"You don't need it," Nell had said as she pulled Camille along.

She'd been charmed. "Oho!" Camille had chortled. "This will be a fine surprise! I'll bet it's in the stables. Is it?"

"Yes, yes," Nell had said, "well, near them. Come on, quickly."

"A colt instead of a ring—or with one," Camille had guessed, laughing. "He knows me so well. That's something to tell the grandchildren." Her laughter had stopped when she heard a commotion behind her, startled voices raised in the salon. A servant had trotted past, ignoring them as he hurried toward the sound.

"He said you have to come quick," Nell had insisted when she felt Camille lagging. She'd tugged at her hand. "It won't be a minute, but it's important, he said." She'd opened the back door and looked out into the darkness. "Hurry," she'd said, taking Camille's hand. "We're late."

Camille had stepped out into the night, looking for Eric's tall form. She'd shivered. It was cold and hard to see her way. A thick layer of clouds obscured the moon.

"Come," Nell kept insisting. "This way!"

Camille had stumbled after her, heading down the back alley. "But the stables are this way," she'd complained, drawing back as Nell dragged her past the turn they had to make to get to the stables. "You're headed toward the street."

"Come," Nell persisted, pulling Camille hard.

Then, Camille remembered, she'd taken alarm. "I'll fall and break my neck," she'd complained, hanging back.

And then she couldn't say another word. She was clutched from behind. She'd turned, too late. Darkness descended. A foul-smelling sack was thrown over her head, and she'd felt herself caught in a strong pair of arms. She'd fought back, trying to free herself, using her knees and teeth instead of her lungs, not wasting her breath in a scream.

"Help me!" a harsh voice had commanded in a hoarse whisper. "She's strong as an ox and fighting like one too. The bitch is kicking . . . Ow!"

"Here, y'damned milksop," another rough voice said. "Aii! She bit me! The mort bit me!"

Aye! And I'll do more, Camille had silently promised, the rancid taste of greasy burlap on her tongue. She remembered struggling against the hands holding her, kicking and snapping at anything she could feel touching her—until a sudden blow to her head made the darkness complete.

And now she was here with an aching head, and even with her eyes closed she knew she wasn't at home. It smelled wrong, and the room was too cold and still, the bed she lay upon too hard. Her memory was complete, the confusion she'd felt on awakening was cleared. But what had happened? And where was Eric? Was he in danger? *Eric!*

Camille snapped open her eyes.

"She's awake," a man's voice said sweetly. "Welcome, Miss Croft."

She tried to sit up, but her head pounded so badly she fell back. She'd seen enough to start shuddering.

She lay upon a cot in a small, plainly furnished room. The light was dim, but she recognized the man looking down into her eyes. He was unforgettable. The destruction of that once handsome face was like a picture from a book of sermons on the dangers of lust and envy, pride and wrath. From this close she could see that Lord Dearborne looked even worse than the last time she'd seen him. The man's clothing was immaculate and fashionable, but it was like expensive wrapping on a corpse. He was gaunt, his cheeks were hollowed, and his color bad. He wore cologne, but it couldn't disguise the stale smell emanating from him. If he wasn't dying of some disease, Camille thought, he was surely sickened unto death by his excesses, which were legendary.

He looked much older than he was, but the century was no longer as young as it had been when he had been remotely acceptable. If morals weren't changing, manners certainly were. Dearborne's exploits had caused his exile from England. Recently returned, forgiven by his long-suffering family, he was nonetheless shunned by polite Society. That was due in large part to the efforts of many of Camille's friends: Gilly Ryder and Rafe Dalton, the earl of Drummond, and . . . and Eric, of course, Eric, she remembered. Rafe had thrashed Dearborne because of what he'd said about Brenna, and she was Eric's sister.

Camille shut her eyes and tried to gather her wits.

"I see you know me," Dearborne said. "Good. I bear you no rancor, Miss Croft, but it is necessary to inconvenience you, I'm afraid. By taking you, I take the wind from a great many sails—even as my sails will carry me far from here. Life is not as pleasant here as I'd hoped it would be. But this, as one of my parting gestures, is delicious. Thank you, Nell."

Camille opened her eyes again. Nell was there too. She hadn't been noticeable in the gloom, because she was dressed in dark colors and sat in a corner in a high-backed chair, hands in her lap, as still and prim as a nun at prayer. She wore a black cloak, and her hair was pulled back severely, exposing her pure profile. Her face was lovely, pale and sad. But then, Camille thought, Nell had always been the very picture of a perfect heroine.

"Well, then!" Dearborne said, straightening. "I think we may leave Miss Croft to her fate. You and I, Nell, still have work to do."

"What fate?" Nell asked.

"Oh, come," Dearborne said, "rather late in the day to worry about that, isn't it?"

"You said you wouldn't hurt her."

"I'm not going to do anything to her," Dearborne answered with a small, satisfied smile. "As I said, I'll leave her to her fate." He turned his attention back to Camille. "I know your head aches," he told her. "It wouldn't ache if you hadn't been such a hoyden. Take off your gown, Miss Croft."

Camille's heart raced. "I can't get up," she said,

pressing her hand to her aching head to buy some time.

"You said you weren't going to hurt her," Nell said again. She didn't sound distressed, Camille noted with sorrow, just curious.

"And so I won't," he snapped. "You're a big, healthy girl," he told Camille, never taking his eyes from her. "You can stand, and stand you shall. Take off your gown, I said, or I'll have someone do it for you. Someone," he added, "less gentle and considerate than I am. My hirelings, the men who brought you here, would love to assist you. They await just outside."

"Why do you want her gown off?" Nell asked. "If you're going to have her, you can't have me. I won't be cheated on before my very eyes."

"What you will or will not have is a matter of small moment to me," Dearborne said curtly, shooting her a warning look. "But I've no intention of having her. She's a fine, healthy creature, but I don't care to ride big brown mares. I like a filly with more thoroughbred lines. However, Miss Croft," he said, looking at Camille again, "my employees don't share my tastes. The ones you fought with are eager to get a bit of their own back, and I don't doubt much of it would be taken out of your flesh. Free yourself of the notion that I want you for anything but revenge."

He picked up a bundle from a nearby table and flung it at her. "Here, put on this on."

Camille slowly sat up. She opened the bundle with shaking hands.

It contained a gown. An old, threadbare gray gown of indeterminate shape and design.

Dearborne nodded at Camille's expression of distaste. "I'm keeping my word," he told Nell over his shoulder. "I only want her gown because it marks her as a lady, one of the quality. Without it, she is instantly anonymous. And actually, were she to wear such finery where she's going, she might be even worse off. They'll take it from her rather than asking nicely, as I have."

"He's only going to take you to Newgate," Nell told Camille.

Camille paled. The word "Newgate" struck terror into her heart. She'd never visited the prisons for diversion, as so many ladies of the *ton* did, but she'd heard about London's vile prisons. Wealthy prisoners could live in somewhat decent circumstances in their own rooms with their own servants and furniture. The poor lived in hellish squalor—if they lived at all. Many went into Newgate and never came out, and not just because of the busy hangman. Hundreds died of jail fever; many more were abused by their jailers as well as by their fellow unfortunates. They might be sending her to prison instead of killing her, but Camille didn't think much of her chances there.

"Don't worry," Nell said. "You'll be home again soon. I wouldn't have let anyone hurt you. It won't be fun, but it won't be for long. This way they'll have to search for you, and by the time we're long gone, you'll be found. Still, at least your family and friends will worry, and that's all he's after. They'll know what he could have done and be grateful to him for not doing that and count themselves lucky. He'll win their respect and their gratitude and his own peace of mind, because they won't have reason to pursue him. But this way, he'll have the last laugh. You see? It's very neat."

"That's nonsense," Camille said firmly.

Her head ached, but it still worked. She didn't believe Nell for a second. But the girl seemed to believe what she said. Her only chance lay in arousing whatever rudimentary conscience Nell still possessed. She was a strange girl, devious and immoral, but she'd lived with Camille. If they hadn't been exactly friends, they'd been companions. She must know she owed something in return for hospitality.

"I'll tell everyone who I am," Camille said. "So what I wear doesn't matter, does it?"

"And they'll believe a great gawky, ugly drab in rags is a well-born, wealthy lady, will they?" Dearborne asked with a sneer. "They have hundreds more who look more like one. You're not precisely the beautiful goose girl whose nobility shines through her rags, Miss Croft. Although you must have some hidden assets," he added with a speculative leer, "or Ford wouldn't have offered for you, would he? Too bad I gave my word to sweet Nell, or I'd have a try and see just what you do that made him so desire your services for life. Of course, it could merely be a matter of manners. He's a friend of your brother, and since Ford has no title, a viscount's sister is a good match, if enough money is thrown in to make measure. They had an earl's daughter set for me, even with my . . . remarkable history."

His expression grew cold. "That is, they did until your brother and his friends, including your dear Lieutenant Ford, sent me into exile again. So there must be reparations, mustn't there? Into your new clothes," he said, "And now."

"Nell?" Camille said, hating how the word came out sounding so quivery and lost.

"At least, let her alone until she gets dressed," Nell said. "She can't escape." She got up, went to Dearborne, and looked up into his ravaged face as though he was Apollo incarnate. "I can calm her down," she whispered to him, her great dark eyes searching his.

"I can have her knocked on the head again. That will keep her calm enough."

"And maybe kill her? That her friends would never forgive. And can you kill those two you brought tonight? If they're caught, those rum touches out there will talk, and they'll say you told them to do it. They'll say it in every tavern in London anyhow, and then they will be caught. You know their sort."

"Not as well as you do, obviously," he said, flicking her cheek with one finger. "Very well, get her dressed and out, and quickly. I'll go," he told Nell with a peculiar smile, "but don't forget, I won't turn my back on you. Half the joy of lying with you as well as dealing with you, sweet slut, is the danger in it. For me and you."

He opened the door and left.

"Nell!" Camille said as soon as the door closed again. "Help me!"

"Well, I wish I could," Nell said, "but it can't be."

"At least tell me if Eric is all right," Camille pleaded, though she assumed he was, otherwise surely Dearborne would have gloated about it.

"He's fine," Nell said too quickly. "And so will you be. Just do as my lord says and it will go even smoother. I'm leaving with him, and we don't want your friends following. This way, he gets to feel that he outfoxed them, and you'll only be inconvenienced for a little while. Believe me, it's best. You ought to have heard some of his other plans!"

"You're leaving with a man like him?" Camille asked in astonishment. "Even knowing what he is?"

Nell smiled her small, secret smile. "Yes. I like him. I know what he is, I know what you said about him too. But he's very rich, and he does please me in other ways. He isn't so bad, once you get to know him. He only hates your brother and his friends because they ruined his face when they pounded on him, he says, as well as his life. He was very vain about his looks. I don't think he looks so bad, but he does."

"Yes, but he did terrible things," Camille said. "He's lucky they used fists and not swords and pistols, or he'd be dead by now. You know that. And it isn't just his nose that changed his appearance, he looks ill, and everyone says it's because of his continuing debaucheries. So how can you think of leaving the country with him? You'll be at his mercy."

"Shall I be?" Nell asked. "That remains to be seen. But what is there for me if I stay here, even if I do become a famous courtesan?"

"Money, you said, and fame," Camille reminded her urgently.

"But not freedom, I see that now," Nell said. "And that's what I said I wanted. I've since come to see that the courtesans I admired are not free either. Men who pay for you feel they own you for however long they keep paying. And in truth, they do. You have to be at their beck and call day and night, and you have to keep pleasing them. Even if you keep replacing protectors, you're just getting the same thing again and again until you're too old for the trade. And what then? Ruby has money, but she still isn't free. She can't go everywhere she wants."

Nell cocked her head to the side. "I needed Dearborne to explain it to me, and he's right. Everyone else, you and my cousin, you all talked about morality. Dearborne showed me reality. See, I want freedom as much as money, and this way I can have it. He's going to America," she told Camille with rising excitement, her eyes shining. "He told me about places like New York and New Orleans. The 'new' he said, is the key. Those are places where a man or woman can be anything and anyone they want to be. If you have money, you can live like a king and get as much respect as one, no matter who you are or what you did to get your fortune. That would suit me."

"And if he tires of you? What will you do all alone in a new country?" Camille asked desperately.

Nell laughed. "If we tire of each other, and I expect we will, that will be fine too. I'll be able to find another protector even faster than I could here, because there are more men than women there."

"But that would be no different from what you'd have here," Camille exclaimed.

"But it is," Nell said complacently. "They don't have Society there, not like here. Or at least, Dearborne says it's just getting started, and I can be part of it. There, it isn't what you were born to be, it's what you're clever enough to make yourself. With manners and money, anyone can pretend to be someone, and so I shall be. Now, get dressed, Cammie," she said, her voice reasonable and calm. "Because he has a terrible temper and he likes to hurt women too. I like it sometimes, but I know you won't."

Camille stripped off her gown and hurriedly donned the old gray one. She did it just in time, because the door opened again, and Dearborne, followed by two brutish-looking men, sauntered in.

"Very good," Dearborne said. "Now, a little ride to Newgate, a shorter one to the docks, and it will be done. Nell?" he said, offering her his arm. "Come along, Miss Croft," he said, "or would you prefer one of my assistants to escort you?"

Camille raised her head, winced at how it still ached, and went out the door with them.

They rode in an undistinguished hired hack. No one spoke.

Nell sat next to Lord Dearborne. One of his hired men drove the hackney. The other sat next to Camille. She sat up against the window, trying to ignore the way the man's thigh touched hers.

Eric was on her trail already, she knew that. Miles too. The earl of Drummond, Rafe, and the others might be following her even now. They had worked for His Majesty, they had influential friends.

That didn't comfort her as much as it should have done.

She was on her way to Newgate Prison, and she didn't know what awaited her there or how soon she'd get out again.

But she had a resilient spirit and the thought of Eric to keep her heart high. Eric mightn't look in Newgate right away, but when he didn't find her anywhere, he'd look everywhere. He'd find her. She had to keep hold of that thought. Nell was wrong about everything but right about one: there were worse fates she could have endured. Even though she'd been mishandled, she hadn't been molested.

So if Camille wasn't exactly comforted by the time the coach at last passed through the heavy gates and rumbled across the cobbles in the inner courtyard of Newgate Prison, she was at least not hysterical with fear. She was only numbed by it.

The coach stopped in a corner of the vast courtyard. It was late, the city was sleeping. Camille had thought even Newgate Prison, king of prisons, would be sleeping too. But when the door opened, Camille heard a babble of voices, the clanking of chains, and shouts. Dearborne alighted from the coach and turned back, holding out a hand.

"Come, Miss Croft," he said. "Time wastes."

Camille refused to take his hand. She went down the steps, blinking against the sudden glare of dozens of torches that punctuated the murky blackness of a fantastic scene. The huge dark space was filled with milling people. Dazed as she was, Camille knew something wasn't right. Why would the people here be out in the night? Was it a rebellion? She could only hope so. She could run.

Her spirits fell when she realized it was orderly chaos. Even in the fitful torchlight she could see hordes of prisoners, men, women and children, being lined up in rows, guards surrounding them. They seemed to be arranged in marching places, as for a journey.

"Moving day," Dearborne said at her ear, as he put a hand on her arm. "Yes, it's to be a short sojourn in Newgate for you, Miss Croft."

Camille began to relax until she realized the other meaning to his words. She stared at him, wide-eyed.

"Now, what would be the point of popping you in somewhere just so your fiancé and brother and their friends can come along and pop you out again?" he asked her, his lips so close to her ear that she shuddered. "I'd something rather more permanent in mind. And this will be. But I'm a man of my word, just like your fiancé, your brother, and all their noble friends. As I told your friend Nell, I won't be the one to harm you. I won't have to.

"It's really brilliant," he said on a soft laugh. "Even if they track you here, they can search every crevice of Newgate until Doomsday and never get a sniff of you. Because Newgate's only a way station for you. They'll never find you now. The man I've paid to take you will never tell for fear of his neck—nor will he be able to, because even he won't know where you're going. It never pays to tell the truth to anyone. Not a word," he said, gripping her upper arm so hard she gasped. "I've yet another surprise. Nell?" Dearborne called. "Come, be polite. See your friend off."

"I'll stay here," Nell said from inside the coach.

Dearborne chuckled. "Faint hearted? I'll swear that's not the sort of wench I want with me on my travels. Come!" he said, like a man bringing a dog to heel, extending his other hand.

Nell, expressionless, slowly descended the carriage steps and came to stand at his side. Dearborne smiled. He reached into his jacket and withdrew a wallet. He raised it in his hand and waved. A guard came hurrying out of the darkness toward him.

"Here she is," Dearborne said. He thrust Camille toward him and handed him the wallet. The guard quickly thrust it into his jacket.

"You have the papers?" Dearborne asked.

"Aye," the man said softly, clasping Camille's wrist in a strong calloused hand. "And the chain." He clipped a cold band of steel attached to a chain around Camille's wrist, released her, and then pulled the chain hard. She staggered. He nodded. "Now give me the other and be gone. I paid some to look the other way, but I can't afford to pay all."

"Very well," Dearborne said. "Nell?" he said sweetly. She stared at him in disbelief. "I'm afraid we'll have to postpone our journey, because there's another you must take. But never fear, you'll still be going on a nice long voyage. I'm off to America. You're bound for Botany Bay, New South Wales, or perhaps Bermuda. It depends upon which line you're put in, I don't know or want to know.

"Yes, you were stupid to believe me," he told Nell. "But you never were as clever as you thought you were. The world is wide and filled with women. Why should you think you had anything to offer that I couldn't find elsewhere? One female's much the same as another, you know. Still, you were a sweet bitch," he told her, chucking her under the chin. "You were a joy. But all joys must end."

He thrust her at the guard so hard that she fell against the man.

Dearborne turned to go back into the carriage. He went up the steps and into the coach and slammed the door. The coach drove the way it came quickly into the London night.

Chapter 18

❧❧

"She's here in London somewhere. I know she lives, I know she's waiting for me," Eric said. He was sitting slouched in a chair in Miles's library. It was the first time he'd allowed himself to rest all day. He'd been coursing through London like a hound on the scent, but every direction he went in came to a dead end. He'd come back to Miles's house to rendezvous with the others, hoping they'd had better luck. They had not.

Now Miles, Drum, and Rafe sat comparing notes with him. There was little to compare. Camille had vanished. Nell was gone too, but they didn't worry about her, believing that she, somehow, was the reason for the disappearance.

"I know it sounds bizarre, even supernatural,"

Eric went on wearily, his long fingers rubbing his aching forehead, "but it's as if I can feel her in my mind. She's frightened but confident that I'll find her. Does that make sense?"

"Yes," Miles said, "and no. It doesn't matter. The whole thing doesn't make sense. It's obvious that Nell's part of this, but why? No one's sent a note. No one knows why they left. It's as though they dropped off the face of the earth."

"She didn't," Eric insisted, dropping his hand and glowering at his old friend. "I'd know if she had. I'm not a fanciful man or a particularly religious one, but damned if I'm not sure of that!"

No one spoke. His other friends glanced away from him.

There was a cough from the doorway.

"Your lordship," the butler said as he stepped into the room. He held out a note to Miles. "This has just been delivered."

The men leapt to their feet and crowded around Miles, trying to read the note he snatched from his butler's hand.

"The boy who brought it began weeping when we detained him," the butler added. "He says he was given a shilling for his services and doesn't know anything else. He's in the kitchen awaiting your pleasure."

"No pleasure in it," Drum said as Miles hissed a curse through his teeth.

"I'll kill him!" Eric said tersely, his eyes scanning the note.

"You and I both," Miles said bleakly. "But we'll have to swim to do it. He says he'll be long gone by the time we read this."

"Yes, Dearborne can wait," Eric said. He raised his head, his eyes were bright, his posture suddenly erect. "The thing is that now that we know who took her, we can find out where he took her."

The others looked at him blankly.

Eric's smile was tight. "A man's desires are his weaknesses," he explained. "Dearborne thought he'd be taunting us, and that helps us. He doesn't ask for ransom. All he wants is his pound of flesh. He wants to hurt and humiliate us. He says he knows where she is and wants us to know he's responsible, but he could have waited to let us know that. The fact that he didn't may make all the difference. I don't think he's gone from England yet. There'd be no point to his revenge if he couldn't savor it."

"Yes!" Miles said eagerly. "That makes sense."

"But it doesn't matter right now," Eric said. "What does, is that we at last have a clue."

The others looked at him blankly.

"It's like the difference between hunting rabbits and foxes," Eric muttered as he began pacing. "Once you know what you're looking for, you have a chance to catch it." He stopped and faced his friends. "Every animal has known traits and habits, every man has a signature. Dearborne has companions, if not friends. His haunts are known, as are his companions. Now at last we know where we can start looking. What taverns does he frequent?

Where does he game? Does he have a mistress? Where does he spend his time? If we can discover those things, we can find those who know him—and we are that much closer to finding Camille."

Drum smiled. "Your intellect is the size of your shoulders, my friend. You're absolutely right. I'll quiz the unfortunate messenger and find out where he was hired, if not who hired him, because I'm sure he doesn't know that. But where he comes from should give us some clues."

Rafe nodded slowly. "Aye. I have some old acquaintances who might know about Dearborne. By God! Gilly must too! That's where I'm bound."

"I'll come with you, Eric," Miles said, as he saw Eric heading toward the door. He paused. "But where are we going?"

"To find Camille," Eric said over his shoulder as he strode from the room. "She's waiting."

Camille never knew so many people could be so still. She was sitting flank to flank with dozens of strangers, and yet all she could hear was the sound of the wagon's wheels going over the cobbles and an occasional muted cough or stifled sob from those in the darkness beside her. She'd been loaded into the wagon along with other wretched, ragged souls, who sat like bags of produce or bales of hay on the bare floorboards.

She sat on the floor of the open wagon as it trundled along the city streets. Her anger and frustration had been too immense for her to notice much else when she'd come aboard. She was cold and frightened, and the night sky above her was as dark as her fears. Her head ached too.

"You can't do this!" she'd shouted as she was led away. "I'm being abducted! My name is Cam—"

A heavy hand struck the side of her head, silencing her. She would have fallen if the guard who had slapped her hadn't been holding the chain attached to her wrist. "Be still, wench!" he snarled, catching her arm and twisting it hard. "Unless you want more."

"This is a new one to me," she'd heard an interested male voice comment through the ringing in her ears. She'd opened her eyes to see herself being eyed by another guard, this one a stout, bewhiskered fellow.

"Yes!" she said eagerly. "Because I don't belong here. I'm not a prisoner, I haven't done anything."

"Oho, lass, who does belong here?" He laughed, lifting a lantern and peering at her. "No one. Just ask any of 'em. No one belongs here but us, according to them we watch over. Howsoever that may be," he added in a low voice, "I can do you a world of good, even where you're bound. I think you can leave this one behind for tonight," he told the guard who held Camille's arm. "She's no beauty, but she's clean and looks healthy as a horse. I like a lass with meat on her bones and some spirit left to her. Don't know how I missed this one. A fine, big girl who can give a fellow a ride to remember."

Camille shrank back.

"Aye, a ride to remember, all right," the guard who held her said bitterly. "This one's for Higgins, on the *Eurydice*. Special order, a gift from a friend. Higgins won't be happy to hear you had a taste of his treat before he did. You know him."

The fat fellow threw up a hand. "Aye, I do! Never mind, then! Well, it's like him to get himself some sport, ain't it?" he said bitterly. "Too bad he don't care for boys, like some of the others on board his ship, there's enough of them there. But he likes his breasts and bums, don't he? What happened to the last lass he requisitioned? She was a lively one. No, on second thought, don't tell me! Least known, less said. Sorry," he told Camille. "Good luck—you'll need it," he added before he walked away.

"Now belt up!" the guard told Camille, pushing her toward the wagon. "Another word and no man will ever make merry with you again. Get in there, and keep your mummer shut!"

The wagon had no seats. It was open to the sky, with a lip made of staves all round that held its unhappy cargo inside. The guard waited until Camille had clambered up into it, then he secured the linked chain he'd been holding to the side of the wagon where she sat and left her, with a curse.

"Ready! You're off!" he called to the driver.

The prisoners around her hunkered down and crouched low as the driver set his four carthorses moving. The great wagon slowly lumbered out of

Newgate and off into the night, a guard up front with the driver and an outrider on either side to keep an eye on its wretched cargo as it moved on.

It was that peculiar hour before dawn when London was momentarily still. The denizens of the night, the nightwalkers and stalkers, the women of the street and men about Town, had all gone to their beds. The early risers, milkmaids, mongers, and lower servants, hadn't yet begun their work. The city smelled fresh, of river and rain, a cold breeze was blowing the clouds away. It was quiet. Even the gulls were still sleeping on the river. The only sounds were the creaking and the turning of the wagon wheels, the horses' hooves clomping, echoing on the cobbles, their fittings and brasses jangling. If anyone in the silent houses around them heard their passage, they didn't look out to see. Theirs was a passage to ignore, like that of the dead wagons as they removed those who had passed on in the night.

Camille took stock. Nell was gone. Where didn't matter, because Camille knew the girl would be able to fend for herself. Now she was on her own.

She shivered. But she wasn't alone, she thought, taking a steadying breath. Eric would find her. She believed it implicitly. Closing her eyes, she could almost feel his presence, feel his big hand covering hers, his warmth and love surrounding her.

Her eyes snapped open. Yes, he'd find her. The problem was what would happen to her until he did. She couldn't just wait for him. She wouldn't. So then, she thought, what now?

She tried to make out faces in the crowd around her. "Where are we bound?" she whispered aloud.

It seemed to her that the night grew even quieter.

A small voice finally spoke in a hushed whisper. "To the *Eurydice*, I thinks."

"It's the hulk they sends the boys to," another voice whispered.

"And then they send you on to Australia?" Camille asked.

She heard a muted choking. It took her a moment to realize it was laughter. "Mebbe some gets to go there," another voice said. "Them what lives. Won't be many."

"But it could be a different ship?"

"It could be," someone else agreed.

"And where is this ship?" Camille whispered, after a moment. "How far away?"

"Shut up back there!" A harsh voice commanded. An outrider trotted up to the wagon, held his lantern high, and glowered at the wretches inside. Satisfied by the sudden breathless quiet, he wheeled his horse around and rode on alongside the wagon.

As Camille's eyes grew accustomed to the darkness, she tried to see how many prisoners shared the wagon with her. She could make out heads and eyes among the welter of rags. There seemed to be at least two dozen souls, all small. She realized they

were all children and youths of many sizes and
ages. She didn't see any other adults or any other
females. She swallowed hard and tried to take further stock of her situation.

The guard up front with the driver seemed to be
dozing. The two outriders sat their horses as
though half asleep themselves as they rode on either side of the heavy wagon as it moved on
through the dreaming city. They didn't have to be
watchful, because there were, after all, three
guards, plenty against helpless children and a female in irons. The boys, Camille noted, were tied to
one another with hemp. She wore her cuff and
chain, perhaps because she was the oldest or because Dearborne had paid for the extra caution.
She moved her wrist and heard the chain clank, and
for the first time realized it was securely fixed to the
outer edge of the wagon, and so, then, was she.

Her heart stuttered, her mouth went dry, her
stomach cold. She'd been hit on the head, carried
off, had woken to nightmare, and still lived in one.
But only now was she afraid. It was as if she hadn't
really believed any of it until this moment. For the
first time she felt a surge of sheer panic, knowing
she was now part of the great lumbering wagon
and so whatever its fate, that would be hers. If it
tipped over, she'd go with it. Where it stopped, she
must too. She was linked to it as sure as she was
linked to an unimaginably hideous future.

Another sudden thought came to her. She took a
quick shuddery breath to keep her heart from leap-

ing out of her throat. They said she was meant for this Higgins fellow on the hulk. She didn't know if he was a reasonable man or a monster, only that she was meant for him. Whatever he was or was not, she was bound for a prison ship. She didn't need much imagination to think about the pain and shame that would await her.

Camille tried to steady her nerves. She could deal with anything, and would until Eric found her. But how would he deal with what might happen to her before he did? Should she expect him to? She felt sick to her stomach and thought for the first time that like any brave soldier, she'd take death before dishonor. But would she even be given that choice? It seemed to her that all her choices were gone, she no longer controlled her destiny.

She wouldn't let that happen. She blinked back debilitating tears and turned her attention to her options. She had to have some. She wriggled her wrist and found the iron circle held fast. She pulled on the chain that held her to the lip of the wagon until it rattled sharply, ringing out in the silent night.

A cold little hand, thin and light as a monkey's, touched hers. "Naw, don't do that, miss," a soft voice said. "It won't do naught but hurt your wrist, and it'll get them vexed with you, which'll hurt more."

She looked down. A thin boy looked up at her sadly.

"I must," she said. "I can't stay here."

"No one wants to."

"But I will not!" she said in a harsh whisper.

"Where would you go?" he asked in a sad, flat voice, no louder than a spider's sigh. The outriders would never hear him. She had to strain to hear him herself. It occurred to her that, young as he was, he must have spent a long time in a prison to learn to speak so softly yet clearly. "Even if you could get free, they'd be on you in a minute," he told her.

"No, they might not," she said. "I'm very strong, and I'm fast and agile, and I'm smart."

He seemed to weigh her before he spoke again. "Aye," he said consideringly. "Mebbe so. But even if you give 'em the slip here in the dark, they'd nab you the minute you set foot back in Lunnon again."

"No, they won't. *They'll* be nabbed, and punished. I was kidnapped. Last night. They stole me away from my home, took my clothes and my name, and sent me here. But my family and friends have money and power. If I can get back to them, I'll be safe."

"Aye, could be," he granted, his head to one side. "I've heard worse tales and some of 'em true. And you speak like a lady, s'truth. But it's too late now, whatever you are," he added with awful resignation.

Camille flexed her wrist, tried to spin the iron band that encircled it, pushed and pulled at it. But though the prisoner's bracelet the guard had clapped on was loose enough to twist, it was too narrow to slip over her hand. It kept getting hung up at the base of her thumb. If she'd had a knife, she'd have cut her thumb off to be free. She looked at her wrist with fury. She felt like bashing it against the floorboards. But she wasn't such a fool. If the metal circle wouldn't budge, then the chain was her only chance.

She was about to tug it again to see if she could slip it off whatever held it fast when she realized that the wagon's wheels were no longer clanging over cobbles but rather seemed to be going over a rutted road. She gritted her teeth against the sudden jouncing. "How much further?" she whispered frantically.

"If it's the nearest ship, we'll be there in twenny minutes," her self-appointed friend whispered back, his small fingers running over her iron bracelet, testing it too. "If it ain't, then an hour, mebbe more. No hurry, miss. We ain't going nowhere after we gets there either, y'know, 'cept on to the hulk. Most of us'll never get off it."

The night was still again. Camille bit back tears. They'd do her no good and would likely terrify the poor child trying to comfort her. She sat still and thought hard. She was doubtless bound for a life of insult and humiliation. She was on her own, with no one to help her, alone in the midst of a pack of helpless boys. It was an impossible situation. She wanted to close her eyes and pray for Eric, her big, strong, capable love.

She sat up straighter. Pray for Eric? Yes, she'd do that—when and if she could find nothing else to do for herself.

Chapter 19

The man was dressed like a gent and looked like a savage. His great fists were bunched, his white teeth were clenched and bared. But it was the expression in his wild eyes that silenced everyone in the tavern. He looked like the kind of man who had raged out of the north and ravaged this island a thousand years before. Even the most ignorant man in the place now suddenly remembered that he knew that bit of history. The fellow might be dressed like a toff in his fine coat and boots, but he was the very image of a berserk Viking. He looked like he should be holding an axe in one hand and a spear in the other instead of just a promise of murder in those blazing eyes of his.

"Yes," the gentleman with him said. He was cool

and arrogant, more easily recognizable, the kind that had ruled men like themselves for hundreds of years.

A silence fell over the taproom.

"My friend's not a patient man," the cool gentleman said. "He wants to kill someone. It was his fiancée who was spirited away last night by a gent who is bound for death and damnation. You all must know about it, as well as of Lord Dearborne, the villain of this piece. There's no mystery, he's confessed to it."

Murmuring filled the room.

"Dearborne? But 'e's loped off, they says," one burly fellow volunteered. "Left Lunnon, entire."

"So he may have. What we want to know is what became of the lady he snatched," the tall, thin gentleman said reasonably. "He didn't do it by himself. Whoever helped him has to be known to some of you. Tell us their names and direction, or tell us what they did with the unfortunate lady, and you'll profit hugely. Come," he said gently. "They'll be found, you know it. It's too foolish a crime. The lady's brother is a viscount, no less. We've a great many influential people involved, and the Runners are already on it. But why should they be the only ones to profit from this?"

The huge man with him made an impatient gesture. "The man who tells us what we want to know will be a deal richer, immediately, and in gold. The man who knows and doesn't tell will wish he had."

His every word was put so plain and grim that

those listening who had knives touched and fingered them secretly where they were hidden in pockets of jackets and trousers. This made the denizens of the tavern look as though they'd suddenly been seized by a plague of fleas. That wasn't unusual, since many of them were already so afflicted.

It was a very low tavern, and fleas were the least of what a man could catch there if he wasn't careful. It was both a hiring hall and a clearinghouse for members of the lower criminal fraternity. Gin and ale, loose women and tips on prizefights, dogfights and cockfights could be had there, along with information about which houses might have a maid willing to leave an upper window open for a price or a kiss and what foolish gent customarily took which route as he reeled home alone after dark. The patrons of the Dog and Bell regularly pinched the weary barmaids' bottoms as well as other citizens' handkerchiefs, hats, horses, laundry, and whatever else they could get their eager hands on. And since all of those things except one were hanging offences, it was a hard-bitten lot who sat there tonight.

They were all members of the same fraternity and didn't trust each other any more than they trusted themselves. But gold was their common goal and god, and the very word caused them all to fall still.

"Dearborne's gone?" one ratlike individual dared say. " 'E's loped off? Well, it may be. But if 'is lordship *ain't* loped off, whoever peaches on 'im will get 'is 'ead *lopped* off, that's certain!"

It was a witticism, and relieved some of the tension. Chuckles were heard, before they slowly trailed off. The big gentleman with murder in his eyes did not laugh.

"Be damned to Dearborne," he growled. "He'll be reckoned with in time, I promise you. The lady was kidnapped. I want to find her and fast. Don't tell me names if you worry about doing that. Right now the who doesn't matter so much as the how. I need only know what was done and where she is. I believe the answer is here because you're wise coves and nothing's ever a secret in these streets. Someone must know something. It will make him rich. Anyone who can tell me what I want to know will be rewarded."

"We understand that it mightn't be prudent to divulge such information in public," the cool gentleman added. "But there's not time for you to come to us. Therefore we'll be outside for the next half-hour. We'll be discreet. You have our word on that. We look forward to hearing from you. Until then, good evening." He tipped his high hat, and, taking his grim friend by the arm, he left, leaving the men in the tavern to look at each other.

One of the two gentlemen was known to them, and they knew his word was his bond. The earl of Drummond had bought their services before, during the long war and after. As for the other? In the way that dogs smell dinner on the wind, they knew what was going on in the better parts of town. So they knew who Eric Ford was too, all about his mission, and that he was good for the money or the punishment he promised.

They looked at each other and away. Some scratched, some spat, some drank. Conversation began again.

"Well," said one fellow eventually, rising from his table, "I got to go piss."

Another looked at him, nodded, and got up as well. "I'd like to have another cup of the creature," he announced, "but my old woman would skin me. She needs me t'home." He plodded to the front door.

Another rose, stretched. "Was up all night on a cloak-twitching lay," he said with a yawn. "I needs to kip out."

In short order ten of them got up and left by the front door and out the back to the alley.

Eric and Drum waited in the cold in front of the tavern. Eric had never felt so useless, weak, and stupid as he did now. He clenched his hands into fists. His Camille was in dire straits, and he could do nothing—but wait. He'd been a good soldier because he'd known how to accept fear and then let it go. Perhaps because of his size and his strength or faith in himself, or his youth when he'd been in battle, he'd never been afraid of much.

Now he realized he'd never been so afraid in his life. He didn't move or speak, because he couldn't. He was nearly paralyzed with fear and frustration.

"Softly, softly," Drum said, laying a hand on his shoulder. "All her friends and ours, as well as the Runners, are working tonight. Someone will find her or word of her. If no one comes to us soon, we'll go on to the next rat hole and have better luck."

Eric looked up at the sky. A muscle moved in his clenched jaw. "The night is growing old," he managed to say through clenched teeth. "And I'm just standing here!"

"There's nothing else to do. We laid bait, we must wait by the trap."

"And you think that we'll learn anything standing here?"

"Oh, I do."

"Honor among thieves?"

"Never that," his friend said on a huff of a laugh. "Dearborne isn't long for this world. He'll soon be finished. The men we just spoke to know that if his sickness doesn't do him in, we will. Our gold is a powerful argument for them talking too. But they'll do it their way, cautiously. Unlike the agents we worked with in the old days, these fellows belong to a fraternity, a guild of sorts. And they have rules. If one man comes to speak with us, others will too, even if they have nothing to say. That way no one can ever say just who it was who peached on Dearborne. It ensures their safety. Patience."

Eric willed himself not to think. But he could feel, and his whole body ached as well as his head and heart. While the minutes ticked by, a freshening breeze began to blow the clouds from the sky. "We were going to announce our engagement at midnight," he suddenly said, the words pouring from the silent roiling fury that was building in his head.

"Yes," Drum said with a small smile. "I know. The worst kept secret in England. I was very glad for you—I *am* very glad for you. In spite of what's happened, I still offer you my congratulations. She's a wonderful woman." His eyes were steady and solemn in the dancing light of the lantern that hung on the door of the Dog and Bell. "You will be merry, Eric, I will dance at your wedding. I was both surprised and delighted when I heard about it."

"Surprised? You think I'm too old and too sick for her?"

"Of course not. It's just that I didn't know events had progressed so far between you two."

"Dearborne did," Eric said bitterly, "because of Nell, no doubt. I curse the day I met her, though I should not. Ironically, it was the same day I realized how I felt about Camille."

He fell silent, as though he'd said too much. His friend didn't prod him to speak. It was all the emotion Eric was trying to bury that would not be suppressed which finally made him go on. "I used to wonder why it was that all my friends were so busily falling in love and marrying and I was the one going on alone. Even hard cases like you met your match, and I remained blithely single. But why?" He shrugged. "I was as puzzled as my poor parents were about that. After all, I'm an easy man to get on with, I think."

"So you are," Drum agreed.

Eric nodded. "I had many friends, both male and female, but though I became interested in decent women, it was only ever that: interest. It never grew to anything more. I told myself it was because I kept admiring the women my friends wound up with. Yes," he said on an embarrassed laugh, "I admired your Alexandria—before she was yours, of course— even though she wasn't small and dark. But I also noticed Annabelle and other dark beauties, though I knew I didn't have a chance with them. Nor they with me, I suppose, since my heart was never involved. In fact, I was beginning to consider a marriage of mutual convenience, as soon, that is, as I could find an amiable female I was attracted to. A fellow has to have something more than children from his marriage. Some men, after all, are not made for love. I believed I could honor a wife well enough, and knew I'd care for my children. I like children.

"That was my predicted fate—at least, it was until that night I met Nell. It was also the night I really met Camille. I rode out with my old friend's sister every morning," Eric said with a small smile, as a fond, far-away expression crept into his eyes. "A lovely young woman. We discussed sports and horses and politics. She wasn't a girl who simpered or flirted. She was as up to date on news and events as any man. I told myself that in time she'd find someone more suitable and forget about me the way a girl forgets about her kindly uncle when she meets a promising young man. I accepted that— until that night.

"Because that night, Drum," he said with wonder, "I came to visit my friend Cammie and instead saw a new woman in her place. She wore a new gown and a new smile. She curtsied to me. It was as though the world tilted on its ear. I always knew she was beautiful, I'm not blind. But that night when I thought about taking her into my arms for a dance, I understood how much more I wanted to do. She wasn't like any of my previous interests. I'd always preferred dark beauties. Camille is fair as a May morning, and she's built along queenly lines, like some lovely, supple lioness. Suddenly, small, dark women looked meager to me, fragile, bird-like, and insignificant. My mate, I realized, could only be a lioness."

He grinned. "I met my match, Drum. I was already half in love with her, but because of my age and possible state of health, I refused to fall the rest of the way. But I had no choice. That," he said, shaking his head, "was what I'd never realized. You don't have a choice when it comes to love. That was what I never knew. I tried to deny it. I tried to escape it. I couldn't. And now," he said, his voice growing grim, "I also don't have a choice. By God, Drum, I cannot stand this!"

"But you will and you must," Drum said. "It will be all right. Dearborne is a coward. He won't do anything to really enrage us, he's just pulling our tails."

"Dearborne is a coward, yes," Eric said, his expression bleak. "But I've heard that he's deathly ill.

This is his last stab at us. When a man is dying, how much of a coward can he be?"

Drum said nothing.

Eric stood silently, thinking of Camille, of all the things they'd done and all the things he wanted to do with her so that he wouldn't think of all the things that might be being done to her. Whatever happened to her, he would find her and heal her and share the rest of his life with her. Because that life wouldn't mean much without her. He thought of her laughter and how she'd returned his kiss. He remembered her tilted smile and the way she'd kissed him. He hadn't told her everything he felt for her, and that hurt him. But he'd wanted what he said to be said perfectly and thought he'd have years to find the right words. And he wished with all his heart that they'd had the time to do more than kiss.

The wind picked up, blowing the dark smell of the river toward them. Men left the tavern and entered it, some nodded good evening to them, some offered them more.

" 'Tis a cold night, gentlemen," one aged fellow said, as he paused at their side. He puffed on his clay pipe as though he hoped the smoke it emitted would hide his face. "Happen I know of a place where the women are warm and cheap."

"If you're interested in fine linens, gents," another furtive fellow whispered, this one already bouncing on one foot, prepared to run. "I knows where there's a shipment, hot off the boat from the

Continent, for sale for next to nothing, at least to gents like you."

One after another they came, offering women, liquors, jewels, French perfumes, and silver plate.

To each offer Drum made polite refusals. And each exchange made Eric's face grimmer.

Then a thin man left the tavern and stayed to chat for a moment. Drum's usually impassive expression grew sharper as he listened, and he exchanged a quick glance with Eric. Eric's eyes widened. He nodded. Drum opened his purse and gave the fellow a handful of something that glinted in the dim lamplight before he quickly shoved it into his own pocket. He handed Drum a small parcel of wadded newssheets, so it would look as though he'd bought something more tangible than information, and then hurried away.

Eric turned to Drum, his eyes ablaze. "Newgate!" he said. "Damn him! It's cruel and it's clever, because I swear I wouldn't have thought of it, and it might have taken weeks to find her. But, by God, now we have it. Let's not leave her there another second!"

He was on his horse and pounding down the street by the time his friend had swung up into his saddle. Eric didn't look back. He rode off into the aging night with a grim but triumphant smile on his face.

Camille saw the great mass of the hulk rising up out of the lingering night long before the wagon would reach it. It was hard not to see it, even in the night. The great ship dominated the little harbor, lights in its upper cabins glaring like the fiery eyes of some gigantic dark beast rising from the water. The huge man-of-war was like an enormous toad squatting in a small puddle, dwarfing everything around it, the cliffs beyond and the other ships before it. The ship had been a monumental engine of war, now it was a black monolith that all but blotted out the setting moon. The size of it took Camille's breath away.

"It ain't the *Eurydice!*" one of the boys breathed.

"That ain't good," another moaned.

There was a stir among them, a quiet agitation, quickly quelled.

"It don't matter, none of them's good nor worse," Taffy, the boy who had befriended Camille, whispered. "S'truth, the *Eurydice*'s for lads, but who's to say it would've been better? Any of you know which one of them it is?"

Silence greeted his question.

"Aye," he said, "it don't matter. Whichever ship it is, we wouldn't get but a glimpse of it. We're bound for the lower decks, where you never see the light. That's where they put the newest ones. They let you out sometimes to work, and they chain you up again at night. Do you live, and if you're lucky, you get to move up a deck at a time. Never to the top, o'course, 'cause that's for the guards 'n officers. But when you gets high enough, and if you lives long enough, you walk in the sunlight every day. Then you might be shipped out off to the antipodes or the West Indies or such."

He stopped talking, because his voice was breaking. He scrubbed his eyes with his sleeve. Prison rat that he was, born in jail and seldom out of it since, still, the thought of exile was worse for him than the thought of death. He hadn't known much of freedom or London, but it was obviously life to him.

"And no one'll ever find you there," another boy said with a thrill of horror, "because you don't get no visitors there. No one never sees you again onct you set foot on a hulk. It's like you're already croaked."

"Mebbe when you gets to the other side of the world, you could have someone write them," a small voice offered with hope.

"If you ever gets there," another said heavily.

The others nodded.

Camille could see them now and hear them better too. They didn't worry about being overheard, because as they neared the ship, the outriders had gone to ride up in front of the wagon close together. They were talking, doubtlessly conferring about how to transfer the prisoners to the hulk when they got there. Dawn was near. She could see the sky turning milky above the cliffs, and what she finally could see of her companions saddened her in many ways.

No wonder the guards weren't worried about them. They were a pathetic collection, the oldest lad perhaps fifteen, and all thin, ragged, and pitiful.

Still, a woman had to work with what she had.

Camille now could also see the long, winding, hilly road they were on and how it led down to the little harbor below. There was a sheer drop-off on the right, hedgerows and trees to the left. A little town lay in tiers in the cliffs above the harbor, a half-cup set in the hollow of the hills. She judged they had ten or fifteen minutes until they began their descent to the harbor below.

She looked at the boys in the growing morning light and took a deep breath. Fifteen more minutes of freedom. She only regretted that she hadn't had a chance to give more than kisses to Eric. She'd been brave enough to fling herself into his arms that first time. Now she wished she'd been brave enough to have more of him. But it was better than nothing. She'd had his declaration of love too, so she had something to take with her, wherever she went, whatever happened.

Now she had to think of what would happen next. There was no more time to think or to pray. She looked at the boys and knew they remembered what she'd said by their watchful expressions as they gazed back at her. They all turned to look at her now, and Taffy's eyes weren't the only ones glittering in the growing light.

"Well, then," she said.

She took a breath, nodded, and stood up in the swaying waggon.

She was ready.

Chapter 20

He'd been riding up the twisting road fast as he dared, but when he got to the top and saw it all happening from afar, Eric almost flung himself off the horse and ran on foot to get there faster. He didn't, but only because he knew that it simply wasn't possible. He had to stay glued to his saddle, bent low, urging the horse on, and watching helplessly as he raced to the scene.

As rising dawn finally showed the sea below, he could see what madness it had been to be riding on such a treacherous road in the dark at all. The drop-off on the right side was sudden, sheer, and deep. He'd been told that, but nothing could have made him sit in an inn and wait for first light. At least now he knew how right he'd been to risk his neck. The lumbering wagon far ahead had been his lighthouse, his beacon. He'd thought himself lucky to find something else moving on the dark road and had been following the bobbing lanterns on its sides for miles now, drawing closer all the time. He'd never guessed that the light that guided him had been the one he'd been seeking since he'd gone pounding out of London in the middle of the night.

But as the dawn came up, like the stage lights at the beginning of the first act of a play, the scene in front of him erupted into frantic action.

Eric saw a figure rise up in the back of the open wagon and then dozens more bob up beside it. He could hear a chorus of shouts and jeers coming from the motley crowd in the wagon even above the steady beating of his horse's hooves. The commotion caused the heavy wagon to slow. Eric saw an outrider come galloping from the front of the wagon toward the back to investigate. There was another outrider on the other side, but he was unable to turn back because of the sheer cliff on his side and instead struggled with his horse as it reared when he tried to turn it.

Eric saw the action as though in shadow play against the rising sun. The first outrider approached the largest figure standing in the back of the wagon. As the rider closed on it, the figure raised an arm and swung a chain that hit him square in the face, sending him reeling back. She— Eric could now see it was a woman wielding the chain, because her hair was blowing in the wind and the profile was unmistakably feminine—struck again as the rider recovered his seat. This time the unlucky rider was toppled from the saddle and went sprawling in the road. His panicked horse spun and raced to the front, almost colliding with the second outrider, who had managed to turn his horse at last. But he was again diverted from the activity in the back of the wagon as he tried to grab the reins of the runaway.

And then, like lice leaving a burning bed, the back of the wagon erupted, spewing what seemed like dozens of ragged little people who went scrambling over the sides and dashing in every direction, filling the road with frantic, fluttering shapes heading toward the hedgerows.

The woman in the back stayed where she was, along with some . . . children, Eric saw now in the growing light. She stood tall and faced the second outrider, swinging the chain on her arm like an angry cat twitching its tail, waiting for him to approach. Eric's heart rose, filled to bursting with pride and fear for her as he raced nearer. An unholy grin creased his face in spite of his worry. Yes! Of course it was his Cammie.

Who else could be so bold, so brave, and so utterly reckless? She didn't see that there was a man crawling over the front seat of the wagon, staying low, so he could grab her from behind. But Eric could see him. And he was finally near enough to fling himself off his horse.

He landed on the road in a rolling crouch and

came up running. He swarmed up over the back of the now motionless wagon and grabbed the creeping man by the collar. He jerked him to his feet so he could hit him properly. One blow was enough. Then Eric dragged the guard upright and shook him like a rat before he raised him high over his head and threw him at the approaching outrider. He leapt after the man he'd thrown and dragged the dazed outrider the rest of the way off his horse so he could pummel him too. Then, scarcely out of breath, the light of battle gleaming in his eyes, Eric turned and went for the driver of the wagon. But his sport was over, because that fellow had seen him coming and jumped out—on the wrong side of the road—and was now rolling end over end down to the sea.

For a moment Eric heard nothing but the sound of his own pounding pulse and harsh breathing. Then he heard early-morning birdsong and the faroff pulse of the sea—and his name called with tentative wonder.

"*Eric?*" Camille cried in glad disbelief.

He put a hand on the wagon and vaulted up beside her, folded her in his arms, and hugged her hard, rocking her against himself.

"Cammie," he said into her hair. "My Cammie," he said thickly. He paused, put her a hand's breadth away so he could look down into her eyes, and then dragged her back so he could kiss her lips, her cheeks, her forehead, and then her lips again.

Too soon for his liking, but because he remembered their danger, he pulled away, still keeping her close in his arms. He looked around to see if anyone else had plans to attack them.

The outriders lay still in the dust, either unconscious or shamming it. The scrambling children in the road were gone. Only three youngsters were left standing in the wagon bed, staring up at him.

Seeing how wide-eyed they were, Camille stepped out of Eric's embrace—but not too far. She rubbed her nose on the back of her hand to keep from crying and said, "They were taking us to the hulks. That one down in the harbor. Dearborne arranged it. He took me to Newgate and then sent me here. Only I would not let it happen. These are *children,* Eric."

She gulped a steadying breath. "So Taffy here"— she motioned to a thin boy—"he found a way to open the lock on my chain. They chained me to the wagon," she added with a thrill of horror. "Taffy knows how to do such things."

Eric saw the fine tremor that shook her when she spoke of being chained and put his arm round her.

"I loosened the rope on the others," she went on, as she fought for composure. "And we waited and took our chances. But if you hadn't come along . . ." She stopped and choked back a sob.

"You'd have done as well," he said. "My God, you were wonderful, Cammie, you were a Valkyrie, a veritable Bodicea, an Amazon queen, a . . ."

"She was a bloody wonder," a little boy standing nearby said with vast admiration.

"A *bloomin'* wonder," another lad hissed at him, "or a *blinkin'* wonder. She's a lady, remember?"

"Beggin' your pardon, miss," the first boy said humbly. "And he, the big one," he said excitedly, "he were a bl-bloomin' wonder too, weren't he?"

"That you were, sir," the boy Camille had named Taffy said. "Thank you."

"So were you," Eric said, bending down to scoop up the padlock to examine it. "How the devil did you get this off her?"

"Well," Taffy said hesitantly, "see, she had a brooch on her . . ."

"When Dearborne made me change my clothing, I kept my brooch," Camille explained. "I certainly wasn't going to hand my pin over to him with my gown. Belle gave it to me for my birthday. So I fastened it to this hideous thing," she held out the skirt of the shapeless gray gown she wore. "But I wore it on the inside, of course, where no one could see it."

Eric's hand tightened on her shoulder when he heard that. He knew, as she obviously didn't, that the inside of her gown was perhaps the least safe place she could have hidden something. She didn't realize how lucky she'd been that there'd been no time for her pin to be discovered—among other, more important things.

"So when Taffy said he could do wonders if he had a pick or a pin or a nail," she went on, "I remembered the pin on my brooch and handed it to him. He had the lock open in a trice."

"That's how I got here," the boy said with a mixture of pride and anxiety. "I'm a dab hand at it. There's no lock I can't fiddle. Nobody would of never nabbed me for it neither, only someone peached on me. Speaking of which, I guess we'd best pike off now."

He looked out at the silent road. There wasn't a child to be seen, and the men in the dust didn't so much as twitch a limb. But Eric thought he saw an outrider's closed eyelids flicker.

"Aye," he agreed with a nod. "Soonest gone, best for all."

Camille gasped. "We can't leave these boys here!" she cried. "They're far from home and will be caught as soon as we leave."

"Don't worry none about us," Taffy said, squaring his narrow shoulders. "We've many a trick betwixt us. We'll do fine."

"No doubt," Eric said smoothly. "But we need help. Do you lads think you might stay on with us until all's clear?"

"I s'pose," Taffy said with just enough reluctance to save his pride, as the other lads nodded their energetic approval.

"Let me just make certain that we've left no one who needs help—little as they deserve it," Eric said. He leapt down and went to examine each rigid figure in the road in turn. All were breathing. Though there might have been a few broken limbs, there was nothing dire. The fellow who had rolled down the hill was sitting on an outcropping far below. Someone would have to haul him up. That someone was not Eric Ford.

Eric stood and studied the prone figures in the road again. He watched carefully and saw one man lying especially rigid. Noting that the fellow's breathing was regular and his color good, Eric went to him, bent on one knee, and whispered low, "Move a muscle in the next hour and you won't have one to move with again. I'm not going far, and I'm meeting friends. Lots of them. After an hour you may get up and go. You may rest until then.

"You are well enough, but your fall affected your memory," Eric told him, watching the closed eyelids fluttering. "Just as well. You'd be in very bad trouble if it were known that a woman and some children outsmarted you. So it's best that you say a gang of their thuggish friends were lying in waiting on the road. Who could deny that? Besides, that is the only healthy thing to say. Anything else would be decidedly unhealthy, trust me on that.

"I do have friends," Eric added, "in high as well as low places. You can lose your position or your life if you don't take care to say what I told you, you and your mates. By the way, you never saw me."

The fellow's Adam's apple bobbed up and down.

"Now open your eyes so I know you understand." Eric said. "Or you won't be able to," he added when the man's eyes remained resolutely closed.

A pair of terrified blue eyes flew open.

Eric nodded. "I'll remember your face," he said. "Now go back to sleep. Then, in an hour, tell your associates how they can stay alive too and that I will remember them too. I have an excellent memory and many friends. Good day." He rose and stalked back to the wagon.

"We'll take the horses," Eric told Camille. "Can any of you ride?" he asked the boys.

"Me," Taffy said.

"An accomplished lad," Eric said approvingly. "I can take a lad with me on my saddle. And you?" he asked Camille.

"I'll take the other one," she said.

"Then let's leave," Eric said. "We've friends to meet."

They rode three of the horses and took the remaining two, which was lucky, because by the time they went back down the road they'd added more children to their party.

Their ragged band left the road soon after and went west over the meadows, through the fields, and into a forest.

"We must talk," Eric told Camille an hour later, when they stopped in a thicket far from the road they'd traveled.

She got down and helped the boys down. "You can stretch or sit," she told them, "but don't go far."

She needn't have bothered telling them that, because they followed after her like a line of ducklings.

"No," she said, turning to caution them with one raised finger. "I must talk with my friend the lieutenant now. You rest here and mind the horses. Don't worry, I won't go far."

"Go far as you want," Taffy said handsomely. "I'll look after 'em, and keep watch too."

"Lieutenant?" Eric asked, raising an eyebrow, when they'd walked until they were out of earshot.

"They need someone in authority," she told him. "A lieutenant will be sure to keep them in line."

"You're their queen," he said, smiling. "You could order them to the battlements and they'd go without blinking." His expression changed. He dragged her close and held her tightly. "Oh, my love," he said, his great chest rising and falling in a mighty sigh, "that was something I never want to experience again!"

She moved in his arms, and he immediately let her go. She might have problems with men right now, he realized. That was something they'd deal with later. His own fears of what those things had been were something he'd deal with later too. This was not the time or place.

She looked embarrassed and stared at her feet before she looked up again. He began to worry over what had happened to her, because his Cammie was never at a loss for words.

"Now," she said, "what are we going to do?"

He was lost for a moment in the beauty of the sunlight reflected in her eyes, striking gold in their depths. Her hair was unkempt, her gown was a fright, and she'd never looked lovelier to him.

"I know we're not meeting friends, as you told the boys," she said, prompting him. "That was for the guards to hear, wasn't it?"

He nodded, still lost in admiration of her.

"Where's Miles?" she asked, her hand flying to her breast. "Is he hurt? I didn't think—but if I was kidnapped—did Dearborne hurt him? Dear Lord, say it isn't so!"

"No, he's fine!" he said quickly, moving to hold her. Then, remembering, he drew back. "He's fine," he reassured her, merely taking her hand in his. "He's on the Brighton road with a Runner, and that lawyer, Nell's cousin, trying to keep up with them. Judging from the speed at which Miles was traveling, I doubt he can. Drum rode out down the Dover road. Ewen and Rafe have taken separate paths to the sea. We practically had to forcibly restrain Belle from joining the hunt and order Alexandria to stay home with threats of death if she stirred from the house. And if it weren't for the fact that Gilly has infant twins and it would be hard for her to drag them with her, she'd be racing hell-bent down to the sea too," he added to lighten Camille's expression.

But she didn't smile.

"We were about to tear Newgate apart," he told her seriously, "but luckily the guards there are as greedy as they are dishonest. They spy on each other. One being bribed made it certain that another would listen and try to get some of the money from him. We were told you'd been sent out with the convicts headed for the hulks. But no one knew which one, because that damned Dearborne had lied even to his associates. The Newgate officials had no record of where you were bound. There'll be some heads rolling there tomorrow, and I don't mean those of the condemned," he added grimly.

"As for the hulks, there are too many of them, and they lie in too many directions. It was only lucky chance that led me to this one and you. I'll send word to Miles and the others as soon as we're safely away, because we'll need all our friends in place to bring this adventure to an end. I don't want your whereabouts known until all's safe and settled."

He frowned. "It's where that 'away' will be that I have to discuss with you now. Things being what they are, with Dearborne still on the loose, I don't trust random inns. And I don't want to cause talk by appearing on a stranger's doorstep. Nor do I want to bring possible danger to a friend. So there's the question of where we go next. You see, we're not safe until we alert the authorities, tell them their misplaced role in all of this, and get them to call off their dogs. You were sent to Newgate and listed as an enemy of His Majesty and then you escaped. So there'll be minions of the law looking for you until they are told to stop. As for the children, I doubt we can ever tell the authorities to stop searching for them, because they are convicted felons."

"But Taffy only opened a door to let his confederates in," Camille protested. "He didn't take a thing. And he's only eight, Eric! Bill's barely six, and all he took was a string of sausages. Jake's—"

"I know," he said, cutting her off, trying to soothe her. "It's monstrous. Even if they didn't tell you the strictest truth, they are only children, whatever they did. But that's the law. That doesn't mean we have to return them to its untender mercies, though. Whatever they did, we can give them a second chance. And so the sooner we have them dressed differently, the better. For now, we have to stay off the main roads and find a safe haven from which to send out word to our friends."

He shook his head. "We can't go to London, because they're likely watching all roads to it. You're innocent, my love, but the plain fact is that a wagonload of convicted prisoners have escaped from His Majesty. That news will stir the authorities. If some of the prisoners remain at liberty, it will be hushed up, but for now, they'll do all they can to sweep in and collect all of them again, and I can't rely on them to think before they act. So even if we could get you there, London's not yet safe. We're too far from your house in the country too. We can reach my family more easily. Will you come home with me?"

She nodded.

He hated the way she avoided his eyes and worried about her new reticence with him. "We'll thrill my parents," he said, trying to cheer her. She still didn't smile. If anything, she looked uneasier.

"All right," he said, making the decision, "that's where we'll go. But though it's closer than your home, we might not be able make it all in one day's ride. Daylight's short this time of year, and after your experience you're bound to be weary by evening. I know a decent and honest inn a few hours from home. I trust its owners completely. I could ride on, but I refuse to leave you there alone. So, Cammie, are you willing to stop for the night with me?"

She gazed at him, obviously puzzled.

"We aren't married," he said. "We're engaged, but no one knows it but us, and I wondered . . ."

She lowered her head and rested her forehead on his chest. "Oh, lud, Eric," she sighed. "I've been kidnapped and sent to Newgate, terrorized and sent to the hulks. Are you thinking about my reputation? I haven't one anymore."

"I'm thinking about you," he said, putting his hand gently on her back.

She immediately stepped away from him.

"Then let's go," she said.

Chapter 21

She never wanted to get out of the bathtub. It was only a waist-high iron tub that she had a hard time wedging herself into, but the water was hot and the soap was scented, and Camille sat folded in on herself until her fingertips grew white puffy ridges and her toes felt tender. It wasn't until the water grew chilly that she finally sighed and rose and, shivering, reached for the towel on the chair next to the tub.

The innkeeper had brought the tub to her room immediately. After that, if it turned out that the inn Eric had brought her to had rodents for waiters and food fit for rats, she wouldn't have cared. She'd longed for a bath all during the long, cold day of riding to get here, and once she had one, she was content.

But her content faded as slowly but surely as her bath water cooled.

The Hungry Horse was a sturdy old inn off the high road, set back in a spinney surrounded by a long meadow. It had once been a priory or a nunnery or a gentleman's retreat, or maybe all three— Camille had only half heard the innkeeper's proud narrative as he'd led her up the narrow stair to her room. She'd been too weary to concentrate or care. It was enough that the place was snug against the increasingly cold night. Her legs ached as she climbed the stairs, and though her bottom was sore from all the day's riding, she was anxious to sit down again. It had been a miserable, long, anxiety-ridden, uncomfortable ride on a sullen gray winter's day.

She hadn't shown her unhappiness, because she didn't want to discourage the children. But now that the boys had been led off to their own dinner and beds, she could at last relax enough to feel terrible.

Eric hadn't complained either. He'd ridden as hard as they had, as well as doing sentry duty, watching the roads and fields before he led them across them on their circuitous path to the sanctuary of the old inn.

"I'll get the boys settled and then send word to Miles and the others," he told her after he'd had conference with the landlord. He urged her to go to her room. "You rest. I'll come tell you when all's done and set. If you want to sleep, I can tell you in the morning."

"I won't sleep until I know," she'd said, and dragged her aching body up the stair.

"It's quiet here," the innkeeper told her as he opened the door for her. "This room faces the fields, not the drive. There's only the roof above and a storage room beneath, so no one will disturb you in the night." It was as kind a way as any to tell her that her enemies couldn't creep up on her unannounced, she thought.

He'd stoked up the fire in the hearth. A tub was dragged up and filled with hot water. Camille threw off her hated gray gown and almost pitched it in the fire before she realized that if she did she'd have nothing to wear when she left the tub. But when a maid came with a last bucket of hot water, she left a dressing gown on the chair along with extra towels.

"The gentleman had this in his saddlebag," the maid said breathlessly, "and he said as how you should wear it until you get another gown, which'll be in the morning, seeing as how Mrs. Cutter in town has a regular store of fabrics and gowns to sell. It's a real shame how the coaching company lost your bags, ma'am, but ain't that always the way? They charge you the earth and don't deliver nothing but grief. Believe me, we hear it all here."

Eric had probably spun a fine tale, Camille thought, as she dried herself in front of the fire, smiling as she wondered how he'd explained the boys. She picked up his dressing gown. It weighed enough to make her stagger. She couldn't help smiling as she shook it out. It was the size of a bedspread, of heavy red silk, with a roaring gold dragon coiling over its breast. It wasn't the sort of thing she'd expect him to wear. He was always well dressed in clothes of a simple military cut. Still, she thought the dressing gown suited him, because he was a vibrant man of substance and unexpected grace.

Camille gratefully slipped her arms into the sleeves and folded it around her. It was much too big, and that felt wonderful. The dressing gown was warm from the fire and smelled of evergreen and spice, just as Eric always did. She cuddled into it and sank to a chair by the fire, careful to keep a towel around her shoulders so that her damp hair wouldn't get his dressing gown wet.

The room was amazingly comfortable. The inn was old but clean, with furnishings that might have been the original ones. They gave added comfort precisely because of their age and air of good use. It was a large room with two chairs and a table, and a tester bed that took up an entire wall. The bed beckoned to Camille. But she knew that if she so much as sat down to try it out she'd fall asleep in it, and she wanted to talk to Eric. There were some things she had to say before more time had passed. She sat back. Her eyes began to close.

When the knock came at the door, she was wak-

ened from a deep and dreamless sleep. She shot upright, momentarily confused and surprised that
she'd drifted off. She stumbled to her feet and went
to the door. The towel slipped from her shoulders.
She went to pull it back and realized her hair was
dry, so she must have been asleep a long while.

"Come in!" she called.

"No," a deep voice said. "That's not the right
answer to a knock on your door."

"Right, right. You're right," she said in embarrassment. "Who is it? is what I should have said,
though I know," she added mutinously, as she
opened the door. "And if anyone was after me they
wouldn't knock, would they?"

"The point is that I could have been anyone," he
said. He filled the doorway and had to duck his
head to clear the lintel but stopped in his tracks
when he saw her tumbled hair, heavy eyes, and
flushed face. "But I woke you. I'm sorry, go back to
sleep, we'll talk tomorrow," he said, backing out
into the hall.

"No, I wanted to be woken!" she cried. "Come
in."

"I was going to invite you to come down to the
parlor and join me in some dinner," he said, his
eyes traveling down his dressing gown to her bare
feet. "I'd better not. I can lend you a robe or a shirt,
but I don't think you'll fit in my boots."

"But I'm hungry!" she wailed.

He laughed. "It doesn't mean you can't eat. I'll
have them send up your dinner."

"Good. Then we can pull a table close to the fire and eat while we talk," she said, "because I must talk to you."

"Cammie," he said, his smile slipping, "we can't. Or rather, I can't. I can't stay up here alone with you."

"Who else do you want to invite?" she asked. She put her hands on her hips. "Eric, this is nonsense. Are you worried about my reputation? Who will ever know? Besides, even if they did, I told you—I haven't a shred of reputation left anyway."

She stood there feet apart, hands on her hips, forgetting, in her agitation, that she hadn't drawn a belt around his dressing gown. He got a glimpse of a long, shapely leg, and more than a glimpse of high, bountiful breasts. They threatened to spill out of his dressing gown where it was parted at the vee of her neck. The contrast between her smooth, matte white skin and the rich red of the silken robe made him wish to see the rest of her breasts. He wondered if they were tipped with the same carmine hue as the robe or were dusky pink or . . .

"Cammie," he said with difficulty, "it's not about your reputation. It's about mine."

"Oh!" she said, seeing the direction of his gaze. "Bother!" She pulled the robe around herself and belted it with such fierce energy he was afraid she'd cut off her circulation. If she thought that would turn the direction of his thoughts, she was wrong, because now the silk outlined her breasts, emphasizing their buoyancy and size.

He sighed.

"Sorry, I'm not used to men's clothing," she muttered. "And such a big man at that. You make me feel dainty." That reminded her of what she had to say, and she scowled. "Still, if I keep myself belted and tucked and tied, I don't see why you can't stay. Come off your high horse and sit down with me. What I have to say can't wait until morning."

She wanted to add she had to say it before she lost the courage. But brave as she was, she lacked enough courage to say even that.

He spread his hands in a gesture of surrender and came into the room, carefully closing the door behind him. He'd hear her out, then leave. They'd each have to enjoy dinner in solitary splendor. Not because of her reputation, but because of his resolve. She'd never looked more tempting. In ordinary times, that might have been all right. He was an honorable man, or so he hoped, but they were engaged, and even if the world didn't know it, they did. But he couldn't forget that she'd had a long and terrifying night and day and she was acting differently toward him. He couldn't impose on her after her harrowing experience. He was too worried about what it had been.

"All right," he said, settling into the other chair by the hearth. "Sit and speak."

She cocked her head to the side. "Sit and speak? Am I a dog?"

"Forgive me, I'm tired," he said, passing a hand over his eyes. "All right, I'll speak first: Woof."

She giggled.

He was pleased he'd defused the situation. "Sit, sit," he said, gesturing to the chair opposite his. "The boys are bathed," he reported as she sat. "That's why I'm so late. The objections were fierce. I'm surprised you didn't hear them up here. In fact, I thought half the lamentations were coming from the fleas we evicted, they were that high-pitched. But eventually the protests ended. I gave them dinner, found them beds in a snug room near the kitchens, and now all the lads are clean and fed, and even our chief rogue, Taffy, is fast asleep."

His expression grew sober. "Lord! They're only children but they've lived harder lives than campaigning soldiers. But I can report that we may only have to travel on with three of them. Not because I drowned the other two, though it was a tempting thought." He smiled at her smile and went on, "But those two expressed interest in staying on here with our landlord. He's a good fellow who needs a pair of likely lads, and they like him. Innkeeping would be a fine trade for them to learn and a good life for them. Taffy and the others will come along to my parents' house. So. Now. Your turn. What is it that you had to talk to me about?"

He didn't expect his question to cause such a vivid response. Her color rose to match the dressing gown. She lowered her gaze and absently picked at a stray coiling thread on a dragon's scale. Eric noted it was very near the tip of an ample breast. He shifted in his seat and tried to look away.

"Eric," she said.

"My name," he agreed.

"Look," she said in the forthright way he remembered, the way she'd won his heart, "I've thought this out. You asked me to marry you and I jumped at the chance. But things have happened since. And so I think I must release you from your agreement with me."

His heart grew cold. "Agreement?" he asked, trying to sound casual. "Seems to me a proposal of a life together is much more than that. Seems to me you once thought so too." He leaned forward, keeping his hands clasped hard together so he couldn't reach out and hold her close as he longed to do. "Cammie. What happened? And why should you think that whatever it was would matter to me? Except of course it would hurt me if it hurt you. But it would be the past, and it's our future I'm thinking of. I think you should be too."

"I am." She cleared her throat but didn't go on.

"Whatever it is, it's damned hard, isn't it?" he murmured. "But it's just me here. Can't you say it?"

She rose in one swift movement and gave him a jerky nod. "Yes. But I think better on my feet."

And that would take her further from him, he thought sadly, watching as she turned to pace, head down. It nearly broke his heart. He loved her because she was valiant and direct. Another woman might be weeping and shrinking away from him now instead of facing the problem. As for what that was, he feared the worst. His hands closed to fists. Who had harmed or shamed his brave girl? He'd kill them of course, but that wouldn't help her now. Only he could do that. He rose to his feet as well.

"Cammie, whatever they did to you doesn't matter to me. Men can be harmed in captivity too. They can be molested. Prisoners of war know that may happen, and yet they expect their wives and sweethearts to welcome them back into their arms, because they know that what happens to the body without consent of the soul in that body is nothing, and—"

"Good Lord!" she said, stopping in her tracks. "I wasn't raped! Not that Dearborne didn't promise that I would be, but no one touched me except to cuff me to shut me up or to chain me to keep me in place." Her voice grew lower, her gaze dropped to the floor again. "Actually, that's just the point."

He was so incredibly relieved at her answer that it took him a minute to understand all she said. "What then?" he asked when he did. "What are you talking about?"

She raised her chin. "Dearborne didn't want any part of me, literally. He told Nell not to be jealous of his being interested in me that way, because though I was a 'fine healthy creature,' he didn't care to ride 'b-b-big brown mares.'" She was shamed by her stammering, took another breath, and went on, "He said he liked a filly with more thoroughbred lines. He also said that I was a great gawky, ugly drab."

She remembered every word Dearborne had said, the accents in which he'd said them, and the expression he'd worn as he had. They were etched in acid in her memory. She also remembered he'd said Eric had wanted her only because of her fortune and his friendship with her brother. The one she knew wasn't true; the other was a thing she'd been thinking about since she'd heard it. It was why she was saying this now.

"Dearborne wasn't the only one," she reported with difficulty. "There was a guard at Newgate who wanted time alone with me because he said I was clean and looked healthy as a horse. Well, so I am. Ironic that we landed here at the Hungry Horse tonight, isn't it?" she asked with a poor attempt at a chuckle.

She squared her shoulders. "Other fellows have offered for me, of course. Because I was a friend and they felt comfortable with me. I can understand that. But I don't know why you offered for me, Eric, because you're so much more than any of them were. My adventures have convinced me that whatever your reasons, they were all the wrong ones. I *am* a great horse of a girl. Plain as a pikestaff, and yes, almost as tall as one. And you? You're . . . you are . . ." She hesitated. How to tell him how big and golden and magnificent he was? She didn't know, so she told him just that, and added, "Any woman would want you, most that I have seen do. Miles is your friend, and you can't have helped seeing how I felt about you. We get on together, true. But that's no reason to marry me."

"You think that's why I want to?" he asked quietly.

"Yes. But it won't do," she said sadly. "You need a lovely wife, Eric, a beautiful woman of fashion like Belle or a pocket Venus like Gilly or a regal beauty like Drum's Alexandria. I've heard you admired them and women who are like them in your time. But me? I'm nothing like that. They're so very desirable."

"You think I don't desire you?"

That chased the sadness from her eyes. "Think it? I know it!" she said angrily. "It took this ugly incident to make me see how deluded I was. I was as humiliated as I was frightened, but it opened my eyes. I've had time to think, and thank goodness there's still time to set things right. This proposed union of ours is not right, at least not for you, and so not for me either. Eric, you offered for me after one kiss!"

"There have been more," he said.

"Well, yes, there have been. But always measured and always controlled. The first were tokens of affection and the last, today, natural relief at finding me alive."

"And the ones before that?" he asked her slowly. "The night I came to tell you that I didn't need three days to make up my mind?"

"Oh, that night under my window?" she said,

her color rising. "You are an honorable man. Now I see you couldn't sleep until the thing was settled and had to resolve matters in order to spare my feelings and respect my brother and behave in a way you felt was right."

"And what I told you?" he asked.

She shook her head. "That doesn't matter, for though you're an honest man, I think you'd dissemble for a good cause. But I don't want to be a good cause! I do believe you have real affection for me. That's not the sort of desire I'm talking about."

"What sort of desire is that?" he asked slowly, his expression unreadable but decidedly peculiar.

"Desire you can't mask or imitate or feign," she said staunchly. "And certainly not keep under control."

"Ah, I see. And you know what that kind of desire is all about?"

"Well, yes, I do," she said. "Because oh, lord, Eric, I so desired you! I kept wanting to touch you every time I saw you. Whenever you kissed me, I lost all sense of time and place. You were the one who always knew when to rein in. I could not. I yearned for you, I swear my stomach actually ached when I thought about touching you, and I couldn't think of much else. But," she said, raising her head, "that doesn't matter. I'll get over it, I daresay. And you have to find yourself a female you want to touch every minute too. These past days have made me think hard. Life's too short for polite love. It would be disastrous for us to marry. For me and for you. Because I'd kill you if you found your true love after we were married. And it would kill me if I knew you wanted her more than me."

She smiled wistfully. "It isn't just that. I ought to have told you this before too, but the fact is that I wouldn't look the other way if my husband took a mistress. I'd murder him and run her out of town. So," she said with decision, "this is for the best for us both, believe me. We can still be friends," she added, when she saw he hadn't moved.

"Of course," he said, "I will always consider you my friend, and I hope you always think of me as such."

She nodded, but it was hard to see him because of the mist that was rising before her eyes. She held her head higher. She could weep all night and probably would, but she'd be damned if she let him see a tear. She refused to let them ruin a fine renunciation speech.

"And I'm glad we had this talk," he added.

"Well, yes," she said as evenly as she could manage. "So I hoped you would be."

"Because it shows me what an idiot I've been," he said.

"I wouldn't say that," she said, anger drying up her incipient tears. "I am a friend, after all, and a fellow could do worse than to marry one. You weren't an idiot, just misguided."

"Definitely," he agreed, and reached for her.

He pulled her into his arms, bent his head, and kissed her. And then there it was again, the incredible taste and scent of her, the feel of her in his arms, electric, thrilling, necessary. Exactly what he needed and what no other woman had ever given him. She fitted him. And that was that. He wanted to tell her so, but he needed to kiss her even more, so he told her with his lips and hands and heart.

She understood. She held him tight and gave him back kiss for kiss and breath for breath, toe to toe and heart to heart, and didn't think it was a strange thing to do after what she had said, because she felt much too much to think at all—except that she wanted more of him.

The slippery silk of his dressing gown made it hard to secure even when it was belted. And so when his hand left off stroking her back and slid in the front to cup her breast, the gown opened wide to him, exposing her from breast to knee. But she never felt so much as a breeze on her skin. She was too busy crowding close to him to feel anything but the heat of his body.

His mouth was warm and searching, his big hand held her breast with exquisitely gentle care. His other hand cupped her bottom, enclosing it completely, holding her close to his arousal. She'd never felt so small, so hugely important, so excited and delighted.

He'd never felt such desire either. But his was not only for her, but also to show her how very beautiful and dear she was to him. And so, with enormous effort, he was able to step away from her.

They stood facing each other. She watched him,

her eyes showing her astonished desire, her lips blushed and swollen. She clutched her dressing gown together again, her hand over her heart where his had been. She wasn't afraid that he didn't want her, not now. That would be impossible. But she wondered why he'd stopped and waited patiently for him to tell her. While she did, she looked at him and filled her heart with him.

He reached out, and she expected to be in his arms again. But he only held her at arm's length, her shoulders in his hands. Slowly, he let his hands drift down the outline of her body, barely touching, as though he were measuring something immeasurably delicate and precious. Her head went back. She closed her eyes. She wanted to cover herself, she wanted him to cover over her. She loved him utterly but couldn't watch him seeing her body. Her big, utilitarian, ungraceful body.

"I was an idiot to keep observing the proprieties," he whispered, "a fool not to show you exactly how much I wanted you and how often. I'm the one who doesn't deserve you. You are everything a man could desire, mind and body. *Never* doubt it. Do you know how hard won that control of mine was? You're everything I could want. Look at me, Cammie."

She opened her eyes, embarrassment and doubt clear to see in them—slowly replaced by wonder and love as she saw his expression clear.

"I don't want a pretty little woman," he said urgently, his hands locking around her waist at last.

"I don't want a regal woman or a pocket Venus, or an Aphrodite in marble or in flesh or in ice or in marzipan or aspic."

She smiled. He nodded, a tiny smile quirking the corner of his wide mouth, before his expression turned deadly serious again.

"I don't want any other woman," he said. "I want *you*, Cammie. As you are, as you were, as you will be. Are you beautiful? Absolutely, you are beautiful to me. Are you larger than some women? Definitely. Smaller than others? Absolutely. Am I bigger than you? What a question. Am I older than you? Unworthy of you? No one could doubt it. But there's a truth that transcends age, size, and shape. I don't know how it happened, I'm only incredibly grateful for it. We are a pair. Come, my love, and see how very well you fit me."

She went gladly into his embrace. She raised her head and reared back from the waist in order to look him fully in the face. Her eyes were fixed on his, but she said nothing.

He cocked his head to the side, listening. He looked into her searching eyes.

He heard nothing but was sure of what she was saying.

Then show me.

He knew it as clearly as if she'd said it.

He raised her up in his arms and walked toward the bed with her, his heart racing, because there was nothing he wanted more, and he wanted nothing to ruin this moment. He hoped he'd said it all right, and he had to do the rest as perfectly, because he needed her pleasure as much as his own.

And then she started laughing.

It stopped him in his tracks.

"Oh, Eric," she said on a ripple of giggles, burying her nose in his neck. "How wonderful to find a man who can pick me up!"

Chapter 22

"**W**retch and witch and utter delight," Eric said as he followed Camille down to the bed where he'd gently placed her.

She grinned.

"First you freeze my heart in my chest with your laughter, and now you stop it by the look of you," he said in a whisper as he leaned over her and gazed down at her. He held her hands in his, their fingers laced together, so that she couldn't secure the dressing gown, which had fallen open again. She saw the direction of his gaze change and saw his expression change as well, from easy laughter to intent surprise. Her fingers twitched, itching to close her gown. She almost turned her head to the side, but then she saw the expression in his eyes, and her heart swelled with pride.

Eric looked at her hungrily. He saw her high, full breasts rise and fall with her excited breathing and watched how they pebbled as though they actually felt his warm gaze upon them. He saw the curve of her waist, the gentle swell of her belly, the triangle of cinnamon curls that covered over the generous mound of her sex, the glorious length of her legs, all revealed to him at last, all perfect in his sight.

She watched his eyes and rejoiced. But even so, a lifetime of doubts was not that easily defeated. She wasn't ashamed of her body, because she knew she wasn't deformed, but she lived in a time of strict definitions. Ladies were supposed to be delicate, elegant and fragile, robust figures were the attribute of whores and peasants. She couldn't forget that, she couldn't stop regretting that.

"I am big," she said softly.

"So am I," he said, as he lowered his head to kiss the puckered nub of her breast.

Her skin was smooth and firm and scented with good soap. It made him dizzy with desire. He released her hands so he could take her in his arms. But she lay too still for him.

He sat back. "And I'm dressed far too formally for the occasion," he said, and unbuttoned his waistcoat.

He pulled his shirt over his head and cast it aside. She stared at his broad bare chest, heavily muscled, covered with fine curling golden hair. She saw how that great chest tapered to a neatly defined waist. Her eyes widened slightly as she looked lower.

He hesitated, his hand on the buttons of his breeches, wondering if for all her bold talk she'd been too sheltered for lovemaking with a naked man. Some ladies, he knew, expected their lovers to come to them clothed, even after years of intimacy.

"I knew you would strip well," she told him with a happy sigh. "I heard you boxed with the best in London, and now I can see why."

He sat back on his heels and roared with laughter.

She blushed all over, he noted with growing interest.

"I can strip to even better," he said, as he hurriedly unbuttoned his breeches. "You'll see, I promise." But when he discarded his breeches, he did so quickly and then as quickly lay down beside her and took her in his arms. There was bold, and there was brash; one was wise, the other foolish. Boxing and lovemaking were very different, and only one was a spectator sport she was likely to have ever seen. He was very aroused. He wasn't sure that was a sight she would sigh to see, at least not until she grew used to him. Because he hadn't lied. He was indeed a very big man.

He kissed her, distracting her before she could see how much he wanted her, pleased because though her manner was shy, her kisses weren't, not even now, when she surely knew what they would

lead to. These weren't the sweet exchanges they'd
shared in the park after she'd accepted his proposal. They were beyond that now. She certainly
knew it, and yet she showed him that she joyously
anticipated whatever else was in store. He had
great plans for that.

She'd been through hell these last few days,
and so he'd hesitated to impose on her in any
way. But Eric had been a soldier, and he knew
how danger and the nearness of death made a
man long to show he was a man, so that he could
feel he was alive and could celebrate that life. His
Camille had proved to be brave as any man, and
so he believed he knew what would be good for
her. He'd already seen how desire chased the
shadows from her eyes and knew that pleasure
would restore her even more. It certainly was doing that for him.

She opened her mouth against his, accepted the
touch of his tongue, and returned it with enthusiasm. She pressed against him, and the sensation of
her naked breasts rubbing against the bare skin of
his chest made him catch his breath. She caught
hers when he bent his head to taste the puckered tip
of one breast and stayed there like a bee at a succu-
lent blossom. Then he covered it with one big hand
and went to address the other one. He cupped her
bottom and devoured her mouth and placed his
lips along the side of her neck, whispering her
name until she shivered. She urged him on, murmuring his name under her breath, running her

hands over his wide shoulders, as though thrilled by his strength and size.

Her ardor was fueled by discovery, and every discovery seemed to delight her. He'd thought his arousal would be intimidating for a girl of her breeding and limited experience. But when she saw him, she was frankly curious instead, then filled with wonder at the extent to which her touch moved him, as it made him groan and grow. She was as astonished as excited by the sight of his arousal.

"Amazing!" she breathed, as he showed her that she could hold him as well as touch him and what motion she could use to best please him. "This is just amazing," she repeated. "Imagine keeping such a thing a secret until you need it!"

Or you do, he almost said with a wicked grin, but at the last minute restrained himself, remembering her age and experience. She was not yet his bride in fact, but she was that in his heart, and nothing about their first night of love could be rude or crude. This act of love must be only that, as well as everything gentle and refined, for her.

She found him amazing? He found it astonishing that she discovered nothing but delight in him. He'd heard such daunting stories about fearful untried young ladies of quality. But she really was quality, he realized, and rejoiced in his good fortune and her eager embrace.

Too soon he found himself fighting against his desire. He couldn't remember ever having a better lover. But then, he'd never loved any lover as he did his Camille.

Nor had Camille ever known anything like these thrilling moments in the night with her Eric. She'd thought she'd be shy when she finally made love with him. She'd worried about this intimacy as much as she'd desired it, if only because she'd been afraid she wouldn't measure up to his expectations. But he seemed delighted with her, and that warmed her heart as much as he fired her body.

And his body! She reveled in it. Though she'd been drawn to his charm and appreciated his cleverness and consideration and a dozen other fine attributes of his, the truth was she'd desired him since the day they'd met, and that because of the way he looked to her. She'd only discovered his warmth and charm later. Now that he was bared to her, she could see how very lucky she was. Many gentlemen of the *ton* had to pad out their legs and chests and arms, but not her Eric. Everything about him was honest and straightforward. He was as magnificent without his clothes as he was in them.

She was charmed to find that his gentle nature and consideration were not diminished by his obvious desire. Even now, alone with her, at ease with her with the door locked behind them, knowing, as he must, that she was his now whatever he did, he was as much of a gentleman as he'd always been. He was also the phantom lover she'd dreamed about. All power, all restraint, all ardor and yet always careful of her, a titan held in check. His body was steel and silk, his touch gentle and demanding. He smelled clean, his skin was clear, he tasted of salt and warmth.

She didn't have to tell him what pleased her. Everything he did pleased her.

He caressed her and then kissed every place he'd caressed. When his hand slid all the way down her body and he finally touched her, low, she stilled. Then, on a strangled groan, she raised herself to him, offering him whatever he wished. There was no way she could be shamed by something that felt so fine. He did more than touch her. His fingers found a slow and steady rhythm against the cleft in her heated flesh as he teased and entered and withdrew again, watching her, kissing her, and watching her again. Soon a slow buzzing pervaded her whole body. She positively hummed with desire. When he saw her head go back and her eyes close, his movements became faster.

She gasped, her body rising hard against his hand. He held her as she shuddered, and then he rose over her, his knee between hers, urging them far apart. She opened her eyes. He smiled down at her tenderly and joined them swiftly.

She caught her breath again as she felt him filling her; she felt herself being stretched, it was uncomfortable, and yet—it was not. It was, she realized, necessary, urgently necessary, so necessary that she lifted herself to help him. When he moved within her, she saw his face transfixed with pleasure, his eyes half closed, distant, his expression intent. She held on to him, rocked with him, watching him strive, feeling his power, beginning to at last feel her own. He pounded against her frantically before he cried out, froze, thrust again and once again, and sank down at last deep within her, now himself shuddering with his release.

She held on to his back, feeling a little confused, a little deprived, somehow as though she'd missed something too. But in all, she felt wonderful, energized, and triumphant.

His breathing slowed. He rolled away and lay beside her. Then he rose up on an elbow. "Are you all right?" he asked worriedly. "Did I hurt you?"

She started to smile and shake her head, but then her body went rigid.

"What?" he asked, feeling her dismay. "What is it?"

She sat straight up and looked down at herself, then scrambled away from him and stared down at the sheets she'd lain upon. "Oh, Eric!" she wailed.

He sat up, looked at her and the bed. There was no blood on the bed or her body, but she looked aghast. A dozen terrible thoughts raced through his mind. He was a huge man and he'd thought she was ready, but had he somehow injured her tender body? What did he know of virgins? She'd been so enthusiastic he'd treated her like an equal in love, but a woman's first experience was crucial. He prayed he hadn't wounded her mind or body and cursed himself silently as he held her shoulders fast in his hands.

"What is it?" he demanded. "Where are you hurt?"

"Well, that's just it," she said, looking at him with wide eyes. "I—I wasn't. And it didn't hurt, not at all, and there isn't any blood or anything, and so now you'll think I . . . But truly, you *are* my first lover, and nothing happened to me in Newgate or with Dearborne or anything and yet how will you believe it now?"

He fell back on the bed with a groan and then reached out and pulled her down on top of him. "Love," he said, "not all women hurt or bleed their first time. Cammie," he said into her ear as he stroked the tangled curls back from her face, "you're a fine horsewoman, you ride like a demon, I've seen it. And you're proud of that, aren't you?"

Her head nodded against his chest.

"And have done since you were a girl?"

She nodded again.

"And you excel at all kinds of sports, many of which your mama despaired of—or so at least your brother told me. Isn't that so? You've jumped your horse over gates and stiles. You've even been caught riding astride, like a boy, when you were out for a gallop at home and thought no one was watching. Haven't you?"

She nodded.

He wanted to keep asking her questions she could say yes to because he liked the feeling of her curls rubbing against his chest, but the sooner he quieted her fears, the better.

"So you see," he said, trying to keep the smile from his voice, because he wouldn't injure her pride any more than he would her body, "the sort of proof you didn't find now was probably given unknowingly to some saddle in some race or at a gallop years ago. Or it's possible you were fortunate enough to be born with no impediment. That happens too. Listen. I know I was your first lover," he added, as he threaded his fingers through her curls and felt them bounce back against the back of his hand. "I'm certainly not sorry I didn't hurt you. Do you think your pain or blood would have made it a better experience for me? Do you think I'm some sort of a monster?"

He felt her head move back and forth as she shook her head in denial. "And why should you think I wouldn't believe you? Ah, why not?" he answered himself. "Well brought up men and women are poorly equipped for the realities of lovemaking, but at least we men can learn a lot in the streets before we gain real experience."

"And even more later," she murmured.

"Yes," he said simply, his hand stilling. "I can't deny that."

"Right," she said after a moment. "So. How did I compare?"

His laughter made his chest rumble so much she had to raise her head. He cupped it in his hands and kissed her thoroughly. "You have no compare," he said against her lips. "And I'm sorry too, but I'm not *that* vastly experienced. Mind, I wasn't a virgin or a monk, but I wasn't constantly seeking available women, because I never sought pleasure for its own sake. Now, of course, I'll never seek it again, because I have you."

After he'd disarmed her of the pillow she was thumping him with, he held her hands still and laughingly protested, "No, no, you know what I meant." His face grew serious. "I meant that since I've found you I want no other woman and never will again. Shall I show you why? You're a very good student. But the first time I think you were too busy watching and learning. Now for some applied knowledge. Are you game?"

She threw herself into his arms. *"Am I?"* she cried.

Then he learned something about love too, discovering it was possible to have it with laughter. Or at least, to have it until the ecstasy overwhelmed the laughter, and then he found there was a pleasure that went on far beyond it or anything he'd ever known.

"Now that," she said with considerable satisfaction when they lay quietly at last, "was something!"

"As are you, my love," he answered with a smile, "as are you."

He didn't speak again until she was drifting off to sleep in his arms. "We'll be home by dinner time tomorrow evening," he said softly. "I've sent word to my parents. They'll be waiting for us. Miles and the others will arrive soon after, I'm sure. So. Do you want to be married at my parents' home by special license in a matter of weeks, or do you want to wait and have a grand wedding in London?"

"Mmmm," she mumbled against his heart.

"Very well," he said on a yawn, as he closed his eyes and held her close. "That's what we'll do."

Chapter 23

The old church was cold, but there were so many guests packed into it that no one noticed, except for those few who had to sit near one of the walls. Not even early spring could take the chill from those ancient stones. Still, no one minded. It was a joyous occasion, and had the church been a great cathedral in the heart of London instead of one of the first the Norman conquerors put up when they arrived on this island, that would have been filled up too. The groom was a very popular man. The bride was not as well known, but her family certainly was.

Every guest there felt it had been well worth the trip into the country. This was indeed a consummation devoutly to be wished by the couple's many friends. And if some few were less than joyous, it was because such a happy union cast light on their own lack of success in love.

Mr. Dana Bartlett, for example, wore a small, sad smile throughout the service. There were some other fellows who looked definitely woeful as they beheld one of their best friends getting married, and it was the groom they were envying. Of course, there were not a few young women who sighed as they saw one of England's most elusive bachelors taking someone else to wife.

Even the two Bow Street Runners who sat in the back of the church were touched by the ceremony, although they didn't know the bride or groom, except professionally. They were only resting after their mad ride from London to tell him and his friends about the man they'd been seeking, Lord Dearborne. They would seek him no more, because he'd gone where they couldn't prosecute him, although everyone was sure he would not remain unpunished. But they'd proof that their prey, Lord Dearborne, had left the ship in which he'd sailed from England in a coffin when it landed in Brazil.

Justice had been done, though the groom and his friends were cheated of doing it themselves. They didn't mind. The sickness of mind and body that had finally felled the late Lord Dearborne seemed a world apart from this happy day, as did any thought of past enemies and sorrows. The future was shining so brightly it cast all thoughts of the unhappy past in the shade.

Arrangements of flowers softened the harsh lines of the old gray church, and the wedding guests were as colorful a lot. Vivid red was a popular color in the congregation, since there were so many men from the military who wore their bright regimental uniforms. Other guests dressed in the latest kick of fashion, since they were wealthy and from the highest reaches of Society. They were not only a handsome group, but also a convivial one. That was helped by the fact that there were so many children invited, many of them babes in arms. The groom's friends, other guests commented, were certainly a prolific lot.

Viscount Sinclair had his family in tow, three boys and a girl, and there was much amusement because of the way his son Max was eyeing Gilly Ryder's beautiful sister, Betsy. Prodigy though he was, Max was a decade younger and a foot shorter than the obvious object of his affection. It looked as though Viscount Hathaway's son from his first marriage had a better chance there, although the bride's brother Bernard was angling for her attention as well. Young Max looked as if he would do far better with the Ryders' flaxen-haired toddler daughter, who was looking up at him as though she'd found her ideal. Everyone was smiling, even the usually composed earl of Drummond was seen beaming broadly at his infant son where he lay in his mama's lap.

Lady Annabelle, the bride's sister-in-law, stood by the happy couple. Her exquisite face was a trifle pale, but the reason for it only made her and her doting husband, Lord Pelham, smile the more. No one felt well in early pregnancy, she'd assured him again this glad morning, although she'd never felt better about anything in her life.

But everyone stopped talking and laughing when the bride appeared.

There wasn't a doubt that she looked beautiful this morning, even if her looks were not the usual. She wore a smile so wide it matched the sweeping hoop of her antique gown as she stepped down the aisle. It was her grandmother's gown, a relic from another generation: tight at the waist, low at the breast, it floated out around her like the bell of an enormous ivory morning glory. It was not at all the fashion to dress in antique clothes, but the style suited her so well many of the young unmarried lady guests vowed to pillage their family attic for their own wedding day. And many young gentlemen there were so impressed by the bride that they'd never be content with whatever bride they chose unless she too looked like a princess from a child's fairy tale.

The groom could not stop smiling either. Big, broad-shouldered, and golden-haired, he made his bride look dainty by comparison and brought his own illumination to the scant sunlight he stood in at the altar, because he glowed with happiness.

After the couple was pronounced man and wife, the massive groom kissed his robust bride, then picked her up and spun her around as she held on to his shoulders and laughed with joy. The happy couple dashed up the aisle in a shower of petals and rice and stepped out into the morning to be further covered by a dusting of snow. They raced to a flower-decked coach, their faces rosy with cold.

They settled into the carriage that would take them the short way to the groom's parents' home for their breakfast reception. Her own mama had said she wasn't up to hosting a reception; his parents had been thrilled to oblige.

"Done!" he said, as he pulled her into his arms. "We've done it, love, you're mine!"

"A wonderful wedding!" the bride crowed, clapping her hands together. "I'm so glad we didn't wait."

"I don't think I could have," the groom confessed, after he took his second kiss as her husband, this one considerably longer.

"Well," she finally said with a mischievous grin, laying her hand on his chest. "I know someone else who couldn't have."

He looked his question at her.

She looked as demure as such a blooming bride could. "It's a very good thing that you're such a big fellow," she said. "And that I'm not petite as well."

"Well, yes, isn't that just what I've always said?" Eric asked, breathing in the scent of the camellias in the floral tiara that perched on her curls.

"Not just because of that, though I thank you for saying it," Camille said mischievously. "But because this way, no one will be surprised when our premature infant turns out to be so big."

Eric blinked. He sat back. He looked as though someone had hit him with a thick plank. Then his eyes lit with glee. "No!" he said. "That's wonderful! Are you sure?"

She nodded. "I just found out myself," she said, "but it's fairly certain. We waited six weeks to marry after we got here, and well, altogether that now makes it two months without me having my courses. You wouldn't have noticed the lack of them," she said on a sly grin, "because there were only a few times when we could steal away and take advantage of it. But be sure I was counting! I know a thing or two, but just to be sure I asked Belle. And she wasn't a bit prim about it either, though she did say it was a lucky thing we decided to go for a country wedding now and not wait until later. Anyway, she had me see her doctor."

Camille smiled beatifically. "It's true! The best guess is that our babe will be a seven month's wonder. But a very big one if he or she takes after either one of us, so there won't be as much comment as there might have been if we weren't so substantial. Are you sorry it will be so soon?"

"Sorry?" he asked, catching her hand in his and pressing it tight. "I'm only sorry we can't ensure it will be twins, so we can get more for the effort, the way Gilly and Damon are building their family. Just think," he said on a smile, "twin fiends like

Gilly! And both boys. They're handsome rascals too, aren't they? We could have a pair of daughters and make splendid matches for them."

"Twins?" Camille said thoughtfully, cocking her head to the side. "Well, I'll try."

They both roared with laughter. Their mirth filled the carriage in just the way it would go on to fill the rest of their long and lively lives together.

Epilogue

The letter arrived at their London house on an autumn morning. Travel stained and wrinkled, it waited on the hall table until the butler put it on the breakfast tray to be brought to his lady in bed. She was feeding her infant son and had to read the letter holding it with one hand. When she was done, she put it down with a sigh.

She showed the missive to her husband that afternoon when they took tea together.

Sunset House, New Prospect Street
New South Wales

My Dear Camille,

I hope you have forgiven me for giving you to Lord D——e, but I had no choice in the matter, and anyway, he said he wouldn't hurt you. I have heard that this was the case, because I have written to my cousin Bartlett and he has replied. I wish you joy in your marriage to Eric Ford. I am glad that he is well too. I gave him only enough of my tonic to disarm him that evening, as instructed. I vow I never meant to do more. He is a very good man and a very large one and so suits you perfectly.

As for me, I have fallen on my feet. I met a man on the ship that brought me to this place and he saw me through the voyage very nicely. As he was a guard in His Majesty's Service, through his good efforts I am now free. I immediately found work here. I have made a great deal of money and many friends. In fact, I have hopes of running this house myself one day, or one very similar, if perhaps a bit more exclusive.

In hopes of your forgiveness, and reminding you that it was through my efforts that you and Eric finally became closer, I remain,

Nell Baynes

Camille wasn't surprised that when Eric finished reading the letter he sighed as she had done.

"Do you think we'll ever see her again?" he asked.

"Only if she needs us for money or favors."

"You've grown very wise, wife."

"Indeed," she said, "I've had a good teacher. But you know, I don't think we will ever see her again. I wonder that she'd dare."

"She'd dare anything. Didn't you read her letter?"

She picked up the letter and folded it carefully. "But she is right. I'll keep it as a souvenir. We can use it to show the children how we *really* met. When they're old enough, of course."

"Children?" he asked with a fond smile, looking at the infant son whom his wife refused to leave with a nurse even for an hour. "With Miles's and Belle's little Gwen here all the time, I feel as though we already have two. Are you thinking of another so soon?"

"Well, at least I think of the process of getting them all the time," she said innocently.

She only stopped laughing when he kissed her.

But she never stopped rejoicing in their kisses, not then, nor during all the rest of their remarkable lifetime together. And neither did he.

Lose yourself in enchanting love stories from Avon Books.
Check out what's coming in December:

HOW TO TREAT A LADY by Karen Hawkins
An Avon Romantic Treasure

Harriet Ward invented a fiance to save her family from ruin, but when the bank wants proof, fate drops a mysterious stranger into her arms, a man she believes has no idea of his own identity. And so she announces that he is her long-awaited betrothed!

A GREEK GOD AT THE LADIES' CLUB by Jenna McKnight
An Avon Contemporary Romance

What if you had created the perfect replica of a gorgeous Greek god, and right before you're about to unveil it to a group of ladies, it comes alive in all its naked glory? What if your creation wanted to reward you by fulfilling your every desire? What if you're tempted to let him . . .

ALMOST PERFECT by Denise Hampton
An Avon Romance

Cassandra wagered a kiss in a card game with rake Lucien Hollier and willingly paid her debt when she lost. Then, desperate for funds, she challenges him again . . . and wins! Taking Lucien's money and fleeing into the night, the surprisingly sweet taste of his kiss still on her lips, Cassie is certain she's seen the last of him . . .

THE DUCHESS DIARIES by Mia Ryan
An Avon Romance

Armed with advice from her late grandmother's diaries, Lady Lara Darling is ready for her first Season. But before she even reaches London, the independent beauty breaks all the rules set forth in the Duchess Diaries when she meets the distractingly handsome Griff Hallsbury.